BLOOD REMAINS

CATHY PEGAU

Bywater
BOOKS

2024

Bywater Books

Copyright © 2024 Cathy Pegau

Print ISBN: 978-1-61294-283-4

Bywater Books First Edition: May 2024

Printed in the United States of America on acid-free paper.

Cover designer: TreeHouse Studio

Bywater Books
PO Box 3671
Ann Arbor MI 48106-3671

www.bywaterbooks.com

To all who seek, find, and provide found families.
The blood of the covenant is thicker than the water of the womb.

CHAPTER ONE

Calliope Payne raised her arm, the contoured handle of the cleaver fitting her palm like it was an extension of her body. The honed blade thwacked into the scarred butcher block counter, separating the joints, cartilage, and soft, red flesh of the slab of lamb ribs like they were butter. She swung again. Thud!

Callie hummed along with the tinny sounds of Duke Ellington coming over the radio playing in the corner. The scent of raw meat and wood shavings filled her nostrils. Strings of sausages hung over the worn white counter. Faded framed prints of farm animals and the cuts of meat they provided adorned the walls. Payne's Meats in the Yesler-Jackson neighborhood of Seattle wasn't anything fancy, but it was home.

This was where she belonged.

Callie finished separating the ribs, wiped her hands on her meat- and fat-stained apron, wrapped the pieces in brown paper, and tied the bundle with white string. The cut and price noted on the paper with a grease pencil, she slid the packet to the woman on the other side of the counter. "Anything else today, Mrs. Kavanaugh?"

Mrs. Kavanaugh smiled back, her pale blue eyes bright. "Nothin' I can t'ink of, Callie." She laid down two dollars in change. "Put whatever's left toward my bill, please."

Callie swept up the coins and opened the till with the

press of a few stiff buttons. A bell within the mass of metal and workings dinged. The cash drawer popped out. "Sure thing, Mrs. K. Have a lovely day."

"You too, dear," the older woman called as she opened the door. The brass overhead jingled merrily. "Tah!"

Callie caught a glimpse of another person coming into the shop, an impression of a hatted female figure in a dark coat, but she wanted to wash up before waiting on the newcomer. "Just a second."

"No hurry," the woman said.

In the workroom behind the main shop, Callie ran water as hot as-she could-tolerate into the sink. Before washing her hands, she raised them to just under her nose and inhaled. The tang of residual blood, faint as it was, danced along her senses, like a fizzy drink on her tongue. Everything sharpened, came into focus and awareness: The background buzz of the radio tubes in the other room that was usually inaudible nearly drowned out the music. The minuscule cracks in the enamel sink became a web of flaws.

The effect was almost dizzying. Callie never felt more alive than when she took in the coppery scent.

Every mage had an affinity for a particular element that strengthened and enhanced spells. Fire, air, water, earth . . .

Hers was blood.

Careful, warned her inner voice.

Callie lowered her hands, taking in fresh air and shaking the sensation out of her head.

Contact with their element was required to cast most spells, but some took it too far. Jemma, her mentor, had warned Callie that blood mages needed to be especially vigilant. Their reputation was often in question to begin with, no matter how regulated and responsible they might be. Allowing your desire—your *need*—for magic and your element to consume you was a troubled path, at the very least. Discipline and the Laws had kept mages relatively safe within society for the last few centuries. That didn't mean practitioners didn't falter.

Callie washed her hands with a bar of Ivory, then dried them on a clean towel, her sensitivity ebbing into quiescence. She straightened her skirt and retied the apron string behind her back. Tucking loose hair into the bun atop her head, she returned to the counter, smiling as she caught the strains of "Someone to Watch Over Me," her favorite Gershwin tune.

"Good morning, what can I get for you?"

The woman had been bent over, perusing the glass case of fresh sausages and hams, the brim of her hat obscuring her face, until she straightened and looked at Callie.

Large, dark eyes and high cheekbones sent an old and familiar zing through her. Smooth brown skin glowed with a hint of blush from rouge, not from the flush of emotion that Callie knew colored her own cheeks. The wicked smile that said this woman knew more about you than you knew yourself struck Callie deep in her gut.

"EJ." Her name left Callie's lips in a soft breath, all she could manage as her heart thumped hard against her sternum and then raced along with the memories that galloped through her brain: the two of them laughing, running from a shop owner, sitting on the roof of Callie's apartment on a hot summer night, practicing the waltz or foxtrot.

"Hullo, Cal. Long time, no see." The bright smile warmed. "How're things?"

Callie took a moment to come to grips with the fact that Eileen "EJ" Jordan was standing in her shop. Her long, fur-trimmed gray coat was open, revealing much of her willowy form in a jade green suit. Wisps of black hair curled from under her hat. Perfectly applied kohl lined eyes that Callie knew could go from soft and laughing to brittle and deadly in a blink.

She knew because as leader of the Jackson Street Roses, the gang of girls Callie had run with as a kid and teenager, EJ Jordan

3

had been a fixture in Callie's life. They'd seen each other nearly every day for over a decade. Then Callie got busy helping with the shop, busy with trying to figure out what she'd do with her life, busy with trying to not feel feelings. Marrying and moving to the other side of the state were supposed to help.

It hadn't.

"I—I'm good." Callie swallowed hard and rubbed damp palms down her apron-covered hips. "What about you?"

Silly question. Everyone in the neighborhood knew how EJ was doing because she owned the most popular dinner club for ten blocks and had her fingers in half the other businesses within the same stretch. Since returning to the neighborhood three months ago, Callie had learned EJ didn't often visit butchers or bakers or candlestick makers. People went to *her*, not the other way around.

"Peachy, thanks," EJ said. She held Callie's gaze for a few seconds longer, making Callie's stomach flutter, then looked down at the neat display of glistening meats in the case. "What do you recommend?"

Callie cleared her throat, adjusting to the safer realm of customer service and wondering what was actually happening. EJ wasn't here to buy sausages, that was certain. "Depends. Are you looking to feed a crew, or having a dinner party?"

"Dinner." She lifted her head and winked. "For two."

Callie ignored the returning funny feeling in her gut and moved to the other case, away from EJ. She felt better having the higher case between them but couldn't figure out why. "We have some lovely bacon-wrapped filet mignons. The T-bones have a nice amount of fat, no gristle."

"Great. Give me two of each."

Callie's head jerked up. Few of her customers ordered her most expensive cuts in such an off-handed manner. In fact, none did. Ever.

"Are you sure?"

EJ reached into an inside coat pocket and removed a leather wallet. "Absolutely."

Weighing the meat then wrapping the cuts in two separate packets, Callie's mind ran with unanswered questions. After more than a decade, her first glimpse of EJ was in the shop she'd taken over now that Pop was gone. EJ hadn't come to his funeral last month, hadn't sat with the other Roses at her wedding a dozen years ago. Not that Callie had sent an official invitation to any of them, but friends who'd spent their formative years running together shouldn't need a special invitation, should they?

Why now? Why was Eileen Jordan, Queen of the Y-J, standing in trampled sawdust, looking amazing, and ordering expensive meat?

"How's your Gran?" EJ asked.

Callie glanced at her, but that was all. It was easier to concentrate when she didn't look right at the other woman. "Good. She's upstairs. Sharp as a tack. Still does the books."

"Wonderful." EJ was silent for a few moments. When she spoke again, her voice was soft and sincere. "I'm sorry about your dad, Callie. He was a good guy."

His loss clutched at Callie's chest and throat. She blinked back tears. "Thanks."

She didn't ask why EJ hadn't come to the funeral or to her wedding. It didn't matter now. Besides, if she asked that, EJ would likely want to know why Callie had left in the first place. The *real* reason she had left.

"And your husband."

EJ's offer of condolences for Nate didn't exactly sound like an afterthought, but it wasn't particularly emotional either. How else did you acknowledge a year-old death?

"Thank you."

"Business is going well?" EJ's tone was lighter now with the change of subject. Thank goodness.

"Well enough."

"Glad to hear it."

Callie set the packets on the counter and worked out the price. She double-checked her math, then jotted the cut and amount on each. The numbers made her nervous, but EJ had asked for the good stuff.

"Would you be available for a drink or something later?"

Callie's head came up again. She swallowed her immediate response of laughing nervously and tucked a loosened strand of hair behind her ear. "What for?"

EJ smiled and shrugged. "Catch up with each other. I have something to talk to you about."

What could she have to say that they hadn't covered already? Plenty.

"Not tonight," Callie said. Not that she was busy. She needed time to gather herself, to figure out a reason *not* to go, if she couldn't gather herself.

"Tomorrow then." EJ's smile softened. "Just talk and some food. The Garden at eight?"

Since EJ owned the club, chances were fair to excellent Callie wouldn't have to drop so much as a nickel for a soda. But a free meal always came with a cost of some kind, didn't it?

What was EJ looking to get from her?

Only one way to find out.

"All right." Callie slid the packets of meat closer to EJ. "Ten dollars, please."

Without hesitation, EJ handed over a ten dollar note. She pocketed the supple leather case and scooped up the packages. "It's good to see you again, Callie. Really good. Looking forward to tomorrow."

EJ swept out of the shop, the brass bell jangling wildly as the door shut.

Callie released her next breath in a long streaming sigh.

Dinner with EJ Jordan. At a fancy supper club. At *her* fancy supper club.

As Callie considered and rejected most of the dresses in her closet, one particular question kept circling her brain: What did EJ want with her?

The next evening, Callie strode down Washington Street in the heart of the Y-J, toward The Garden, past stores and businesses with apartments on the upper levels. A working-class neighborhood that wanted to be swankier. At least EJ was pushing it in that direction as best she could.

Her heels hit the sidewalk with sharp staccato beats, and the lower half of her wool coat flapped open. She wasn't quite running, not wanting to jostle other pedestrians, but definitely moving faster than necessary.

Slow down before you sweat through your good dress or snap a heel.

Taking a breath of exhaust-tinged air, Callie deliberately slowed her step. Was she just anxious to get the meeting over with, or was there something else making her heart race?

Cars passed, rubber tires hissing on the wet, black road. Few of the vehicles were late models, though she knew of several year-old 1930 Model A's in the area. Despite the Depression, Mr. Ford was probably doing all right for himself. As were the few local individuals who could afford new cars. No one in the neighborhood openly wondered where such income originated. There were plenty of opportunities—magic-influenced or otherwise—for those who didn't mind laws. Mages were free to do what magic they could to make a living and get ahead, like any other skilled person. Within reason.

"Harm invoked is harm thrice returned" was the singular Law mages lived by. That magic wasn't 100 percent guaranteed, could potentially take a hefty toll on mental and physical well-being of the wielder, and often needed to be very specific, kept most mages from pressing the limits. Even if you were working for the greater good, there was a chance of harm caused somewhere to someone. The universe was keen on balance. Intentional harm was forbidden by the Covenant, but there could still be repercussions for accidental injury.

Magic couldn't prevent things like war and economic downfalls, but often helped mitigate the outcome. Grand world events were too much for a mage or even a group of mages to wrangle and control. As Gran always said, they were mages, not miracle workers.

Callie took in the storefronts as she passed. She knew EJ ran some sketchy enterprises here and there, along with her legitimate businesses, and likely employed mages somewhere along the line. Hobson's Laundry and Dry Cleaners housed a bookie in a back room, and Callie knew for a fact that Hobson was a decent water mage. Martinelli's Shoe Repair did top-notch work while they ran a numbers game for EJ that was coded in the *Seattle Times*. There was also, supposedly, a "members only" gambling den somewhere in covered-over roads and old businesses beneath Pioneer Square. Other bosses had similar enterprises throughout the city. As far as Callie knew, EJ wasn't threatening or underhanded or cruel like some she could name. At least not *as* bad. Or she hadn't been.

No one in the criminal world made it to EJ's level without breaking laws and doing some sort of damage somewhere. Even before Callie married Nate twelve years ago and moved away, EJ had graduated from running their gang to running errands and small schemes for Darren Scott, a significant dweller of the Seattle crime syndicate. EJ was destined for greater things than the petty thefts and minor shakedowns they'd enacted as kids. The Lady Gangster was a moniker they'd joked about, knowing none of them would ever be "ladies." But it looked like EJ was achieving her goal.

The rest of Roses had mostly grown up and moved on,

though some had gotten themselves into deep trouble and were spending five to ten on the state's dime. EJ had managed to avoid the long arm of the law. A night in lockup for drunk and disorderly had been the worst thing on her sheet back then.

If she had been in for anything more serious, Callie would have heard about it. Though to be fair, leaving town had cut ties to those deep in the know, namely the Roses. Ties she missed, she realized.

Her own fault. Trying to live the life she'd thought she'd wanted hadn't worked out as she'd imagined. Go figure. She could blame Nate and his bigoted parents, but it was on her, plain and simple.

So what if now and again she longed to cast a spell to ease a bit of work? So what if the spring butchering brought both excitement and fear of being found out because the scent of blood sparked her magic? Taking to her bed for a few days claiming "woman problems" garnered some looks and grumbles about a butcher's kid being squeamish, but they had left her alone.

"Good evening, miss."

The smooth, deep voice snapped Callie's attention away from the bubble of grief and resentment that had started to form. A tall Black man stood at the door of The Garden, his broad shoulders perfectly filling out his suit coat. His hair was straightened and slicked down in the current fashion, and a thin moustache graced his upper lip. Doorman or bouncer? Perhaps a bit of both.

"Good evening," Callie said. "I—" Recognition hit. "Mason Jennings, is that you?"

Mason grinned and a flood of memories of a skinny kid hanging around the Roses came back to Callie. Most of them included his beautiful smile. "It seems to be. How are you, Callie?"

Callie threw herself into his arms, hugging him tight and

taking in the citrus scent of his cologne. He "umphed" but returned the hug with a laugh.

"My gosh, it's been forever," Callie said.

She let him go. He made sure she was steady on her feet before lowering his arms.

"It has," he said. "Heard you were back. How's your Gran? Haven't seen much of her recently."

"She's good. Getting her piss and vinegar back."

Gran had been taking care of Pop in his last months, downplaying the severity of his illness, and it had taken its toll before Callie returned.

"Good to hear." Mason laughed again, then grew sober. "Sorry about your dad. I was out of town and missed the funeral. And about your husband, um . . ."

"Nate," she managed with a nod in appreciation of his sympathy. After a moment, she asked, "How's the family?"

Mason's father was a plumber, as were his two brothers. Mrs. Jennings was a nurse and cared for some of the neighbors when she wasn't pulling shifts at the hospital. The elder Mr. Jennings had tried to get Mason interested in the plumbing trade, but his youngest son preferred cars to clogs.

"Dad's still working hard as ever, and Mama keeps buggin' about grandkids. Lucky for me and Jeff, Kenny is married, so she focuses on him mostly." Mason checked his watch, then grasped the door handle of one of The Garden's double doors. "EJ said to be on the lookout for you. We'll catch up later. Stella will show you to your table."

That Mason was working for EJ didn't surprise Callie. With jobs in town being scarce the last few years, the mostly white employers leaned toward hiring whites. In the Y-J, with its array of people of all backgrounds, folks knew the color of their skin was less of an issue. Besides, hiring friends was a neighborhood tradition, especially when you needed people you trusted.

"Thanks. I definitely want to catch up." Callie rose on her

toes to peck him on the cheek. "It's really great to see you again, Mason."

"You too," he said, smiling. He gestured for her to enter the club.

The sounds of a piano and a trumpet playing a slow, delicate tune wafted into the front room from deeper within. The entry was decorated with enough living plants to support the name of the establishment, but not cross over into implying a jungle. EJ employed either a talented plant mage or a heck of a gardener.

Wing-backed upholstered chairs and a few low tables gave patrons a comfortable place to wait while their dining tables were readied. No one occupied them at the moment. A young woman read a magazine behind the coat check counter. An archway led into the dining room, where Callie saw a number of cloth-covered tables and a low stage where the band played. Delectable food smells drifted in with the music.

A woman with shoulder-length blond hair set in stylish waves came around the archway and stopped at the podium with an open reservations book. She wore a burgundy halter gown that showed off her pale shoulders and ample bosom. Callie immediately felt underdressed.

"Good evening. May I help you?"

"I'm Callie Payne. Miss Jordan—EJ is expecting me."

Stella, Callie assumed, smiled. "Of course. If you'll come this way. Let me take your hat and coat."

Stella deposited her things with the coat check girl and handed over the ticket. Callie stashed it in her clutch, then followed Stella through the archway. Half of the dozen or so tables were occupied. Not bad for a Wednesday night. Everyone was dressed to the nines, or what was considered dressed up for the neighborhood. Her own long-sleeved violet dress was not as swanky as Stella's gown, but it would do among the other patrons.

Stella led her to a side booth that was set for two with thin white-china plates and sparkling crystal. Indigo linen napkins and tablecloths added to the subtle richness. Perfumes, colognes, and food aromas vied for her attention. The band had switched to a different song, and though none of the four musicians were using it, a microphone stood at the front of the stage.

"Can I get you a drink?" Stella asked as Callie slid across the soft black leather seat of the booth.

"A lime seltzer, please." Callie smiled at the woman's quirked eyebrow, a hint that there was more to be had than fizzy water and juice. "Just that. Thanks."

She was well aware that Prohibition was mostly a technicality in clubs, but Callie wasn't much of a drinker anymore.

Stella nodded and sashayed away.

Servers wearing white shirts with dark waistcoats and ties weaved between tables with trays large and small, depositing plates of food and colorful drinks in an array of shaped glassware. The band finished a piece, garnering a round of polite applause before conversation filled the void. The musicians quietly left the stage to take a break.

The Garden was a reprieve from the hard scrabble of life outside its doors. Clean, quiet, comfortable. Callie settled back against the leather seat. She had to hand it to EJ. This was not the sort of establishment she would have expected from the brash girl she'd grown up with.

Movement from the corner of her eye grabbed Callie's attention.

"Lime seltzer? Really?" EJ slid the tall glass in front of Callie as she sat on the opposite side of the table. The gleam in her eye was all too familiar. All too enticing. "I have other things to offer, you know."

Tonight, EJ wore a sapphire blue suit, her blouse buttoned to the top with an ivory brooch in the shape of a rose pinned at her throat. She had applied rouge to her lips and cheekbones, with kohl emphasizing her bright brown eyes.

"I like lime," Callie said, grinning.

"I'll keep that in mind." EJ smiled in return, and Callie felt the flush rise on her chest and neck.

"This place is gorgeous." She took a sip of the drink to moisten her suddenly dry mouth.

EJ looked around at the dining room, clearly proud of what she'd done. "Thank you. A lot of work went into it."

"It was nice to see Mason out front."

EJ laughed and turned her attention back to Callie. "He likes to stand out there, no matter the weather. I think he enjoys chatting it up with folks who pass by."

"Mason was always the friendly type."

"He is friendly," EJ agreed, "until he isn't. I'm grateful to have him only a step away if things get rough."

So he was more than a doorman.

Callie tilted her head. "Do they? Get rough, I mean?"

EJ didn't respond for a few moments as she was forming her answer. What went on in The Garden that might turn rough? Could be anything. It didn't seem to take much to get people riled these days.

"Now and again," EJ finally said. "Hazard of the business."

Right. The business. EJ's sort of business. How hazardous did it get?

A black-clad waiter stopped at the table and deposited small plates of salad in front of each of them. He took another lime seltzer off the tray for Callie and something amber in a squat glass for EJ. Without a word, he tucked the tray under his arm and strode toward a set of swinging doors that marked the kitchen.

"I hope you don't mind," EJ said, "but I took the liberty of having our meal prepared already."

Callie spread the dark blue napkin across her lap and picked up her salad fork. "That's fine. I'm sure whatever it is will be delicious."

"Guaranteed." EJ winked at her and ate a forkful of greens.

The band returned to the stage. The trumpet player and trombonist did their best to prepare their instruments without making too much noise. The piano player arranged music and quietly conferred with the drummer.

The salad was fresh, the dressing tangy with vinegar and subtle spices.

"I'm glad I caught you at the shop. Did you keep Eddie on?" EJ asked. Her direct gaze didn't so much as hint at what she was thinking.

"We did, but only part-time these days. He's working at Stillman's Market mostly. Gran's glad I'm back, though. Eddie's cuts aren't up to her standards."

EJ grinned. "No one has your skills, Callie."

Callie knew that was mostly true, but she had the feeling EJ didn't mean her ability to debone a chicken or create beautiful crown roasts.

When she was old enough, Pop had taught her how to butcher the lamb, beef, and pork they received from local farms and ranches. Magic enhanced the cleaver and knife skills she'd learned, and neither talent failed her when she needed them. Not that she used her magic all that often, especially in the last decade.

While magic was useful, Callie and her folks didn't advertise her, her mother's or her grandmother's abilities. Not that they didn't want her to employ her skills to succeed—plenty used magic in businesses, including the Paynes—but there was often a fine line between success, abuse, and exploitation.

She was a rare breed, being a blood mage, and not willing to break the Laws set down generations ago that regulated what those with magic could and couldn't do. Funny how many who learned of her skills, if not her affinity, wanted to hire her to harm another. Pain and suffering were forbidden. Everyone knew it. It was an insult really, to be considered little more than a weapon by some.

"Is that what this meeting is about? My skills?" Callie absentmindedly picked up her steak knife and tapped the end of the handle on the table. "And here I thought you just wanted to chat about old times."

"That too."

All right then. At least she now knew why EJ had come to see her. But Callie wasn't ready to go there yet. She'd get the ball rolling on a somewhat safer topic.

"You've stayed in touch with the others, of course."

EJ nodded as she sipped her drink. "Of course. Well, with the exception of those who are doing time or moved away." Her sloe-eyed gaze revealed nothing about her feelings on Callie having moved away. "But Ruth, Marian, and Bette are still around."

Over the course of their growing-up years, there had been a dozen or so official members of the Roses while some had only hung around the periphery, like Gloria Burns and the Lang sisters. But EJ, Callie, Ruth Cheng, Marian Calder, and Bette Nelson had been the heart of the gang.

And Janie Underwood.

Callie pushed the image of Janie's sad smile and soulful gaze out of her head.

"I should have been better about staying in touch," she said with a wince of guilt. "How are they?"

"Marian married Ralph Gaynor."

"The theater's popcorn kid, right? Gran had mentioned it in one of her letters. Marian was always sweet on him."

EJ laughed. "Still is. He runs the Palace now. They have three kids."

"Good for them. And Bette?"

"Helping her mom, working at the five-and-dime. Still nicking the odd candy bar."

Callie chuckled. How many times had Bette come away

15

from the five-and-dime with treats or movie magazines for the Roses to share? It was ironic that she was now employed there, but not surprising considering her fresh-faced girl next door appearance and charm, which she likely used on the owner.

"You'll see Ruth soon," EJ said. "Her folks still have the store down on the east end of Washington Street."

Callie hadn't expected to meet with any of the others tonight, but this was EJ's gathering.

"And you, EJ?"

She grinned, a proud glint in her dark eyes. "I have this," she said, gesturing at the Garden, "and a few other things to keep me busy."

"Other things" that weren't as nice or legal as the supper club.

"Why didn't you stay in touch?" EJ asked. There was nothing on her face that indicated anything more than curiosity, but then again, EJ was the master of appearing unfazed while hitting like a freight train.

"I—" Excuses caught in Callie's throat. "I was busy at the ranch. The few times I came back to visit Gran and Pop were quick trips."

After moving to eastern Washington and into Nate's family home, she'd managed to keep her ability from her in-laws. Nate had said they were nervous about mages in general and, like many, downright fearful of blood mages. So, Callie tried to establish herself as a rancher's wife rather than a poor butcher's kid who used magic that most others would be afraid of.

Her relationship with Nate hadn't been bad, but it didn't take long for them to figure out they weren't really as in love as they'd thought. Friends, sure, cared for each other of course, but that was about as far as it went. And Nate's parents had made it clear how they felt about magic, so they made sure his folks never found out. For years, she denied who she really was, because . . . because that was what she thought would make things easier, better, normal.

But she wasn't about to tell EJ all that.

"What kept you there so long, after he died, I mean?" Now a furrow between EJ's eyes made itself present. Curiosity? Irritation?

"His folks needed help, and I had to deal with some legal things."

The fib came easier than she'd expected.

Her in-laws had allowed her to stay at the ranch for nearly a year after Nate died while she settled his affairs and continued to help where she could. It was a good excuse to avoid returning to the Y-J with all the expectations of a new widow. But without Nate around to keep on her, to remind her that she didn't have to do "that stuff" anymore, Callie had started practicing again. Little things, like spells to light the stove or to move heavy furniture. Things that required barely a drop of blood, if any, yet buoyed her as she grieved. No one was the wiser.

Until her mother-in-law caught her. Once they learned she was a mage, Nate's parents were all too happy to show Callie the door. Her father's illness made the decision to return to Seattle absolute.

In the long run, it was probably for the best for all of them. She'd thought she wanted different. Now she knew. Being with Gran in the old neighborhood was all she needed and wanted. Comfort. Familiarity. Safety.

The waiter returned with two plates that were each filled to the rim with a gorgeous T-bone, green beans, and fluffy mashed potatoes. Callie shook her head. Leave it to EJ to serve her meat from her own shop. She gave EJ a smirk of recognition.

"Figured you'd appreciate the way Valerie cooks it better than anyone else could," EJ said.

"You didn't even ask how I like it prepared."

She answered immediately. "Medium rare, salt and not too much pepper, a touch of garlic butter. Let the product speak for itself."

She wasn't wrong, about Callie's preferred preparation or her philosophy.

As tempting as the meal before her was, something turned in Callie's stomach. EJ knew her well, even after all this time. Or thought she knew her.

Callie set down her knife. "What do you want, EJ?"

EJ cut into her steak. The interior was perfectly cooked, dark pink with a hint of juice. "Eat first. We'll talk after. Here comes Ruth."

Callie turned toward the archway leading from the lobby into the dining room, expecting to see Ruth Cheng, but no one was there. Instead, the tall, full-figured woman sauntered from the wings of the stage to a smattering of applause. Black bobbed hair shining under the lights, dark eyes lined with kohl to emphasize her heritage, lips and cheeks rouged, Ruth smiled at the audience as she took her place before the microphone. Stage lights danced off her pearlescent sequined dress.

The band played the introduction to "Dream a Little Dream," and Ruth began to sing. Her throaty alto infused the lyrics with a sexiness Callie had never heard in the song. It wouldn't surprise her if a little mood magic had gone into the tune, and Ruth's ability as an air mage allowed her to hold notes longer with more purity.

Ruth had mastered manipulating air itself, a skill that mages strived for but that could prove tricky, as elements resisted such control. Using them for a spell was one thing, but bending them to your will was a whole other ball of wax sometime fraught with unwanted results.

Seeing the "baby sister" of the Roses all grown up and doing what she loved most delighted Callie. Ruth had come a long way from the skinny, scared little kid hovering at the edge of the Roses' activities, insisting she was a girl like them despite what others may have seen and expected. It hadn't taken long for EJ, Callie, and the others to take her completely under their protection and make Ruth one of their own. Over the years, the acceptance of Ruth as Ruth was never questioned in the Y-J.

"Eat," EJ encouraged when she saw Callie hadn't touched her food yet. "You can be mad at me later."

There was no sense letting a perfectly good meal go to waste, so Callie complied, pretty damn sure she would be mad. Her tongue all but danced at the first bite of beef. EJ was right about her cook doing the cut justice. Everything on the plate was simple and delicious.

Ruth accepted applause with quiet thank yous, then started singing "All of Me." As much as Callie wanted to just sit and listen to her old friend, she needed to address EJ's scheme, whatever it was.

"Tell me what you want, EJ."

EJ sipped her drink, then gently blotted her lips with the napkin from her lap. "It can wait. Let's enjoy the show."

EJ was used to getting her way.

Callie set her cutlery down and moved her napkin from her lap to the table. She started toward the edge of the bench seat, determined to leave.

EJ laid her hand on Callie's arm, stopping her. She glanced around the room as if making sure no one was paying attention to them. They weren't. The booth was off to the side, far enough from the closest patron that they'd have to have super-human hearing. "Paul Underwood."

The name immediately knotted anger and grief in Callie's chest. She hoped EJ was about to tell her he was dead, but she would have heard that bit of cheery news by now. She had to swallow several times before speaking. "What about him?"

EJ traced a line through the condensation beading on her glass. "He's causing trouble. I want him gone."

"Causing *you* trouble, you mean." Callie shook her head. EJ wanted to use her, just like others had. "I don't hurt people. I can't. You know that. I don't want to get involved in your business dealings."

Running with the Roses had been exhilarating when they were teens, and a necessary sense of family for most of them. But things were different now. She had Gran to take care of and her own business to run.

"I don't need you to hurt him, just get him out of the Y-J." EJ's brow furrowed. "He's threatening people, Cal. Friends. He's already run off the Parkers. His goons beat up Mr. P. over some imagined insult after Parker refused to accept their 'protection.' I won't have that in my territory."

Her territory.

"This is a battle for territory?" Callie edged toward the end of the seat again. "No, EJ, I told you, I won't—"

"He's responsible for Janie, like we always thought."

Callie froze, her breath caught and her heart stumbling, rendering her speechless.

"And we can get him for it, Cal."

CHAPTER TWO

Callie closed her eyes, grimacing as if she'd been struck. EJ watched her face go pale and hoped to hell she didn't pass out.

When Callie looked at her again, EJ still saw the shock, but was sure she wouldn't faint. Well, pretty sure. Callie might be a blood mage, but what had happened to Janie had been horrible. And that was only what Janie had told them or what they'd figured out for themselves from her bruises. EJ knew bringing Janie up like this would shock Callie, had counted on it even. She felt a little guilty, but not enough to toss her plan out the window.

"How do you know?"

"Come on," EJ said, rising and coming around the table. "Let's talk in my office."

She offered a hand to Callie and was surprised it was accepted. Callie closed her fingers around EJ's and stood. Years of working in the butcher shop and on her late husband's ranch had made her strong, her hands calloused, and EJ appreciated the thrill that zinged through her from the contact.

With Ruth's sultry tones and gestures captivating the audience, no one gave them so much as a glance as EJ led Callie along the side of the dining room and through a door marked "Private." The music became muffled, but not completely silenced, as the door shut behind them. A couple of plain light fixtures illuminated the corridor. They followed the hallway to the back of the building, where an exterior door led to the alley and a narrow set of stairs led up to her office and a storeroom.

EJ went up first, her hand still in Callie's. At the top, she turned left toward her office. Digging a key from her pocket, she unlocked the door, felt for the switch on the wall to turn on the light, and gestured for Callie to go in.

The office furnishings were a few years old, but in decent shape. The heavy oak desk, cabinets, and brocade-upholstered chair and chaise cost a pretty penny but were meant to last generations. A far cry from the flimsy crap she'd grown up with. These pieces were an indulgence, but she spent most of her money where it counted: where the public could pay for the privilege of experiencing lush furnishings and delightful décor.

"Have a seat," EJ said, pointing at the chaise. She went around to the business side of the desk and took a bottle and two tumblers from a bottom drawer.

"I don't drink," Callie said as she sat on the edge of the chaise.

EJ poured a finger of dark amber liquid into each glass, corked the bottle, and set it on the desk. She took both glasses over to the chaise and held one out as she sat beside Callie. "Just hold it for now."

Callie accepted the tumbler. Grasped between her hands, she rested the glass on her lap. "Tell me what you're talking about, EJ. How do you know Underwood was responsible?"

EJ sipped her drink and let the whiskey infiltrate her senses before swallowing. The Canadians made a decent product; it hardly burned at all.

"A few weeks ago, a guy came in here and got a bit deep into his cups. When Mason made to throw him out, he started yammering about being one of Underwood's men or something. He looked familiar, and I wanted some dirt on Underwood, so I brought him into a corner and started asking questions."

Defying the Prohibition law was one thing. Letting some mook get drunk and cause trouble was another.

"Who was it?"

EJ wasn't sure if Callie was up on the Underwood organization, but the name she was about to reveal would certainly hit another nerve. She downed a mouthful of whiskey before answering. "Ned Winslow."

Callie paled again, her hands white-knuckled as they tightened around the glass.

Over twenty years ago, Doctor Edwin "Ned" Winslow had been called in when Janie got sick. Or that's what Auntie Kay and Uncle Paul Underwood had claimed at the time. No one recalled seeing Winslow go up to their apartment, nor did they see the Underwoods taking Janie to see him in his office above the drug store. The Roses had been keeping a sharp eye out, because you didn't leave one of your own to fend for herself when she'd been telling you about how her family had been treating her for the last four years.

Yeah? And what did you do about it, huh?

EJ gulped another mouthful of booze.

Callie opened her mouth to say something, but nothing came out. With shaky hands, she lifted the glass to her lips and took a modest sip. EJ wasn't sure what had prompted her to quit drinking, but she wasn't one to judge.

"What did he say to you?" she asked.

"That Underwood owed him for taking care of Janie, whatever that means since she died." EJ slugged back the rest of the whiskey in her glass. It kept the anger and sadness under control. Mostly. The sudden jolt of alcohol felt good. "That if it wasn't for him, there would have been trouble."

Callie narrowed her eyes. "He was drunk. You can't trust him."

EJ stood and strode to the desk. She poured another finger—

made it two—into the glass. "Not that drunk. And we both know Underwood didn't ever do shit for Janie except smack her."

"We should talk to Winslow when he's sober."

The swallow of whiskey didn't help this time. Anger and frustration heated EJ's neck and face. "Would if we could. He conveniently fell off a curb in front of a speeding truck last week. Hit and run."

Callie's mouth dropped open into a little O of shock. EJ dragged her gaze from those perfectly pink lips back to her sapphire blue eyes. Shit. That didn't help either. She took another slug of her drink.

"You don't think it was an accident."

EJ swallowed as she shook her head. "No. I think someone saw me talking to him and told Underwood. I think he was given a shove, but of course there are no witnesses or proof. Underwood is pretty damn good at cleaning up his messes."

"Did he say Underwood was responsible for J-janie?" The name of their long-gone friend caught in Callie's throat.

EJ grimaced. She hadn't expected the pain of the girl's memory to affect her so much either, but it had. The only thing equal to it was the anger at the Underwoods, especially Paul.

"Not in so many words."

"There's no proof, EJ." Callie took another small sip and shook her head. "We can't."

EJ slammed the glass down on her desk. Callie jumped, her eyes wide before she frowned at EJ. The sturdy tumbler didn't break, thankfully, or EJ would have had a handful of shards and blood.

"We *know*, Callie. We've *always* known. Now we can do something about it." The specter of revenge, of justice, mixed with the alcohol nearly made her giddy. "We can't go back and save Janie; we can't even get him for what he did, but we can make him pay in other ways."

EJ pushed aside the veiled hints of aggressions Janie had

shared with them but never came right out and said. Her stomach had turned then and turned now, churning the whiskey that threatened to come up. She'd been unable to do anything when they were kids. But she wasn't a kid anymore. Unlike Janie, who would forever be a sweet-faced, sad-eyed girl who had just wanted to be loved.

Callie stood, tossed back the last of the liquid in her glass, and then set it down on the desk. Her eyes locked with EJ's. "Harm invoked is harm thrice returned. It isn't just a quaint saying. It's Law. More than that, it's the balance of energies. It may not come back on a witch immediately, but it *will* come back somehow and some way. I can't kill him, not outright, not even for her."

Those last words came out in a strangled whisper. She wanted to get back at Underwood, EJ could sense that. *She* wanted him dead, but getting him the fuck out of her face forever while bringing him down a few notches would work too.

She reached out and took Callie's cool, strong hand in hers. "But we can do other things, things that will screw up his business or otherwise make him miserable, right?"

EJ knew she was right. You didn't grow up with mages around without gleaning a little information. And EJ made it her business to have as much information as she could gather. Mages had their limits, legal and otherwise, but could do more than advertised. She just needed Callie to agree.

Callie looked down at their clasped hands. Her gaze came up again. "I don't know."

Hope flared in EJ's chest. It wasn't a no.

"Think about it." She gave Callie's hand a light squeeze. "Come on. I'll have Mason drive you home."

Still holding her hand, EJ led Callie back down the stairs, through the dining room, and into the lobby. Stella quirked a slender eyebrow, but EJ gave her a slight shake of her head. They collected Callie's hat and coat at the window. EJ held the garment out for her. Callie slid her arms in. Under the pretense of smoothing the material, EJ caressed Callie's shoulders. How had she gotten more good-looking in the last ten years?

"Wait here while I get Mason to bring the car around."

Callie nodded, almost distracted.

Let her work it out. She was never one to make rash decisions. Other than marrying that rancher anyway.

A brief image of Callie in her white wedding dress standing next to Norm or Nate or whatever the hell his name was flashed in EJ's brain. She hadn't officially attended the ceremony or the reception, but couldn't resist slipping in and sneaking a peek at Callie. She'd made a beautiful bride. She made a beautiful anything, actually.

EJ opened the door, letting the cold air shoo away the memory.

A gentle rain made the streetlights seem all the more dazzling against the dark night. Windows glowed in residences above nearby businesses. EJ grinned as a peal of masculine laughter echoed from next door. Mr. Escobar's Wednesday euchre game.

Mason turned at the sound of the door. "What's up?"

"Can you bring the car around and take Callie home? It's not far, but it's getting late." She would have driven Callie herself, but EJ got the feeling being in close proximity even for a short time might be detrimental to her cause. Callie needed time away from her, time to think without even a hint of pressure.

Mason gave her a quick nod and headed toward the side alley. The car was parked behind The Garden. She could have had Callie go back there, but the area was mucky and not a little stinky. Besides, with the car pulled up out front now and again, EJ got to show the neighborhood how she was doing. Her success was a message she promoted at every turn. If she was successful, associating with her might mean their success as well. Stick with EJ Jordan and you'd do well.

She'd gotten the neighborhood to accept her when Darren

Scott retired, and she wasn't about to let Underwood screw it up for her or them.

EJ ducked back inside, rubbing her arms. Callie was buttoned up, waiting. Stella was nowhere to be seen, and the hat check girl, Verna, had gone back to flipping through her movie magazine.

"It'll just be a few minutes," EJ said.

She stood in front of Callie, trying to read her expression. Still pensive and slightly disturbed, it seemed. Couldn't blame her there.

"I know it's a lot to take in, Cal." She purposely kept the conversation vague. There was no one but Verna around, but you couldn't be too careful.

Callie nodded slowly. "It is. I hadn't really thought about Janie for a long time. Too painful. Still trying to get over it, I suppose. Know what I mean?"

She did. But how do you get over the death of a friend you'd sworn to protect?

You didn't. Even decades later.

Maybe they could make up for it in some way now while getting rid of a pain in EJ's ass.

After EJ saw Callie off, she returned to the dining room as Ruth finished the last song of her set. The crowd gave appreciative applause, and Ruth smiled brightly. She turned and acknowledged the band. More applause. With a double-handed wave and several blown kisses, the singer made her way from the dais to EJ's table. Just as she sat down, a server deposited a tall glass of water with a slice of lemon in front of her.

"Thanks, Johnny," Ruth said.

He looked at EJ expectantly. She shook her head.

Johnny gave a nod and hurried to a table where a man waved him over.

"You sounded great tonight," EJ said.

"Don't I always?" Ruth winked, her false eyelashes nearly

brushing her cheeks.

EJ grinned. "Of course."

The singer sipped her water, eyeing EJ over the rim. Her pearl-white gown shimmered in the soft light of the room. The neck-high front and plunging back were enticing, but while EJ appreciated women's curves, Ruth was more friend than flirt fodder.

"I'm sorry I didn't get to chat with Callie."

A slight twinge of guilt warmed EJ's cheeks. "I should have had you sit down with us. Sorry. We got to talking about Winslow. Shook her a bit."

More than a bit.

Ruth nodded. She'd joined the Roses just before Janie died and knew plenty about Underwood's activities over the years. She ran a fingertip down the side of the glass, through the beads of condensation. "Is she in?"

"Not yet." Ruth's arched eyebrow made EJ shrug. "Yeah, I know. Arrogant of me to assume. But she loved Janie as much as the rest of us. More, maybe. Give her a chance to work through it and she'll come around."

"I hope you're right. We need her. Nothing we can do would come close to what a blood mage would be capable of."

Ruth's air talent was great for her singing ability, and she could probably suffocate someone given enough of a chance and disregard for the Laws, but her spell use, from what she'd told EJ, wasn't nearly as strong or reliable as a blood mage. Callie was the only blood mage they knew. Her added personal and emotional stake wouldn't hurt either.

"She won't hurt him physically." There was still a twinge of disappointment there, but EJ understood Callie's point. If she was responsible for any sort of assault, the punishment was harsh. Society as a whole might tolerate magic, even enjoy the benefits, but cross the line and you paid a steep price.

In her own business dealings, it was get caught crossing the line and you paid for it. But they'd need more than brute force for what she had in mind for Underwood. At least for now. She wanted him gone. She wanted him humiliated and ruined. If he couldn't be offed, she wanted him to suffer as much as humanly possible. Hell, that might be even better than killing him.

"Of course not. She's more cautious than the rest of us. Maybe a little too cautious, but you can't blame her for that." Ruth swirled the contents of her glass. "What if we all get together and talk to her?"

EJ made a face. "I don't want to pressure her. Once she agrees, we'll meet and go through details."

"If she agrees," Ruth said, reminding EJ that Callie wasn't a sure thing.

"If."

But if Callie didn't help her, EJ's options for stopping Underwood from intimidating, bullying, and tearing his way into her territory were at their limits. No amount of magic would save her from what she'd need to do then. There would be more than "harm" from either side.

It would be all-out war.

CHAPTER THREE

Friday and Saturday were busy at the butcher shop. Those who had paychecks figured it out down to the penny for groceries and expenses for the week ahead. Callie made sure to have plenty of affordable cuts available. By the time she turned the sign in the window to "Closed" and threw the bolt on Saturday evening, she was ready to sleep for the rest of the weekend.

Not all of her exhaustion was due to work. After meeting with EJ on Wednesday, she hadn't slept more than a couple of hours at a time, either never really getting her mind settled or waking to nightmares of Janie calling out and Callie being unable to find her friend.

If EJ was right, if the Underwoods had been directly responsible for Janie's death, then she owed it to the girl's memory to deliver some sort of justice. What good was having such powerful magic inside you if you couldn't use it for important things like that?

But how?

The covenants against harm were clear. She would need to get some advice without revealing what was going on.

Callie brought the displayed meats back to the cool room, secured the doors to the shop, wiped down the cases, mopped the floors, and went upstairs to the apartment she shared with her grandmother.

The yellow Swiss dotted curtain covering the plain glass of the door jiggled on its spring frame as Callie opened the door. She made a mental note to tighten the hardware. The aroma of simmering stew and biscuits baking made her stomach rumble.

Callie took her shoes off and set them on the woven mat beside the door, under the coats, scarves, and hats on their hooks. The wood floor was cool beneath her stocking feet. She crossed the small dining room and into the tiled kitchen, right to the stove. Simultaneously grabbing a spoon off the counter and lifting the lid of the pot, Callie sighed as the steamy aromas warmed her from nose to toes. She spooned up some gravy and a chunk of beef. Delicious, as always.

"Pull out them biscuits while you're there," Gran said as she came in from the hall that led to the bedrooms and bathroom.

Callie set the lid back on the pot and the spoon on the counter. She slid an oven mitt on and opened the oven door. Another assault of aromas that made her feel warm and happy. She took the flat sheet out and carefully placed it on the stovetop. The biscuits were perfectly shaped golden-brown circles.

"You sure you're a water witch, Gran, and not a kitchen witch?" The terms were as old-fashioned as the woman she addressed.

"Just got a lot of practice cooking." Gran's dark blue dress with its small rose pattern and white collar was dated but well maintained. She wore dark stockings and house slippers. Despite no plans to leave the house today, she was primped and dressed, her white hair in a neat bun.

Callie resisted taking one of the piping hot biscuits. That would only get a smack from Gran and burned fingers. "I'll go get cleaned up."

She hurried into the tiny bathroom, situated between her room and Gran's, smiling despite the pang she felt as she passed the closed door of her parents' bedroom. The cracking rubber

31

plug didn't quite fit right in the sink anymore, but the water would remain in the basin long enough for a quick wash. After dinner, she'd fill the claw-foot tub and take a nice leisurely bath.

Oh, the excitement of her Saturday nights.

Callie chuckled to herself, content with how her life was going for the most part. With the exception of EJ's plan, that is.

Her good feeling evaporated, and Callie frowned at her reflection. What was she going to do about EJ? About Paul Underwood?

She dried her hands on a towel hanging beside the sink and returned to the dining room. The sitting room windows, facing the front of the building, showed the fading early October day. She would spend the evening reading, or in Gran's case knitting, while listening to the radio or phonograph.

Gran was at the stove, ladling stew into white china bowls with blue and yellow flowers along the flat rim. The biscuits were under a tea towel on the table.

"Let me get those, Gran." Callie carried the full bowls to the table. She set one down at each place, then poured water into glasses.

Gran took her seat across from Callie. They put their napkins on their laps and dug in. While she ate, Callie's thoughts wandered back to her meeting with EJ. She assumed EJ's idea of what to do would skate the edge of legal, at the very least. That wasn't the problem. It was getting Paul Underwood to pay for what he'd done, some way, somehow, that excited Callie more than it should have. He needed to pay. She *wanted* him to pay. Yes, there were rules and Laws to follow, but . . .

But this would be for Janie.

After a few minutes of silent eating, Gran dabbed at her lips and asked, "What's on your mind, Callie-girl?"

Callie swallowed the lump of potato and guilt. "What makes you think there's something on my mind?"

Gran gave her the look of someone who had known Callie

all of her life and knew when she was trying to pull a fast one. Rather than draw out the interrogation that would only end in her telling Gran anyway, Callie sipped her water and decided advice would be appreciated.

"My dinner with EJ the other night."

Gran pursed her lips. She had constantly warned Callie away from running with "that gang of hooligans" when they were kids, but had never punished her for it. In fact, she suspected Gran had a bit of a soft spot for most of the girls and for EJ in particular. Callie had never asked for details. "How is Eileen doing?"

Callie couldn't help but grin. Gran never called her EJ, always Eileen. And she was the only one EJ allowed to do it. "She's doing well. Have you been to The Garden?"

Gran shook her head. "Haven't had the pleasure."

"It's nice. Ruth sings there."

At that, Gran cocked her head and smiled a little. "Ruthie has a lovely voice. Always did. Though she doesn't go to church these days."

A few of the Roses went to church or temple as kids, Callie recalled, herself included when she couldn't escape the house early enough on Sundays. She hadn't seen them there on the couple of occasions she'd accompanied Gran since moving back to Seattle. Ruth had sung in the choir for several years, and though she was the most talented member—even before her magic ability proved useful there—she was often passed over for solos. Callie suspected more than a little racism was at play, accompanied by favoritism for the pastor's daughter.

"But you didn't go to The Garden to hear Ruth sing," Gran said knowingly.

Might as well spill.

"No." Callie took another sip of water. "EJ wants me to help her with something. To use my magic. I'm not sure if I can."

More like she wasn't sure she'd be able to resist doing harm to Paul Underwood, but Gran didn't need to know that part.

"Is what she's asking against the Laws?"

Her grandmother didn't just mean the laws of the country, state, or city, but the Laws of the Covenant. For generations, those who were gifted—or cursed, depending on your interpretation—with magic ability had to abide by certain rules of behavior. As with any society, there were also rogues, those who did whatever they pleased, whenever they pleased, but the Laws worked to prevent chaos and to protect everyone. They were generation-old agreements between witches, who were an almost negligible percentage of the population, and the uninitiated, those who wouldn't or couldn't practice, a decidedly larger number. The arrangement allowed for magic to be utilized for the good of all as well as consequences for using magic for illegal or harmful purposes. Keeping the agreement intact was worth it to prevent another horror like the Salem witch trials.

"I don't know," Callie admitted. "I don't think so. She understands I wouldn't go against the Covenant. Even if she isn't exactly following the laws of the land herself."

Gran snorted a little at that. She knew exactly what EJ was about.

"I want to help her on one level," Callie continued, "but I'm afraid I might see this as an opportunity to do something that isn't permitted and have the Tribunal after me."

A look of concerned curiosity raised Gran's eyebrows. "Not permitted and something harmful you'd *want* to do?"

Heat rose on Callie's neck, to her cheeks. "Yes," she said, her voice small.

Gran had always been a stickler for following the Laws, especially once Callie decided to practice. It was a witch's greatest responsibility, she often reminded Callie.

"Care to explain?" Gran buttered a biscuit without meeting Callie's eyes.

"It has to do with maintaining the neighborhood."

Gran took a bite, nodding as she chewed, then swallowed. "You mean Eileen's trying to keep someone from strong-arming their way into her territory." Callie couldn't help the wide-eyed surprise on her face. Gran shrugged. "I know how things work around here. You youngsters aren't the only ones with ears and connections. You think the Y-J was created out of thin air the day you were born?"

She scoffed at the assumptions of youth, and Callie grinned.

"No, of course not. I've heard plenty of your stories. And Pop's too. You were quite the hellion back in your day."

Which is likely why she had a secret soft spot for EJ and the Roses.

"Maybe so," Gran said, "but we knew our responsibilities and limits. And we helped where we could, like during the fire and rebuilding the city."

The fire of 1889 had devastated Seattle's downtown area, but it could have been much worse were it not for the few but tireless fire and water mages. Sure the damage had been significant, but not a life was lost. And when the city decided to rebuild and take the opportunity to raise the streets with soil fill from the hills, the community's earth and water mages stepped in where they could, speeding up the process to get businesses back on track.

They also managed to create a warren of under-the-street passageways used by locals for all manner of activities. EJ wasn't the only one to take advantage of that setup.

Folks had been grateful for the mages then, but memories were short if you hurt someone.

"There is little excuse or leeway when it comes to causing harm," Gran continued.

Callie took a breath, releasing it slowly. "Yeah, I know."

Gran covered Callie's hand with her own, her dark eyes softening. "I think I know you well enough, Callie-girl, to guess this means a lot to you." She squeezed Callie's fingers gently. "I can't advocate breaking the law or Laws, but I understand.

Whatever you do, however you do it, do it for the right reasons."

Callie squeezed back and offered her grandmother a wry grin. "I was hoping you'd tell me not to do it. That way I could go back to EJ and just say no."

Gran laughed and patted her hand. "We aren't always in the position to be so black and white, my girl. Now eat your dinner before it gets cold."

EJ parked above the access to the private dock of a warehouse used by Finn's Produce. She shut off the engine and gave herself a minute to scope out the area around the waterfront. Though outside of town a ways, having deliveries made here was easier and safer than at the public dock. The Coast Guard patrolled the Strait of Juan de Fuca and all around the islands, keen on catching rumrunners. It took a skilled captain to avoid being boarded or shot at as they came down from Canada.

EJ could have driven farther down the dock, but she wasn't a fan of having a single option for departing. Besides, it gave her a chance to stretch her legs. A walk in the chilly, salty night air could do wonders for strained nerves.

Long coat cinched, she made her way along the approach and kept an ear out for unusual activity. The rumble of idling engines, the thud of cargo hitting wood planks, and similar sounds echoed across the water from the larger commercial docks half a mile north as the crow flies. All normal noises that could cover a lot of not normal activity. Well, not legal activity, at any rate.

Tall pole lights provided murky pools for unloading vessels, creating blacker than black shadows where they didn't reach. Her nose itched with the tang of oil and diesel fuel, exhaust and salt, seaweed and dead fish.

A bland and unassuming panel truck with a faded "Finn's

Produce" sign painted on either side wasn't far from the finger dock where she was headed. However, Finn's produce wasn't the only thing it transported.

She veered away from the main dock, heading to the long creaking float where smaller boats were tied up. The lighting here was even dimmer, which suited EJ and her associates just fine.

Two men in caps, wool jackets, and work clothes stood on the dock beside the forty-foot vessel that fished for salmon in the warmer months and ran back and forth to Canada when fishing was slow. From what she understood, the engine bay housed a beast of modern machinery that could outrun most Coast Guard vessels. The men took sturdy boxes from a deckhand and placed them on a wheeled cart.

EJ greeted them when she was close enough not to have her voice carry too far. "Hey, Dom. Jocko. How's it going?"

Dom, the beefier of the two, nodded in her direction. EJ could just see the stub of cigar between his lips. "Hey, boss. Almost done." He aimed a thumb at Jocko. "If Jocko'd gotten his ass in gear, we'd'a been out of here half an hour ago."

Jocko took a box from the man on deck and swung it onto the pile of a dozen or so others on the cart. "Shut your pie hole," he grumbled, then addressed EJ. "That's the last of it, boss."

"No problems?" There was always a chance cops or someone would have seen the boat tie up in the middle of the night and guess what was going on.

"All good." Dom started to push the cart while Jocko walked ahead pulling on a rope tied to the front. Going up the angled ramp to the main dock required extra effort.

"Smitty said something about a jump in patrols coming the next few weeks," Dom said, referring the boat captain. "Might be a delay in deliveries."

EJ trusted Smitty to know his way around the Canadian authorities, the USCG, and their schedules. With the holiday

37

season starting in another month, they'd need to stock up on booze for merrymakers. "Okay, we'll order a bit extra next time then lay low for a while."

They reached the ramp, which was just wide enough for the cart, and EJ dropped behind Dom. At the top, Jocko tossed the line over the crates and jogged to the back of the panel truck. Before he reached it, the rear door flew open. Three loud pops rang out across the dock, echoing against warehouse walls.

Jocko stumbled back, clutching his chest.

Adrenaline and instinct kicked in. EJ dove behind an old crane armature. She hit the damp pier hard and rolled into the shadows, scrambling for her gun. More shots rang out. Closer. Dom? The other guy? How many were there?

Heart racing, she crouched behind the cement and steel base. No sign of Dom, but he was smart and likely using the cart of crated booze for cover. The doors of the truck were open.

How many had been hiding in there and where were they now?

The crunch of shoes on gravel from behind her had EJ pivot on her heels. In a split second, she determined it wasn't Dom—too skinny—and fired. The *pop!* of her assailant's gun sounded at the same time pain burrowed into her left arm.

"Fuck!" She jerked back and fell to the side.

A wet thud and a groan came from the man's direction, barely heard over the roar in her ears.

Calm down before you bleed out.

Yeah, easier said than done.

Her teeth clenched, EJ rolled to her feet and made her way to him. His gun lay near his right hand. He grunted and reached for the grip.

I don't think so. Grimacing in pain, anger, and disgust, EJ aimed her gun at the back of his head and pulled the trigger. Bits of skin, hair, brain, and blood blew back onto her shoes and pantlegs. Her dry cleaning bill was going to be outrageous this week.

His body twitched; then he lay still. Blood pooled beneath him, spreading across the tarred wood. As the gunshot echoes died, silence descended on the secluded dock. It wouldn't last long. Someone in a nearby warehouse could have heard and would be calling the cops.

Taking a life wasn't "business as usual" for her, but she'd be damned if she'd hold back when openly threatened.

"Dom!" It was a risk to let a potential second man know where she was, but EJ needed to figure out her odds. From the fiery pain and the warmth of blood seeping out of her arm, "not good" was her first thought. She pulled the tie from around her neck and fashioned a crude tourniquet. "Dom!"

"Over here, boss." He didn't sound hurt, but Dom wasn't one to let weakness show.

EJ peered around the crane base. No movement. She scurried behind the cart to find Dom beside another dead man.

"Olmstead's?" she asked, referring to Seattle's biggest bootlegger. But Roy had given her the go-ahead to make her own arrangements as long as he got a cut. Besides, his boys didn't pack heat.

"Nah. This one is Underwood's man Mickey Harlow," Dom said kicking the body. "Fucking loser."

EJ glanced behind her to the man she'd shot. "I think I've seen the other guy around, but I can't be sure." She turned back to Dom. "Clean 'em out and get Smitty to dump 'em."

Dom nodded. His head came up, and he looked toward the truck. His brow furrowed. EJ followed his gaze. Jocko lay sprawled on the wet ground. Fuck fuck FUCK!

Each step toward Jocko jostled her wounded arm. Pain and anger boiled as she stood over her man. There were three holes in his coat, and blood stained his shirt, trickled from his mouth. He stared up into the night, dead eyes surprised.

Damn it.

No time for emotions. The cops were likely on their way,

and the people responsible were dead. At least those directly responsible. She'd deal with that later. Right now, they needed to get the hell out of there.

EJ closed his eyes. "We'll make them pay, Jocko," she whispered. "I promise."

Careful of her injury, she climbed into the back of the truck, making a mental note to remind her people to lock vehicles or keep watch from now on. Was the ambush merely an opportunity to steal from her, or was it some sort of message from Underwood?

She'd bet her last buck it was a bit of both.

Muted voices and heavy burdens scraping on wood, then footsteps coming closer told her Dom and Smitty had finished with the bodies. Smitty fired up the engines and pulled away from the dock. He'd find a good place to dump them where they wouldn't wash ashore too soon.

EJ searched for something to help them with Jocko. An old blanket used to cushion cargo would suffice to keep his blood from seeping into the truck bed.

Dom took the blanket from her and she jumped down from the truck, immediately regretting the decision as pain shot through her arm.

"You need that looked at," he said, laying the blanket out beside Jocko.

"Let's take care of him first."

"So you can bleed out? Lemme get something else around that."

Dom found some rags to tie over her wound. Cinching it tight brought tears to her eyes. She blinked them away as she pulled her coat back on.

EJ helped where she could, but with one arm she was almost useless. Luckily, Dom was big and Jocko wasn't. Dom got his friend into the truck. Then they transferred the crates from the cart to join the rest of her cargo.

"My car's out front," she said as they climbed into the cab of the truck. Dom started the engine and got going just as a siren could be heard in the distance. "We'll take him to Lowe's and go tell Mary."

The funeral home in the neighborhood did a nice job. They'd clean up Jocko's wounds and make him look peaceful.

Telling his wife set EJ on edge, but he was her man, her responsibility, as was his family now. She'd set up a monthly payment through her accountant.

"We can wait to tell Mary," Dom said as they pulled up beside her car. "No reason to wake her and the kids in the middle of the night."

He had a point.

Before getting out, she laid a hand on his arm. "I'm sorry, Dom."

He and Jocko had been friends for decades. They had worked for her old boss, Darren Scott, since they were young men and had joined her when Scott retired to California. For as much as they bickered like an old married couple, they were close.

"We all know the risks." He lifted his hat and smoothed back his thinning hair, cigar clamped between his teeth. "Get that looked at sooner rather than later. We'll go talk to Mary tomorrow. Meet me at their place at nine?"

EJ nodded and patted his arm before getting out of the car. "Yeah. Okay. Thanks, Dom."

He drove off.

EJ could count on Dom to take care of the crates and his friend. He wanted to grieve in his way, alone. She got that. Tomorrow, she'd get an envelope together for Mary and make sure Lowe's was taken care of as well.

As she reached for the car door handle, her arm screamed at her. Clenching her jaws, EJ got in and headed to the one person she could trust to help.

Callie startled awake, blinking at the unexpected lamp light as she became aware that she was on the sitting room sofa and not in bed. The book she'd been reading lay on her chest. The clock on the shelf showed it to be nearly two in the morning.

A quick double knock on the door shot her heart into her throat. No one knocked on someone's door at this hour with good news.

She jumped up, ignoring that she'd lost her place in the book as it tumbled to the floor, and hurried to the other room before Gran woke. A flick of the curtain over the window showed EJ standing in the dim stairwell. Callie turned on the light, unlocked the door, and yanked it open.

"What's wrong?" She spoke quietly despite the quiver in her chest.

"Just dropping by to say hello." EJ smirked, but the lines around her eyes and the ashiness of her pallor spoke volumes.

Callie narrowed her gaze as the scent of blood tickled her nose and twitched her gut. "You're hurt."

"Just a scratch."

"Liar. Get in here and tell me what happened."

EJ stepped over the threshold and into the dining area of the kitchen. Callie watched her closely as she shut and locked the door. There, as EJ tried to shuck her coat, Callie saw the wince and the awkward way she moved her arm.

Callie helped her with her coat. The burst of blood scent hit her, sending vibrations of awakening magic through her. The hastily tied bandage around EJ's upper arm, as well as her shirt sleeve to the elbow, were stained dark red.

"I'm fine," EJ said, the words in complete opposition to what Callie was seeing and sensing. "But if you could help me . . ."

Callie steered her to a kitchen chair and gently pushed down on her shoulder to have her sit. "You are not fine. And of course I'll help."

She went to the cupboard where Gran kept the medical supplies. Though Pop had been careful and professional, being a butcher meant the occasional slip of a knife or sharp bone. Bandages, scissors, an enamel bowl, clean clothes, but also tinctures, balms, bundles of herbs, and a flask of sterile water. Callie took all she needed and returned to the table.

"Tell me what happened." She picked up the scissors to cut away the makeshift bandage and the ruined cotton sleeve.

"Damn it, I just bought this shirt," EJ muttered as the scissor zipped through the cloth.

"Stop stalling."

With little emotion, EJ described her visit to the dock to see about the booze shipment and the subsequent shoot-out with Underwood's men. Though she described the awfulness of seeing her man Jocko shot with a steady voice, Callie heard the quiver of anger and sadness.

A shoot-out on the docks. Three dead. EJ could easily have been a fourth. A shudder ran through Callie. They'd done some less than safe things as kids, but there hadn't been violence, not really. They weren't kids anymore, though, were they? When did EJ start carrying a gun?

"I'm sorry about Jocko." Callie winced as she exposed the wound. "This is more than a scratch, EJ."

There was only the entry wound. The bullet was still in EJ's arm. A bullet. This was no scraped knee or gashed head from a scuffle on a street corner.

"Yeah." EJ swallowed hard. "Can you do something?"

"Why didn't you go to the hospital or a doctor?"

The other woman quirked an eyebrow at her. "You have to ask?"

"Right. Too many questions. But Doctor Evans would have patched you up." Lydia Evans had been in the neighborhood for ages, fixing everything from snotty noses to broken arms and ribs and then some.

Another strained grin from EJ didn't reassure Callie she wasn't in pain. "Evans is out of town. Besides you're nicer and easier on the eyes."

Callie shook her head and purposely tilted her face away from EJ's gaze to view the wound. How had such cheesy comments caused her cheeks to flame? But the lightness left her mood as she took a closer look.

"Jesus, EJ, this is not good."

"Being shot rarely is, though I thankfully have little experience with it."

Blood oozed steadily from the wound. Callie splashed sterile water on a clean cloth and held it gently against EJ's arm. She took a breath and closed her eyes to settle herself. Not because the sight of blood or wounds bothered her. Quite the opposite. She had to keep her head clear so she could do this right and not get caught up in the intoxicating sensation of being so intimate with EJ's blood.

"All right. Here's what we need to do." She made sure EJ was looking at her. She needed to understand exactly what coming to Callie for help meant. "I can get the bullet out and use some of Gran's ointments to heal you."

EJ's jaw tightened. "With magic."

Callie almost laughed. "Well, yes. That shouldn't be a surprise."

The other woman looked chagrined. "I suppose not. But . . ."

"I need to use a spell to make sure it comes out without causing more damage." Callie moistened her lips. "But that means using blood. Your blood."

Despite the pain and wariness in her eyes, EJ grinned. "Got enough of that available."

Callie didn't smile back. This was serious, and EJ needed to take it as such. "A blood mage typically uses their own blood for spells. Something like this, when another person's blood is

44

involved as well, that takes it to an entirely different level. The spell will be more effective, which will aid in the healing, but it also creates a connection between the caster and the recipient."

The smile left EJ's eyes. "What, you'll be . . . linked to me somehow? Able to read my mind or make me do things, like a puppet of some sort?"

Callie shook her head. "No, of course not. I'll be more sensitive to your moods. You'll be a bit more sensitive to my magic if I do things around you. Otherwise, you won't notice a difference. You won't be affected by my magic unless it's directed at you, which it won't be without your permission."

She waited a moment, making sure her words sunk in and made sense. Not everyone who asked for magical assistance understood what it entailed—why personal, intimate magic wasn't something to trifle with.

"I swear to you, Eileen Jordan, no harm will come to you in any manner, at any time, by my hand. Do you consent to the spells I'm about to initiate using your blood?"

EJ searched Callie's face, a heavy silence between them. The scant handful of times she'd enacted any sort of healing spell, this was usually the point where the person balked or hesitated. And for one of her father's former assistants who had neglected to sharpen his knife, passed out.

Finally, EJ nodded.

"You have to say it." Callie would explain the verbal requirements for positive energies in spells like this at another time. Right now, she wanted to get EJ healed up.

"I-I do," she said. She lifted her chin and spoke again, her voice stronger. "I trust you, Calliope Payne. I, Eileen Jordan, give my consent."

Relief and appreciation made Callie smile. "Thank you. Okay, relax. Close your eyes." EJ did as she was told. Callie kept her tone soft and soothing. "No harm will come to you here. I'm going to ease the bullet out. Relax your shoulders, your arms, your neck."

She felt EJ's muscles soften slightly beneath her touch.

Callie swiped her thumb gently along the edge of the wound, smearing a trail of EJ's blood across her skin in a pattern of protective runes she'd learned in her girlhood. She whispered the simple words of a telekinesis spell—something mages learn early on and didn't require their element to perform—infusing it with gentleness and delicacy. The bullet needed to retrace its path to minimize further damage. As she spoke, she gathered more of EJ's blood. It seemed to tingle on her finger, shimmering with life and energy. She didn't often use another's blood and hadn't in a number of years. She needed to be careful.

She drew a steadying breath and let it out slowly as she felt the magic begin to seep into EJ's skin.

EJ gasped, closed eyes squeezing tighter.

"It's just me," Callie said, reassuring her.

EJ settled once more.

Callie rubbed EJ's blood on her skin, then gathered more on her own forefinger, taking in the slick-tackiness of it. She picked up a needle from the kit on the table and pricked her thumb. A drop welled up. Callie mixed their blood on the tips of her finger and thumb. Doctor Evans and any other medical professional would have had kittens seeing blood mixed anywhere near an open wound, but blood mages had a certain amount of immunity from blood-borne illness, as did their patients for a short time.

As their blood combined, magic shivered through her, raising goosebumps along her limbs, heating her skin. At the same time, she sent more soothing thoughts to EJ, to herself. The magic within a person's blood was the most powerful force an individual held, even if they weren't mages themselves. Gaining their consent and trust increased that sense of ultimate control ten-fold. Combining the two made the magic stronger, the connection stronger.

It also increased the mage's responsibility toward the other.

She had to make sure her own craving for magic didn't overwhelm either of them. The desire to take the potential power of another's blood wormed through her. It would be so easy to take advantage, and some did. Those mages were a danger to them all.

Callie soothed that base desire with assurances of satiation, of her vow to do no harm. Contact with EJ's blood would quell the need without violating the Law or EJ's trust.

Callie gently grasped EJ's upper arm with her unbloodied hand. She brushed red-stained fingertips over the wound, feeling the foreignness of the lead bullet embedded in EJ's muscle. Bolstered by her magic, she visualized the bullet slowly reversing its path.

The bit of metal started to move. EJ hissed in pain. Callie spoke the soothing component of the spell, gently retracing the blood runes on EJ's skin that numbed the area and aided in removal. She focused on the bullet again, on easing it out with minimal harm.

Blood oozed from the wound, the scent perfuming the air between them. The bullet continued its path, turning slightly. Soon, the blood-streaked bit of lead emerged from the torn flesh.

Callie pinched the edge of the slug and gently pulled it free. The wound began to bleed. She set the bullet down on a cloth and scooped up two fingerfuls of the healing ointment Gran used for everything from kitchen burns to lacerations though the concoction hadn't been used on so serious a wound until now. With the ointment plugging the hole, she poured sterilized water into the enamel bowl and used a clean cloth to wipe blood from EJ's arm. She washed her own hands as well, leaving the water deep pink.

"Almost done." Clean bandages and a final word of desire for successful healing finished the job. "There. You shouldn't scar too badly."

EJ looked down at her arm, then at Callie. Though she

seemed weary, the pain was gone from her dark eyes, replaced by a glint of playfulness. "A scar might make me look tough."

"You're tough enough." Callie smiled. "But I bet the girls will swoon."

The playful grin turned wicked. "Will they? Good to know."

Heat flooded Callie's cheeks then traveled south. She cleared her throat and started cleaning up. "You should go lie down. The effects of magic can be draining."

She was paradoxically tired yet energized.

"I'm fine." EJ rose, but when she tried to take a step, she stumbled. "Whoa."

Callie stood and took her uninjured arm. "I wish you'd believe me the first time. Come on over to the sofa. I'll bring you some tea."

"Whiskey would be better." EJ allowed her to take her into the sitting room.

"No alcohol. It messes with the magic."

"Darn. So many rules."

"Tell me about it."

EJ settled onto the sofa, head leaning back. She looked tired, but pain free.

"Thanks," she said softly, and closed her eyes. "You always know how to make me feel better, Cal. Even when we were kids, when my dad was shit and I was so scared, I knew you'd be there for me. Don't know what I'd do without you."

Callie remembered those times, how she'd admired EJ's strength in leading the Roses, yet sympathized with her situation at home. "You're doing fine now."

"I have to meet Dom at Mary and Jocko's by nine." The words came out half mumbled. The soothing, somnolent magic Callie had included in the spell was taking effect. "Then figure out what to do about this bullshit."

She meant the escalation of attacks on Underwood's part. Things would only get worse.

"I promise you'll be at Mary's on time. I'll get that tea." Callie went back to the table and finished cleaning up, not bothering to put on water or preparing a cup. When she returned to the sitting room, EJ was, as expected, snoring quietly, shoes off, curled on her side.

Callie retrieved the lap blanket from the back of Gran's chair and draped it over the sleeping woman.

She looks so innocent.

Considering that Callie had just pulled a bullet from her arm, that three men were dead due to EJ's business dealings, she knew looks could be deceiving. But still . . . If Callie could help keep people alive, shouldn't she?

Leaving a table lamp on the other side of the room burning, Callie went to bed, rubbing the tips of her fingers together, still energized by the residual effects of their blood and her magic. She'd definitely need to deal with that before falling asleep.

CHAPTER FOUR

Callie sent a note over to The Garden later that Sunday, paying one of the neighborhood kids a dime for their messenger services. The response to her "All right. What next?" was "Meeting with the Roses tomorrow at my place. Mason will come for you at 3pm" with an address on Fourth Street, near Main.

Were all the Roses involved with EJ's organization? Had they been all this time?

That Callie had been so out of touch with the people she'd once considered more family than friends gave her a hint of sadness. Like herself, some had married, moved away. Babies were born, parents and elders had died. She had missed so much in the past ten years.

The next day, Mason drove Callie to a brick apartment building. The three-story Federal-style home had been renovated and divided into six apartments, two on each floor. It had once been a stately home to one of Seattle's elite families, but the recession in October of '29 hadn't done them any favors.

It could have been much worse but for the witches who had quietly alerted the government ahead of time that something was amiss. One of those who'd had the government's ear was an economist who knew both their magical and non-magical stuff.

Some had asked why there hadn't been earlier warnings to

help avoid such a terrible impact on the country, on the world. Wrangling magic to see the future was difficult, fraught with pitfalls such as blindness—both literal and magical—and wildly unreliable. If it hadn't been, there would be more winners of horse races and other gambling endeavors. Even with notice, people had lost money and jobs. Luckily, things were starting to look up with employment programs and a stabilizing economy.

Fourth Street wasn't as bustling as Jackson a few blocks away, having only the occasional car passing. On a Monday afternoon, the sidewalks were nearly empty, with folks being at work or school. Callie could have walked from her place with ease, but she sensed EJ wanted to make sure she was safe more than that she was showing off.

Callie smiled at the man in the driver's seat. "Thanks for the lift, Mason. Are you coming up?"

Mason had been as much a part of the Roses as any of them back in the day until he found some boys to run with. Callie wondered if nostalgia or necessity had brought him back to EJ.

He grinned. "Nah. I'm sitting out this meeting. EJ'll fill me in. I'll be around when you need me."

Callie patted his hand where it rested on the steering wheel. "Okay. I'll see you later."

She got out, shut the passenger door behind her, then waved to Mason before going up the steps to the main door. He drove off.

Callie went into the foyer. There was a closed door to her left with a simple "1A" on it and a staircase to her right. Down the hall was another door, presumably marked with a "1B." EJ was on the top floor. No elevator, Mason had informed her. She climbed the carpeted stairs.

The polished wood rails and wainscoting, fresh paint, and sparkling windows gave the old home a luxurious feel. It was definitely better than the apartments any of the Roses had grown up in. EJ Jordan had done all right for herself.

Callie reached the top floor. She strode down the carpeted hall, noticing the etched glass-enclosed light above each of the doors on either side and the framed prints along the walls. At 3B she stopped and took a deep breath. EJ hadn't said how many of the Roses would be involved, though Callie assumed Ruth would be among them.

The only way to find out was to go in.

She pressed the doorbell and took another calming breath.

The door swung open. EJ stood there in a pair of dark trousers and a white, long-sleeved shirt buttoned to her sternum. The narrow triangle of brown skin made Callie's mouth dry. Pale blue smoke rose from a Chesterfield EJ held between her fingers. Behind her, beyond the short hall that made up the foyer, voices and the clinking of glasses and silverware told Callie the others had already arrived.

EJ smiled and stepped aside. "Hi. Come on in. Let me take your coat."

She put the cigarette between her rouged lips and held out her hands.

Callie entered the apartment, closed the door behind her, and turned her coat and hat over to EJ. While EJ hung her things in the closet, Callie nervously patted her hair. She'd let the bob she'd worn grow out over the last few years and had settled for as neat a bun as she could manage. EJ's sleek black pin curls perfectly framed her oval face as usual.

"The others are waiting." EJ said. "Everyone's looking forward to seeing you."

Were they? Callie had had to spend more time at the shop as a teenager when her father lost his assistant. Then she'd gone and gotten married to the son of one of the ranchers who supplied beef at a reasonable price, moving to the other side of Washington with barely a word. She'd felt as if she'd abandoned the Roses. Wouldn't they feel the same?

As they entered the main room, raucous laughter greeted

them, making Callie smile. Even before she saw the women, she knew she'd been right about one of the Roses being present; that was definitely Ruth. The three of them sat around a cocktail table covered with glasses, a coffeepot, cups and saucers, and a plate of shortbread cookies.

Bette, Marian, and Ruth looked up at Callie. Ruth jumped up from her place on the floor, her delighted squeal at least an octave higher than her sultry singing voice. She wasn't glammed up as she'd been the other night at the Garden, but was wearing a forest green dress and dark hose, her shoes tossed aside. She hurried over to Callie and threw her arms around her. Callie inhaled her floral perfume, laughing.

"I've missed you, Sissy," Ruth murmured into Callie's neck.

Tears sprang to Callie's eyes at the nickname. "Missed you too, Baby Girl."

As the youngest, Ruth had balked at the moniker when they were kids, but she'd quickly learned that it came from a place of love and protection.

Ruth squeezed her tight, and Callie forced back the waterworks. When they finally let each other go, Callie saw the other two women were now on their feet.

Bette Nelson, the blonde and blue-eyed girl next door. As sweet and innocent as they came. Except for her penchant for stealing. As they'd grown up, Bette became quite the pickpocket. On the rare occasion her target realized what was happening, Bette's charms kept her from getting hauled off to the police station.

She came up to Callie, arms wide. "Long time, no see."

The two embraced. "A dog's age. How's your mom and Ben?"

Bette's mom had worked the custodial night shift at the hospital for years and picked up cleaning jobs on her days off, leaving Bette and her kid brother on their own. Mr. Nelson had returned from the Great War with part of a hand missing and a short temper. Bette often met the Roses sporting some bruise.

He disappeared one day and the Nelson family had been a lot happier and healthier ever since.

"They're good," Bette said, though there was a sadness behind her eyes that made Callie wonder if that was the truth of it. "Mom's still working, Ben's down in California. How's your Gran? Still making cookies?"

Despite her disapproval of the Roses' activities, Gran often had sugar cookies on hand for Callie to share with them.

"She is. I'll bring some next time."

Bette gave her one more squeeze then stepped aside. Marian Calder stood before her, giving Callie the up and down with one eyebrow arched, like a mother inspecting her kid before they walked out the door for church. Marian was the only girl among her siblings and had often helped her mother keep her brothers in line. She did the same with the Roses. EJ may have been the leader of the gang, but Marian had been the heart, reminding them they were family even when tempers flared.

Marian took a step toward her, arms open, smiling. Emotion caught in her throat, Callie stifled a sob and embraced her, sinking into the other woman's warmth. She was thinner than Callie remembered as Marian's strong arms encircled her, but otherwise her smooth brown skin was as dewy as a teenager's.

"Missed you, Callie-girl."

Only Marian and Gran called her that.

Callie swallowed hard. "Missed you too."

Why had she turned away from them? What had made her think marrying Nate and moving to Spokane would make her happy?

No, not happy. Normal, like her folks. But marrying and moving hadn't changed who she was, had it? It hadn't changed who she cared about.

Marian released her. "It's been too long, for sure."

"My fault," Callie said. She glanced at EJ and the others, then back to EJ. There was a strange expression on her face, like she was bothered by something but sad as well. Like she could tell what Callie was thinking. Was that just EJ being the perceptive person she was, or was their new bond from the other night to blame? How much could EJ sense? Callie felt her cheeks heat.

EJ shook off whatever was on her mind and strode to the table. "Let's get some drinks poured. Callie, you want coffee or something stronger?"

Callie sat in one of the unoccupied chairs. "Coffee, please."

Ruth resumed her seat on the floor, while Marian, Bette, and EJ settled on the loveseat and another chair. EJ passed Callie a cup and saucer. Her finger brushed the side of EJ's hand. The frisson that traveled up her arm made Callie's breath hitch.

EJ startled, her dark eyes flashing something unreadable. "M-milk's in the little pitcher. Sugar's in the covered dish."

More awareness due to the connection Callie had spoken of? Maybe, but it wasn't magic that caused Callie's reaction to EJ's touch.

Callie busied herself spooning sugar and pouring milk. The others got their refreshments squared away. After everyone finished their drink preparations, EJ sat back in her chair, one leg crossed over the other. She appeared to be more settled. More than Callie, at any rate.

"It's been forever," Callie said glancing at each of the Roses in turn, "and I'm sorry. Tell me what's going on. Marian, EJ said you married Ralph the popcorn guy?"

Marian smiled and nodded. "Yep. That sweet boy became a helluva man, let me tell you. We have three kids. Twins'll be four in December and our oldest, Glory, turned six this past June."

"I'd love to meet them sometime."

Marian's smile widened. "I'd love for you to meet them too, Callie-girl."

Bette and Ruth shared what they'd been up to as well and how their families were faring. Bette hadn't settled down, preferring to date different types of men and simply enjoying herself. Ruth worked in her parents' store when she wasn't singing at The Garden, and had been dating a policeman for several month.

"A policeman?" Callie couldn't keep the shock from her voice. The police were not known for their tolerance of most in the Y-J or anyone not fitting in, which the Roses certainly did not for various reasons. "You used to run from cops, like the rest of us."

Color rose on Ruth's cheeks and she shrugged, a shy smile hinting at a girl in love. "Joe treats me like a lady. He's good people."

That was all Ruth had wanted from the time she started hanging around the Roses, and Callie was particularly happy she'd found it, even if it was in the form of one of Seattle's finest.

"Yeah, Joe's okay," EJ said. Then with a wink for Ruth, "For a cop."

They all chuckled at that.

"And how are you holding up, Callie?" Marian asked.

Callie gave her a small smile. "Good. The shop's been busy, so that helps."

She had seen the Roses at the back of the church during Pop's service, but had felt awkward approaching them, as they must have felt about approaching her. There hadn't been a good time to reach out since returning to Seattle, had there?

"We heard about Nate last year," Bette said while picking at a loose thread on her skirt. "Sorry for your loss."

"Thanks." To be fair, Callie wasn't quite sure how she should feel about Nate, or losing him. She'd realized early in their marriage that it wasn't love, at least not passion. They'd liked each other well enough, had enjoyed each other's company. She missed him and was saddened by his passing, but she hadn't been devastated by his death the way a widow should have been.

No one spoke for a handful of heartbeats. Should she say something else? What? That she'd married Nate not for love she could admit now to herself at least, but to try to be something she wasn't?

EJ cleared her throat, getting their attention. "Okay, let's get down to it. Bottom line, Paul Underwood is trying to expand his territory, and he'll do it in any way he can."

She told them what had happened at the docks on Saturday night, leaving out the part about getting shot herself. There was no indication by her movements that EJ had been injured. Callie's spell must have worked as expected, which was a relief. The Roses in turn expressed concern, grief for the loss of Jocko, and anger at Underwood.

"My parents have been visited by a couple of his boys," Ruth said. "Nothing threatening, just walking around the store like they were assessing it, checking the inventory or something, you know what I mean?"

Even if EJ was in the habit of garnering "protection" money from establishments, she wouldn't have subjected the Chengs to any sort of deal, seeing how Ruth was one of hers. It went without saying, however, that the Chengs were under EJ's purview. Everyone would know it. A visit by Underwood's men was a clear message to EJ.

"Has anyone else been hurt?" Callie asked.

"Other than Jocko and Winslow?" EJ sipped her coffee. The other Roses exchanged significant glances, telling Callie they'd been privy to the doctor's rant at The Garden and his subsequent accident. "Not that he was one of mine, but he was talking about things he shouldn't have been as far as Underwood is concerned. Before the other night, a couple of my drivers had been beaten up, and some cases of hooch have gone missing. There have been retaliations of a similar nature on Underwood's interests. Normal stuff." Her expression darkened. "But nothing intentionally fatal."

Marian refilled her coffee cup. "What have you done up till now?"

EJ shrugged. "Same as him mostly. Posturing, threats. Got hold of one of his smaller shipments of cocaine and poured it into the sound."

Callie wasn't surprised EJ had dumped the drugs rather than sold them herself. EJ wouldn't be involved with the narcotics trade. Not after seeing what it had done to her father and a number of friends.

"Injuries?" Marian asked, an eyebrow quirked.

"Other than his two men who ambushed Jocko and Dom, nothing permanent from my side." EJ hesitated for just a second. "Yet."

Her tone suggested that was on the table now with the shooting of Jocko.

If Callie could enact a spell that would prevent a bloodbath, she would have to give it a try. Even if deep down she wanted to do more.

Involvement in Janie's death was certainly enough to seek revenge, but a tribunal would want more than their gut feeling and the second-hand account of an unreliable yammering now-dead drunk. The Roses needed a solid reason for going after him. Going on the offensive in case Underwood retaliated for Saturday night wouldn't wash with the Covenant. Protecting EJ's interests with a nonfatal spell could be sufficient and acceptable.

EJ leaned over to splash a bit of whiskey into her coffee. She sat back and sipped, eyes on Callie. Lowering the cup to the saucer she rested on her knee, EJ moistened her lips and said, "He's after The Garden."

Ruth stiffened, eyes about popping out of her head. Bette gasped.

"What do you mean, he's after it?" Marian asked.

EJ took another calm sip, but Callie noticed a slight quiver in her hand. She was holding back rage—for Jocko, for her business. "He's been scaring away customers. Profits are down, and not just due to the economy. There are rumors that he's working on the bank that holds the mortgage. If they think—or are made to think—something shady is going on, they can call in the feds and I'm screwed."

"He wants to shut down The Garden?" Callie asked.

Anger flashed in EJ's eyes. Not at her, Callie knew, but at Underwood. "He wants me out of town. Whatever I've got going, my numbers, my gambling place, my booze deal, he wants. Made an offer that was laughable. Now he's poking around, causing trouble. He's unpredictable, and I'm afraid the other night's shooting is just the beginning. Nothing I've tried so far to discourage him has worked."

The implication that there could very well be more serious injuries or deaths as a result of EJ and Underwood's battle wasn't lost on any of them. No one had any delusions about violence, but it would be best to prevent an all-out turf war. Innocent people tended to get caught in the crossfire of those. While any bystander EJ hurt would be unintentional, she hoped, no one would put it past Underwood to accidentally-on-purpose hurt or kill someone just because they were in the neighborhood.

"Underwood's in debt up to his eyeballs, from what I hear," EJ continued. "But if he can get me out of the way, he can make a decent profit in a short amount of time."

"Why bust your chops?" Bette asked. "There are plenty of small-time bosses to go after."

"'Cause I'm fucking Goldilocks," EJ said with a wry smile.

Callie didn't quite understand.

"A big enough organization to be worthwhile, but small enough for him to possibly succeed," Marian explained. "Just right for the taking."

"Over my dead body," EJ growled. "If we can get him off my back, he'd have to find another way to pay up. His options are limited there, so with any luck he'd be screwed."

Ruth smiled with more than a hint of malevolence. "Shame, that."

59

EJ made eye contact with them all in turn. When she spoke, her voice was quiet rage. "We can't get him directly for Janie, but we can get him."

There was silence among them for a dozen heartbeats. They could do this, Callie realized. She could do this. For Janie.

"We need to get Underwood to lose interest in you and the Y-J." Callie's mental catalog of spells and incantations ran through her brain. There were a number of them, some more effective than others, some more permanent, some more dangerous. And a few that would have her severely punished by the Tribunal as well as in standard courts.

"You have ideas." EJ's eyes glinted with anticipation.

"What can we do to help?" Ruth asked.

The others stared at Callie, their anticipation clear. The Roses had each other's backs, and they owed it to Janie.

In all their years together, not once had any of them asked Callie to use her magic for anything. Not in a serious way at least. Because they understood how difficult and how dangerous it could be if something went awry. But now they needed her, and she was willing to do what was necessary to stop Underwood from hurting anyone else. To get back at him.

"I'll research an appropriate spell," Callie said. The women hung on her words, so focused on her she was surprised her voice wasn't shaking. This was important, perhaps the biggest thing she'd ever do. "All spells that target a person require a personal item from the subject. The more personal and long used, the better."

"Like a comb or a toothbrush?" Bette suggested.

Callie nodded. "Yes, exactly. Something he's touched intimately and often if possible."

"He might miss something *that* personal." EJ smirked and made a rude gesture of her fist pumping near her crotch.

Callie couldn't help but grin. "Very funny. But if that's our option, I'm out."

The others laughed. It felt good to be with them again, even under these circumstances. Their connection had been so strong for so long, they had been closer than some families. Hell, for some the Roses were the only family life they'd enjoyed. Callie hadn't fully realized how much she'd missed them all until that moment. A lump of emotion rose in her throat.

EJ watched her from the other side of the cocktail table, her features going from mirth to concern. As Callie got herself under control, EJ relaxed.

"What else do you need?" she asked soberly.

"I'm not sure yet. I'll get a list together. Nothing terribly unusual, I don't think. It's having the right spell and the right conditions that will matter most of all."

The leader of the Roses nodded. "All right then. How do we get something of Underwood's?"

"Something that intimate," Marian reminded them. "It's not like he'll invite one of us to dinner so we can swipe his fork."

There was silence for a few moments, and then EJ perked up. "Their anniversary is coming up. Big shindig. Kay Underwood's been all over town blathering about it."

"Ma used to clean house for them." Bette rolled her eyes. "Our invitation musta gotten lost in the mail."

Ruth snorted a laugh.

"Mine too, seeing as he's inviting a bunch of business pals," EJ quipped. "They're having it catered. And caterers need servers."

"One of us goes in, serves a few canapes and ginger ales, pops up into his bathroom, and grabs his toothbrush." Ruth dusted her hands together. "Easy peasy."

"I'll find out who's catering the party and get them to hire you on," EJ said.

Ruth's mouth dropped open. "Me? The overly tall Chinese girl? I stand out like a sore thumb."

"I'll do it," Bette said. "It's more along the line of my hobbies anyways."

Another round of chuckles and smiles. Bette's "sticky fingers" had benefited them often as kids. It was little surprise she'd kept her skills honed into adulthood.

"I think we have ourselves a plan." Leaning forward, EJ raised her coffee cup, and they all touched their cups and glasses together.

After another hour of catching up, Marian, Bette, and Ruth gathered their things. Marian had to get dinner on the table for her family, and Bette and Ruth needed to check on their parents. Callie also started to get ready to leave, but moved slowly as if distracted.

EJ touched her lightly on the shoulder. "Stay a minute?"

She wanted to let her hand linger, but lowered it to her side.

Callie stared at her, questions clear in her blue eyes. "Um, sure."

They both bid good-bye to the other Roses, and EJ shut the door. She returned to Callie in the living room.

"What's up?" she asked.

EJ opened her mouth to say . . . something, but her mind blanked. She gestured for Callie to sit down, giving herself a little more time to gather her thoughts. EJ sat on the edge of the chair she'd previously occupied, leaning forward with elbows on knees and hands clasped.

"I just wanted to thank you for agreeing to do this. I know it's a risk, in a lot of ways. I'm going to do everything possible to keep you safe before, during, and after."

Color rose on Callie's cheeks. "I-Thanks. I appreciate that."

"Anything you need you let me know and we'll get it."

Callie nodded and looked down at the table.

Was she reconsidering?

"What is it, Callie?"

She brought her gaze back up to EJ, her eyes wide and full of worry. "I've never done anything like this before. Nothing this involved. I want to help you, to get back at Underwood for Janie, but . . . I'm a little nervous. What if something goes wrong?"

Callie had seemed sure of herself while the Roses were gathered, laying out what would be needed, even if she had to temper it with reminders that magic could be iffy. Admitting she had worries revealed a trust she had in EJ that EJ hadn't expected. It was a trust she appreciated and knew she had to return.

As leader of the Roses and boss of the Y-J, it was EJ's responsibility to take care of her own. As someone who wanted Callie Payne to know she was more than just a means to an end, keeping her safe and happy was of utmost concern.

EJ got up and sat beside Callie on the loveseat. She put her hand on Callie's knee, ignoring how nice it felt to be close to the other woman, and concentrated on making her feel better. "You'll do great. We're all with you. Take what time you need to get ready."

But hopefully not too much time, she thought. If Underwood wasn't stopped soon, there was a greater chance of him escalating, especially after the other night. Enough people had been hurt or killed; enough profit had been lost. She wasn't one to start trouble these days, but she'd sure as hell see it finished.

Callie covered EJ's hand with hers, sending tingles dancing across EJ's skin. "I don't want to involve Gran in this, but I'm going to need to tell her something. She can't be part of it otherwise." She turned her head, her mouth a scant couple of inches from EJ's. EJ bit down on the inside of her cheek to keep from leaning forward. "Will you help me keep her safe?"

"Of course. Like I said, whatever you need."

Growing up, EJ knew Callie's Gran hadn't cared for her much, and with good reason. She'd gotten Callie more than a few scoldings by keeping her out late or just skirting serious trouble. But EJ appreciated the older woman for her dedication to her family, and the concern she had for the Roses when she learned of rough patches some were going through. Like Gran's quiet help with EJ's home life that even Callie didn't know about. Having the older woman step in with food and personal items had been both embarrassing and met with great relief for young EJ.

"While we do this, I want Gran out of town. I'd like her to go visit her sister in Portland. Can you help me with that? I-I don't have the money."

The color on her face deepened. Embarrassment this time, EJ surmised.

She squeezed Callie's knee. "Leave that to me. Tell me when, and I'll get Gran a first-class train ticket. Count on it."

Callie smiled and EJ's heart skipped. "Thanks, EJ. I wouldn't ask if it wasn't important."

"I know you wouldn't. I don't trust Underwood to leave anyone alone. He has never been one to keep business as business, the rotten bastard. Better that Gran is safely away from here."

She nodded, then parted her lips as if to speak but didn't say anything for a few heart beats. EJ imagined kissing those lips. What would she taste like? Sweetened coffee and shortbread? Jesus, all she had to do was lean forward ...

Something made Callie startle and she rose. "I should get home."

EJ got to her feet as well. Had their connection through Callie's magic given away her thoughts? Shit. She needed to stop those sorts of ideas before they got started anyway. It wasn't good for anyone she cared about that she consider such things. At least not until Underwood and his tendency to go after others was put to rest. "Mason should be downstairs soon. He's taking the others home."

They headed to the foyer. EJ retrieved Callie's hat and coat;

then they walked down the three flights of stairs. The street was empty, the air chilly. While they waited for Mason, EJ made a point not to talk "business" or let her thoughts wander onto Callie herself. But what was a safe topic? What do you think of the Marx Brothers? How about them Yankees? Certainly not the next thing that popped into EJ's head: Why did you marry Nate?

That would go over like a fingernail in pudding.

"Do you remember that paper you had us sign?" Callie suddenly asked. "You, me, Janie, Marian, Ruth, Bette."

EJ's mind went blank for a moment before it came to her. The oath she'd come up with when they were barely teens. "Oh, yeah. I'd read it in some book, about signing your name in blood to make a promise of loyalty. But I didn't think you and the others would go for that."

Callie shook her head, smiling. "No. Especially not Bette. She was always a little squeamish. You let us sign with a pen because it was more permanent than pencil and only made us dab a dot of blood after our names."

"A silly thing," EJ said, waving off her childish actions. "I think one of the lines in the story was 'blood is thicker than water,' but I learned that meant something about your family, so it was wrong anyway."

Callie's smile softened to something else. Something wistful and nostalgic. "Actually, you were right. The actual quote is 'blood of the covenant is thicker than the water of the womb.' Meaning, the bonds we make with those we *choose* to be with are stronger than who we are related to by dumb luck."

EJ thought about the decades of her relationship with the Roses versus her old man, of the new connection she had with Callie through her magical healing, and of their shared desires to fix what had happened ages ago as well as more recent troubles.

"I had been worried that leaving here had broken those bonds," Callie said quietly. "That I'd lost you and the others.

But this afternoon made me think that the blood oath remains, doesn't it, no matter how many years have passed?"

"It does." EJ's voice was equally subdued. "Did—did we perform some sort of magic that day?"

She was a blood mage, after all, even if she hadn't started practicing at that point.

Callie shook her head. "No, not in the sense you're thinking, EJ. The power was in our care and our promise to be there for each other."

Her expression flickered, showing a hint of apprehension. She had thought she'd gone back on that promise by leaving.

EJ reached out and took her hand, gently squeezing her fingers. "The paper is long gone, but the blood remains, Cal."

Her blue eyes held EJ's as she squeezed back. "I suppose it does. I—"

Mason pulled up, tapping the horn, interrupting whatever she was going to say. With the engine running, he got out and came around to open the passenger door for Callie.

Callie waved at him, then turned to EJ. "I'm glad we've been able to get back together. I-I mean all of us."

EJ grinned. "Once a Rose, always a Rose." The returned smile sent shivers through EJ. "We should go to the movies sometime. Something fun, like a Marx Brothers film. After all this, that is."

Callie stared at her for a moment, then she smiled that sweet smile that made EJ's knees wobble. "Yeah, I'd like that. Good night, EJ. I'll let you know what I need as soon as I can."

"Good night, Cal."

Callie descended the stairs, and as she lowered herself onto the passenger seat, waved at EJ.

EJ waved back, grinning like a fool. She caught Mason's eye after he shut the door and made his way to the driver's side. His smirk and arched eyebrow told her he could read her like one of his well-worn detective novels. She waved him off and went back inside, cheeks aching all the way to her apartment.

CHAPTER FIVE

Callie let herself into the apartment just as Gran took the roast chicken out of the pan and set it on the wood cutting board atop the counter. The aroma of meat and vegetables should have made Callie's stomach growl in appreciation, but instead her gut tightened.

"Just in time," Gran said. "How was your visit?"

Callie shut the door and hung up her hat and coat. She toed off her heels. "Good. The girls say hello."

Ladling vegetables onto a platter, Gran shook her head. "I used to think they were a bad influence on you. Especially Eileen."

A flicker of wariness went through Callie. EJ had been a delinquent back in the day, no doubt about it, but she had always been honest and loyal to Callie and the Roses. Gran knew that; it had been Callie's defense of her friend for ages. "And now?"

Gran carved the chicken as she spoke. "Now, I can't say I agree with all the things Eileen Jordan does, but she and the others are doing their best. Considering what she's up against, I suppose I can forgive some . . . indiscretions."

Callie wondered if Gran actually knew what EJ's business dealings were like. She sat at the kitchen table, at one of the places not set for dinner. What did Gran know about the happenings with EJ and Underwood? And why hadn't she spoken to Callie about it?

"You know what's been going on?"

Gran shrugged and brought the platter of food to the table. "I hear things. Are you eating?"

She didn't want to insult Gran, but Callie's stomach wasn't up to it. "Sorry, no. Why didn't you tell me?"

Gran retrieved the vegetables and set them down. She took her seat, opened her napkin on her lap, and filled her water glass. Just because she was the only one eating didn't mean she would skimp on dinner formalities.

"Figured you'd catch wind of it sooner or later. Was that why you were with Eileen and the Roses? Talking about what to do?"

"Yes." The knot in Callie's gut tightened. "I need to find the right spell. I'll have to talk to Jemma."

Her mentor had been part teacher and part aunt for several years while she taught Callie about spells, the Covenant, and ways not to accidentally hurt herself or others. Gran had taught her quite a bit, but she didn't have near the power of the fire mage. Callie had needed someone who understood her magic better.

Gran filled her plate. "Good. What can I help with?"

This next part would not go over well. "I need you to go visit Aunt Vivian for a couple of weeks."

The fork in Gran's hand stopped halfway to her mouth. She narrowed her eyes. "What, now?"

Callie swallowed hard. "What we need to do might be dangerous. I want you somewhere safe."

Gran sighed and set the fork down. She laced her fingers together, her sharp gaze penetrating Callie. "What do you plan on doing, Calliope Anne?"

Adult Callie felt the same twinge of dread Child Callie had at the use of her full name. But she was an adult now, and keeping Gran safe was more important than facing her wrath.

"I don't think it matters what we do. If Paul Underwood finds out I'm helping EJ in any way, shape, or form, he'll come after me. That means you'd be in danger too. I can't let that happen, Gran."

Gran's fingers tightened around each other, the knuckles turning white. "Paul Underwood is a pissant coward who thinks fear and intimidation will get him the respect he desperately and pathetically wants. I'm not afraid of him."

"I am," Callie admitted. "Please, Gran. I have to do this, and I'm nervous enough as it is. If I have to worry about you as well, I'm afraid I'll mess it up."

As a witch, Gran would understand how critical concentration was for a spell.

As a protective grandmother and a woman unafraid of anyone like Underwood, she'd want to stay close.

Callie hoped the former would win out.

The pride and annoyance left Gran's face, replaced by resignation. "When?"

"We want to start within the week. Once I find the right spell, I'll need to get a list of items and ingredients together."

Gran nodded and picked up her fork. "I'll help you prepare where I can. I can wire Vivian tomorrow."

Relived and suddenly exhausted, Callie got to her feet. She came around the table and hugged Gran from behind, kissing her wrinkled cheek. "Thank you. I think I'll just go to my room."

Gran grasped her hand, prompting Callie to meet her gaze. "I understand why you're doing this, Callie, but you have to be careful. Underwood is a weasel, but weasels are dangerous when cornered."

Callie squeezed her hand. "I'll be careful."

She went down the hall to her room, closing the door behind her.

The room hadn't changed much since she'd left it more than ten years ago. Some of her childhood things had been kept out, like the rag doll posed on the bookshelf, and a music box that had been her mother's. The narrow single bed had the same white sheets and thick daisy motif quilt. The linens were a little worn, but they were soft and familiar.

Callie unbuttoned her dress as she walked to the closet, realizing a headache had started behind her left eye. Ignoring it as best she could, she pulled her dress off and hung it up. Her slip and brassiere followed, tossed into the basket on the floor. Chilled, but enjoying the cool air on her bare skin, she pulled her nightgown from under her pillow and put it on. She sat on the edge of her bed and carefully rolled her stockings off. They were one of her few pairs without runs. She'd hand wash them later.

Kneeling on the hardwood floor, Callie reached under the bed for a sturdy wooden box. She sat with her back against the bed frame, legs crossed, and set the box in her lap. It was heavier than it appeared. The chestnut brown varnish had been worn off around the corners, revealing the yellowish beige of the wood. She pressed her thumb to the gold filigree medallion on the front. There was a small sound as a tiny needle jabbed her finger then retreated. She was surprised she hadn't jumped, though the prick stung a little. Callie put her thumb in her mouth to soothe the slight injury while she waited for the box to recognize her. The salty metallic taste of blood perked her up.

Within a few seconds another soft click sounded. She lifted the lid.

Inside, the black leather-bound book filled most of the space. The box had been constructed solely for it, as Callie understood to be the case. There was no title or name on the cover, though there were signs of many hands having used it. The leather was gray and soft in places, the spine creased and supple with age. The book had belonged to Callie's mother, and her mother before, passed to the oldest child for generations. Each man and woman had used the book even as they attempted to assimilate into "standard" society. The laws of the country and of the Covenant required anyone with ability to be registered and recognized, even if they didn't seek or find formal training. Most adhered to that requirement, just as most refrained from using their magic to harm.

Callie lifted the book out of the box. A fraying, blue silk ribbon marked a page. She set the box on the floor. With the book in her lap, she drew her fingertips over the cover. She had taken it with her to Nate's family ranch outside of Spokane, but hadn't opened the box until after he'd died. She'd tried to be "normal" for Nate's sake, so his folks wouldn't look at her with suspicion or worry or fear. Fat lot of good being "normal" had done for her there.

Now here she was, back where she'd started. But at least she felt more like herself.

Callie opened the cover. The first leaf was a long list of family members, mostly women who, like herself, had sworn to never use their magic to harm another. Well, not directly. That she wished to have all the terrible things happen to Paul Underwood for how he'd treated Janie was another matter. Wishes weren't admissible in standard court or at a Tribunal. At least as long as any magic she enacted didn't reflect them. Intent of the spell held more weight than feelings between mage and subject. The trick would be to keep those thoughts out of her magic. If there was no proof she actively wished harm to come to Underwood, she'd likely be cleared if it came to that.

She ran her finger down the familiar names, wondering if her distant relatives had ever faced such dilemmas. Probably. They were only human, after all, with human emotions and foibles, human needs for justice and fairness.

She stopped at her own name, the last on the list. Calliope Anne Payne. She hadn't entered her married name, nor had any of the women before her, though she knew most of them had been married and went by their husbands' names in public. A few she knew to be mother and daughter had the same last name, suggesting there was no father figure deemed necessary or worthy to bestow his name on the child.

A pang of sadness twinged in Callie's chest. Her parents had loved each other, had loved her, and her father had been honored, he'd said, to have Callie share his name. God, she missed them so much. She would have loved to consult with her mother about the spell, about life. And to chat with Dad as they worked in the shop or listened to the radio.

Wiping at moisture forming near the corner of her eye, Callie flipped through the thin pages of the book. Surely there was something in here that could help. Spells were often shared, with each mage or witch or whatever moniker the person used modifying a basic incantation depending on their elemental affinity. Components such as herbs or other physical items were fairly standard. Notations in the margins added helpful hints, though sometimes there were jottings of frowning faces or multiple exclamation points left for the reader to interpret.

There were numerous spells for urging fortune, love, and health. Those were the staples of safe and acceptable magic consultation. There were also minor hexes that invoked annoyance more than any sort of damaging or permanent harm. She'd used a few in her youth to help the Roses or her family. A pinprick of blood worked well enough for small, off the cuff spells that hadn't been studied and so ingrained as to be considered "mental" magic, such as minor telekinesis or unlocking. Those didn't require a mage's element and utilized no more energy than a brisk walk.

But nothing more significant quite fit what EJ wanted her to do to Underwood.

Unless a modified reversal could be performed.

Reversal of fortune. Though not magic-induced, that had caused more than a few to take their own lives a few years ago. The Covenant wouldn't look kindly upon the use of such a spell.

Reversal of love. Even if she could pinpoint anyone

Underwood actually loved, similar results could occur.

Reversal of health.

That last one sent an ominous shiver through Callie. Definitely needed to stay away from that. There had to be something useful. She would consult with Jemma, though the fewer who knew what she was doing, the better. Claiming ignorance of Callie's intentions would go a long way in any court, if it ever came to that. She'd do her best to protect Gran and Jemma and the Roses, if it came down to such a situation.

Callie skimmed a few more pages. Just as she was about to set the book aside, to give her eyes and brain a break, a word practically jumped off the page at her. Rebuff. That was it. The idea was to influence Underwood's desire for EJ's property and business. He needed to be rebuffed in the way an unwanted suitor needed to be turned aside. It would cause no physical harm to Underwood. She read through the spell, formally known as Standler's Lament, twice, slowly, carefully.

This might work.

The list of spell components wasn't terribly outlandish, though getting poke root this time of year might be tricky. Surely someone in the Seattle area had it. Malmo's Nursery, perhaps, or maybe the plant-loving earth mage who worked on The Garden would have some if not all of the components.

She'd speak with Jemma, for sure.

Callie placed the blue ribbon between the appropriate pages and closed the book. Her limbs were heavy with relief. They'd be able to deter Underwood without going against the Covenant. She couldn't wait to tell EJ.

EJ sat at her desk, a cup of strong coffee at her elbow and a ledger book opened flat before her. Things were nice and quiet at The Garden, it being Wednesday morning. The club was closed, but the books needed balancing and bills needed to be paid. The weekend receipts were secure in the wall safe behind her. After lunch she'd head to the bank and make a deposit. One of the keys to being successful in not-so-legitimate enterprises was carrying out legitimate ones. Unfortunately, legit ones didn't always do that great.

Everything in the ledger looked good, arithmetically speaking anyway. That the club was barely breaking even made EJ's gut churn. She'd started The Garden with money gained from her numbers games and gambling operations, but she needed it to be on the up-and-up in order to cover her ass with the state and feds. Plus, it was her baby, her flagship, her stamp on the neighborhood. If it went down because of Underwood's shit, she could lose her hold on her other businesses as well as her reputation.

And then what? Become some other boss's lackey? Go back to the petty thefts of her youth? Living hand to mouth in a shithole apartment, or in the basement of some building hoping not to be attacked?

No fucking way. Never again.

EJ slammed the ledger closed and got to her feet. She was pacing behind the desk, anxious to release some energy, when someone knocked on the door.

"What?" she snapped out, stopping in her tracks, hands fisted.

The door opened and Callie poked her head around the edge. "This a bad time?"

The anxiety drained from EJ like a plug had been pulled in a filled tub. Seeing Callie was a balm, a soothing caress across her heated spirit. She smiled. "Not at all. Come in. Sit. Want some coffee?"

Callie came in, her coat draped over one arm and still wearing her hat. The subtle flower-patterned dress she wore was buttoned to her throat. Thick stockings covered her shapely legs, and her low heels were more practical than pretty. Jesus, she was gorgeous.

"Mason let me in. I hope that's okay." Callie shut the door behind her.

EJ busied herself at the desk, retrieving a dusty cup from a drawer rather than staring at Callie. "Of course it is. Any time you want to see me is fine."

She wiped the dust out of the cup with her unused handkerchief, poured from the pot, and added a little milk and sugar, just the way Callie liked it. She gestured toward the chaise.

Callie accepted the cup and sat on the edge of the seat, knees together, ankles crossed and slightly angled to the side. "Thank you."

EJ leaned her backside on the edge of the desk. "What's up?"

Callie sipped her coffee and smiled. "I found a spell I think will work."

Anticipation sent EJ's heart racing. "You did? What do you need? When can we start? Whatever you want me to do, Callie, I'll do it."

The other woman gave a little laugh. "I do have to find some poke root, among other things, and was hoping I could contact the mage who keeps your plants thriving downstairs."

EJ nodded. "Sure. I have Ruth's cousin Henry taking care of the front for me. I'll ask her to contact him."

"Good. Dried would work, but fresh is much better for some things. The better the quality, the more powerful the spell. In theory."

There was still something going on with her.

"We'll get the best money can buy. Anything else?" EJ tilted her head. "You okay?"

Callie laughed again, but this time the nervousness was evident. "Yeah, I'm good. Just want to do this right. I need to talk to Jemma. I promise not to tell her any more than necessary."

EJ had met Jemma McAndrews when Callie started taking

her magic seriously, which made sense as a blood mage. From what little EJ understood, having that particular affinity was nothing to be cavalier about. The older woman was strict and had required almost daily lessons for Callie.

"If talking to her will help, then sure," EJ said. "I appreciate the discretion. If Underwood gets wind of what we're doing, he'll either go on the offensive or flee. At least for a short time."

"Right. He needs to stay in town," Callie said. She sipped more coffee. "My range isn't that great."

"We'll make sure he stays put." EJ made a mental note to put a few more eyes and ears on Underwood where she could. "What else can I do to help?"

Before Callie could answer, another knock on her door took EJ's attention away from her friend. She strode to the door and opened it. Bette stood in the hall, wearing her hat and coat and out of breath, as if she'd run up the stairs. Had EJ been so distracted by Callie she hadn't heard Bette's approach? That was a bit disconcerting. She needed to stay on her toes.

"We have a problem," Bette said, slipping past EJ. She gave a quick hello to Callie and stood in the middle of the room.

Shit.

EJ shut the door. "What's wrong?"

"Mom and I went out for breakfast this morning. It's her birthday and I wanted to treat her to something special before she left for her shift. Took her to that new café on James Street." Bette's hands curled into fists. "We ran into Kay Underwood."

Double shit.

"She knew Mom, of course, from when she used to clean for the Underwoods. And she remembered me as a kid. I don't think it would be smart of me to go to their place the night of the party, EJ. I'm sorry."

If Kay Underwood saw Bette there, she could become suspicious. Curious at the very least. And odds were good Kay would mention it to Paul. If Paul Underwood was anything like

EJ, he wouldn't believe it was an innocent coincidence. Or take that chance anyway.

"Fuck." EJ crossed the room and threw herself into her chair behind the desk.

"I'm sorry," Bette repeated, sinking down beside Callie. "It was just one of those things."

EJ leaned forward, elbow on her desk as she rubbed her forehead. "Not your fault, Bette."

"You couldn't have known she'd be there," Callie said, her hand on Bette's shoulder.

Always the soother, Callie was. That's why most of the Roses saw her as a sister, someone they could go to when troubled. Hell, wasn't that partially why EJ had gone to her? She knew Callie would want to help, especially if it meant getting back at Underwood for what he did to Janie.

"So what do we do?" Bette asked.

"Can Ruth or Marian go?" Callie wondered.

EJ shook her head. "Ruth made a good point yesterday. She is too recognizable. And Marian has family coming for dinner."

That left one option.

EJ quirked an eyebrow at Callie.

Callie sighed. "Damn."

"You're the only one left I'd trust here, Cal," EJ said. "I know you're doing a lot, but . . ."

Callie pinched the bridge of her nose between her fingers and winced a little, as if a headache was coming on. "Yeah, I get it."

"We can get you a wig so there's less of a chance the Underwoods would recognize you," Bette offered. "Maybe some makeup to have you look older or—"

"Let's not make a production of this," EJ said. Bette was a big fan of the movies. She and Ruth could chat for hours about the latest film to come out or celebrity gossip. "Just get her set up with the caterers and get it done."

"Right." Bette stood. "I'll bring you the uniform and the name of who you need to contact."

"Thanks," Callie said, her hint of sarcasm making EJ grin despite the wrinkle in the plan.

Bette headed to the door. "I better skedaddle. See you later."

She left the office, and EJ heard her high heels patter all the way down the stairs.

EJ and Callie's gazes met.

"This isn't my thing, EJ."

"You nabbed the occasional piece of candy, as I recall."

The reminder of childhood escapades garnered a smile from Callie. "Yeah, but you or one of the others were always there to distract the owner or keep lookout."

EJ rose and went to sit beside Callie. She put her arm around her. "You'll do fine," she said. "I have faith in you."

"Glad someone does."

Jemma McAndrews opened the door to her fifth-floor apartment and Callie was immediately hit with the combined aromas of at least six different scents. Patchouli, rosemary, basil, cinnamon, pepper, sage, and others she couldn't suss out made her nose twitch. Jemma smiled and spread her arms wide for a hug. As Callie embraced her, a familiar feeling of warmth and strength enveloped her.

"Come in, come in," Jemma said, stepping aside and waving her in, stacked silver bangles on her wrist giving off a soft ringing. Her turquoise lounging pajamas accented her tall, slender body. The blond hair of her youth—however long ago that was—had turned snowy white. The fashionable bob should have seemed wrong for such a woman, but it fit Jemma just fine.

Callie crossed the threshold, unbuttoning her coat. The apartment took up half of the top floor of the building. The other half was occupied by an old man who was rarely seen, though over the years strains of operatic music could be heard, and the delectable aromas of cooking came through the gap beneath his door. Jemma closed the door, then took Callie's coat and hat to hang in the closet.

"Come sit down. I've made tea."

"I'm always up for your tea." Callie followed her mentor into the living room.

The furniture was older, but sturdy and comfortable. Every horizontal surface held a statue or vase or framed photograph. The walls were covered in art pieces from around the world. The subject matter was all the same: animals, from domestic to fantastic. Cats, dogs, bears, ravens, dragons, griffins, and everything in between. Jemma was a fire mage with a deep love for animals yet she kept none. Over the years, there had been birds, cats, and dogs that came to her, but she allowed them to move about as they wished. Some stayed longer than others, always by choice.

On the low table before the sofa, a tea set of white with blue birds along the rims sat on a tray. A plate of shortbread cookies was nearby. Callie took a seat.

Jemma settled beside her, dark eyes sparkling. "I was hoping you'd come see me."

Callie tilted her head. "We've seen each other regularly since I came back."

The older woman looked amused. "Yes, but there's something specific on your mind."

It wasn't a question. Callie should have known that Jemma would know there was a reason behind her visit.

"I've known you almost all your life," Jemma said. She picked up the teapot and poured out two cups, then offered Callie the plate of cookies. "I can tell when you're on edge."

Callie took one of the still-warm disks off the top of the pile and set it on her saucer. "I do have something to ask you."

Jemma added sugar to her tea and stirred. The small spoon made delicate tinkling sounds against the china. She sat back and crossed her ankles, saucer on her knee. She lifted her teacup and sipped, watching Callie over the rim with bright anticipation in her eyes.

"I've been asked to enact a spell and I need some advice."

"You've already decided to proceed."

Callie nodded. "It's . . . important. The spell that I'm thinking will work is fairly straight forward, though I could use some assurance that I chose the correct one."

The other woman waited for her to continue. She knew there was more.

Callie took a fortifying breath. "I want to do this for all the right reasons, but also for some not so right ones."

Jemma set the teacup on the saucer, her eyes never leaving Callie. "Are you intending to hurt someone?"

The first tenet of the Covenant: do no harm.

"Not physically." Despite how much she wanted to punch Paul Underwood in the face repeatedly to pay for what he did, she wouldn't mete out that particular punishment.

Jemma cocked a plucked eyebrow at her.

"It's intended to keep him from pursuing a path in business. He may suffer some financial difficulties, but nothing specifically targeted to ruin him."

Though EJ would love for her to do it, Callie couldn't pull that one off without considerable power, which she didn't have.

"What do you have in mind?" Jemma asked.

Callie shifted on her seat. She hadn't reached the level of relief or assurance she needed from her mentor. Could she get it without telling Jemma everything? She'd promised EJ to avoid specifics, and while she'd never lie to Jemma, she couldn't bring herself to lay it all out yet. Explanation and justification would have to suffice for now.

"A dissuasion spell. Something akin to what you'd cast to

turn away an unwanted suitor."

Jemma's brow furrowed. "Standler's Lament?"

"Yes. It was the closest one I could find in my spell book for what's necessary."

"That's a good one, though I think there may be something better." Jemma drained her teacup and set it on the table with her saucer. "Let's look."

She rose and strutted toward the back of the apartment. Callie hurried to keep up. She hadn't been in Jemma's incantation room in ages.

They passed Jemma's bedroom as well as a guest room and a bathroom, the plush carpet muting their footsteps. Outside of a plain-looking door—the only closed one along the long hall—Jemma toed her shoes off. Callie did the same. Then Jemma laid her palm flat on the surface, closed her eyes, and tilted her head slightly. She murmured several words that Callie felt more than heard. Nothing obvious occurred, but Jemma opened her eyes and reached for the cut glass knob.

Inside, the room was dim and windowless. Light from the hall allowed Callie to see the cupboards along the walls and the hint of a protective circle etched into the hardwood floor. Spaced around the periphery, several small braziers glowing with banked coals flared to dancing orange life when Jemma entered.

Callie knew the symbols and words on the floor as if they were part of her, because they were. She had assisted Jemma with renewing the protection spells each solstice she had been in town. The next casting would come in a couple of months.

Jemma waved a hand and two electric wall sconces were turned on. Such a feat looked impressive, making one think Jemma had control over electricity, but in reality she merely flipped the switch on the wall. Telekinesis was a minor mental trick for most mages, Callie included. Anything more involved would require concentration and tapping into your particular affinity. Complex incantations, like the one Callie was going to do for EJ, would need those plus time and components.

"Set up the podium, if you would, dear," Jemma instructed.

Callie was already on her way to the corner where the elaborately carved wooden structure resided when not in use. Calling up a little magical assistance that made her skin goose-pimple as if chilled, she shifted each side of the solid piece in an alternating motion to "walk" it closer to the center of the room. She didn't need to place it within the protective circle as they weren't going to enact a spell. It was merely easier to read her book if it was on the stand and in better light.

Jemma knelt before a trunk. As with the door, she rested her palm on the smooth wood top and closed her eyes. This time Callie saw a distinctive shimmer of magic. A stronger spell protected the contents of the trunk than the one that secured the room, and with good reason. Sure, there were special items in the room, but a personal spell book in the hands of the wrong person could be dangerous.

Jemma opened the lid and withdrew a heavy, white silk-wrapped bundle, which she rested on her lap. Murmuring words that were part request, part assurance, and part identification, she revealed the contents as she loosened each looping layer. The leather-bound spell book reminded Callie of the huge dictionary at the public library, the one that was always on display upon a stand in the reference room.

With an audible "Umf," Jemma rose, cradling the book in her arms. She walked to the podium and set the tome down.

"Let's see what we can come up with." Jemma skimmed the thick pages of flowing script, carefully folding over each leaf.

Callie stood beside her, reading along. She was aware of a number of the spells in Jemma's book, had enacted a few of them, but there were plenty she'd never learned. There were also ingredients listed that she had never heard of. What was powdered dragon tail?

"Ah." Jemma had stopped at a page with dense paragraphs

of instruction. "I think this one will work better than Standler's."

She stepped aside to let Callie read. "Repel. Simple title."

"Simple is often the best way to approach things. This one isn't, particularly. It uses some of the same herbal components as Standler's, but also requires several days of repeated invocation and the assistance of others to create a stronger energy."

The Roses.

"I have people."

Jemma drew a well-manicured finger down the page. "Affinity matters in this spell. As a blood mage, you'll be powerful enough to sufficiently complete it and have it hold."

That was reassuring. Still, Callie's cheeks warmed, and not from being too close to the brazier. Being a blood mage wasn't a choice of course. Affinity not only affected a spell's strength and duration, but the power and limitations of the mage themself.

Where blood mages generally had strong magic, they were inherently prone to greater and greater reliance on their element for the simplest of spells.

Fire mages were also strong, but their element wasn't always easy to contain. Though she had a gorgeous silver and gold Zippo on hand when she went out, Jemma did most of her incantations in this room with her braziers to avoid unintentionally setting something ablaze.

Earth magic was more stable and durable, but effective spells were limited in number. Some spells an earth mage enacted were irreversible where another sort of mage's might be.

Water mages, like Gran, had trouble with predictability so they tended to keep things simple.

Air mages were provided with a virtually unlimited supply of their element, but the magic itself wasn't particularly durable. Fleeting but impactful was how Ruth described it.

Jemma made a hum of consideration and pointed to a middle paragraph. "You'll need something of personal use, of course. Can you get that?"

"I already figured as much. We have a plan." Callie skimmed further down. "'Refrain from alcohol and sexual congress for the duration of the spell.' Well, that should be easy enough."

Jemma patted her shoulder in sympathetic understanding. She went over to the cupboard and opened it. After riffling around for a moment, she returned to Callie with a fountain pen and thick paper. "Copy the spell and notes word for word. Don't leave anything out, or who knows what might happen."

Callie took the implements from her, smiling. "I remember doing this when you first took me on. My hands were cramped for hours."

"Builds character," Jemma said. "When you're done, come back into the sitting room. You'll want to see Neil Pasternik for the herbs required. He's the best in the business. I have something I need returned to him anyway. You can bring it with you."

She'd never met Pasternik, though word was he tended to be as prickly as some of his offerings.

When she returned home, Callie would transcribe the spell into her own book, assuring its power and protection. For now, she got to work.

CHAPTER SIX

Callie carried the tray of hors d'oeuvres from the kitchen of the Underwoods' Renton Hill apartment to the living room, pausing by the small groups and pairs of guests as they chatted. The jazz music on the phonograph was loud and scratchy, competing with the growing volume of the guests as they drank.

The fake glasses and mousy brown wig she'd borrowed from Bette weren't the best disguise, especially upon close scrutiny, but it helped her blend into the background and be ignored. People took the sausage rolls and skewered pickles and cheese off her tray with barely a glance at her. She deliberately kept her back to Paul and Kay Underwood as much as humanly possible. For a few extra dollars the other server agreed to keep herself in their view.

As she made her way around the room, heart pounding, Callie kept an eye out for anyone she might recognize. A few of the women were members of committees and charity groups who got their pictures in the papers now and again. The men ran businesses that Paul Underwood probably had some sort of interest in, or vice versa. These sorts of parties tended to be a display of who mattered to the hosts, not necessarily who they cared about.

Thomas Greer stood by the makeshift bar, swirling his

martini, and ogling the front of a woman's snug pink dress as he spoke to her. The woman was turned away from Callie, so she couldn't tell if the staring was noticed or appreciated or irksome. Her jutted hip and the waving of the cigarette in her hand as she spoke were vaguely familiar, but probably because Callie had seen a thousand women like her in real life or on the silver screen.

Greer was a muckety-muck lawyer, complete with slicked-back hair and overpriced shiny shoes. He glanced at Callie, but showed no sign of recognition. Not surprising. Heck, she could have ditched the glasses and wig and he still wouldn't know her. It wasn't as if they ran in the same circles. Callie only knew him because Greer made sure *everyone* knew who he was: Underwood's lawyer.

Since the Underwoods had moved out of the heart of the Y-J, their social circle had changed, thankfully. She'd seen some of the others around, but they were of her parents' generation and hadn't socialized with Callie and her friends. Far from it. Having been gone for over ten years and wearing her disguise kept any of them from associating the scurrying server with Callie Payne, blood mage.

Callie circulated through the rooms with the anonymity of a servant, getting the layout of the apartment. Once she figured out where the Underwoods' bathroom was, and how people flowed into and out of the rooms, Callie would find a suitable time to switch out Paul's toothbrush for the one in her uniform pocket.

When the last sausage roll had been plucked from her tray, she turned as if going back to the kitchen where the staff from Alonzo's had set up. She'd already been through a few times, trading her empty tray for one filled with bite-sized delights. Normally, her stomach would have growled at the thought of the delicious food, but nerves outstripped hunger.

Instead of skirting the group in the living room and then

the smaller gathering in the dining room, Callie checked that no one was heading her way or watching as she ducked down the short hall that led to the bathroom and the bedrooms. Once inside the bathroom, she shut and locked the door and felt for the light switch. The overhead frosted globe revealed a well-kept, impersonal facility. A claw-foot tub sat against the back wall, a toilet beside it. A double sink and vanity dominated the room. All the white and chrome fixtures sparkled. Embroidered hand towels and fancy, molded, flowery-smelling soaps were laid out between the sinks. No slippery bar of Ivory in a dish for the Underwoods. The normal day-to-day items you'd expect to be at hand weren't cluttering the counter.

Listening for any commotion or trouble at the door, Callie opened one of the two mirrored medicine cabinets above the vanity. The top two shelves held a variety of tins and bottles of popular ointments and remedies. A small glass with a white toothbrush sat on the lowest of the three shelves beside a tube of Colgate. For a moment, Callie's heart leapt in anticipation of the deed to come. Then she saw the three tubes of lipstick and a bottle of ladies' tablets on the next shelf up. This side had to belong to Mrs. Underwood.

She gently closed the cabinet door and opened the other one.

Ah, this was more like it. A few jars and tubes of drug store products. Brylcreem and some sort of antifungal foot ointment. *Ew.* The same type of toothbrush sat in a glass, but there was no paste. They must share. Beside the glass was a safety razor, a small cardboard box of extra blades, and a shaving soap stick.

Callie wiped her damp hands on her upper thighs. She withdrew a new toothbrush from her pocket. She had wrapped it in a handkerchief and would wrap Paul's in the same handkerchief to keep it from getting contaminated by someone else's touch.

When she opened the white cotton, Callie's breath caught.

The toothbrushes weren't the same.

They were almost the same, but Paul's had a red stripe down the back of the handle while the new one had a blue stripe. And the bristles of the old brush were much more worn and splayed.

Damn damn damn.

There was no option but to switch them out and hope Paul didn't notice such things or would assume Kay had replaced his old brush.

Callie pressed the bristles of the new toothbrush against her leg and moved it back and forth, hoping to get close to the visual condition of the old one. Good enough. She dropped the new brush into the glass and picked up the old one with the handkerchief, stuffing it into her pocket. As she was about to shut the cabinet door, the razor and blades caught her eye.

Underwood was such a terrible person. Word of his meanness and arrogance, his strong-arm tactics against anyone who dared to defy him, had been known to Callie and the Roses since childhood. The things Janie implied he'd done only made them want to antagonize him that much more, but they knew Janie would face the brunt of it, so they'd kept quiet. They'd kept quiet, and then Janie had died.

Underwood deserved every unfortunate thing Callie could wish upon him. But that sort of retribution was out of the question.

What if she could just plague him with minor troubles?

Would that count?

Even if it did, it would be worth the punishment, worth whatever the universe would return to her three-fold.

Callie grabbed the box of new razor blades and worked one out of the package. She set it on the edge of the sink while she put the box back, then twisted the handle of Underwood's safety razor, opening the housing. The blade inside looked new, but she wasn't interested in that blade. She took up the one she'd pulled out and began a hex for things to not go quite as planned, for miscues and minor ill luck. Nothing fatal, just inconvenient.

As she spoke, she slit the tip of her finger just enough to allow a bead of blood to gather. Magic bubbled through her, a pleasant sensation that increased with the intensity and frequency of use. She had to be careful, like someone prone to too much drink. The desire could tip from pleasurable to dependency before she realized it. The more an incantation required from the mage, the higher the probability of falling off that edge.

Chanting the simple words under her breath, Callie smeared the drop on the inside of the razor housing and along the handle, nowhere near the edge that would touch Underwood, and just enough to carry the spell. The blood would rinse away, but the magic would be imbued within the instrument. Every shave Underwood attempted would not be as close as he wanted and would result in a nick or two, no matter how new the blade.

It was petty, a waste of her magic, yet admittedly satisfying.

Callie returned the razor to its proper place then dropped the blade she'd used through the narrow slit at the back of the cabinet, where it would join its aged and rusted brethren within the wall of the apartment building. The hex wasn't going to ruin Underwood or cause him great harm, but it would be annoying as hell, and that was fine too.

A vigorous knock on the door made her jump, closing the medicine cabinet with more force and louder sound than she'd wanted.

"You done in there?" a man called. "Some of us gotta go."

Shit.

She had hoped to be able to slip out as easily as she'd slipped in.

Callie wiped her damp hands down her hips and adjusted the fake glasses. Just as she reached for the knob, she heard a click within the lock mechanism. Someone had a key to the bathroom?

The door opened.

A younger version of Paul Underwood stood there, Brylcreemed brown hair flopping over his eyes, tie askew. Bert. Paul and Kay's son. Janie's cousin. Callie took an involuntary step back. So did Bert. He missed his jacket pocket in an attempt to put something shiny in it, then managed on the next try. The bleariness in his eyes and slight sway of his body indicated he was drunk, or close to it. Small favor there.

He squinted at her. "Don't I know you?"

"No." Callie ducked her head and slipped past him. "Sorry."

"Help don't use this bathroom," he called after her. "Go piss in the alley."

The closing bathroom door muted his cackling laughter.

Ass.

Bert had been an annoying kid, constantly bothering Janie and wanting to tag along when she was with the Roses. If he was rebuffed, and he always was, he'd find some way to bug her at home. Janie, who was nice to everyone, couldn't stand him. Aging hadn't made him any more mature or likeable.

Callie attempted to beeline toward the kitchen, but partiers stood in her way. It would be faster, but riskier, to go through the living room. Keeping her head down, she hurried through the crowd. The bark of Paul Underwood's laugh caught her attention. She glanced over to the group where he held court. Mostly men. Kay Underwood stood just behind his right shoulder. She smiled tightly. Then as she turned away from her husband and raised her glass to take a drink, her face contorted into a brief sneer.

Callie pushed open the kitchen door. She weaved her way past the caterers who were filling more trays, snatching her coat off the back of a chair as she passed. No one bothered her as she went out the back door and down the stairs. Alfonso's knew she was there for something other than serving. EJ had paid them to not ask questions and to let her go about her business. It worked out well for all involved.

Hurrying past the landings of the next three floors, Callie exited through the ground floor door that led to an alley. The stench of garbage and piss hit her full in the face. Even the more well-to-do couldn't completely escape the realities of city life.

She pushed the door shut behind her and did a quick walk to the end of the dark alley. Only the streetlight on the main road lit the narrow space between buildings. The sound of tires hissing on the pavement eventually became as loud as her pounding heart.

She'd done it.

Now came the hard part.

CHAPTER SEVEN

Callie got out of EJ's car and regarded the vine-covered cottage surrounded by lush green grass. Window boxes bloomed in colors she couldn't name. If you didn't know any better, and if it wasn't October, many would assume the occupant had been blessed with a green thumb. Callie knew there was more to the vines than met the eye.

The drive had taken about an hour along several small back roads. EJ had handled her car with ease and a few curses as she steered around potholes on the last stretch. They had filled the time with light conversation and debating the directions Jemma had given Callie. After a couple of wrong turns, she was confident they were in the right place.

EJ slammed the driver's side door and came around the front of the car. "I expected something larger."

Callie took in the humble, verdant home. The air seemed cleaner with a hint of the nearby sea, but mostly the aroma of damp earth and growing things surrounded them. Mountains blurred in the distance. "He's an earth mage who has a special talent for plants, not a captain of industry. Come on."

They walked up the slate path to the front of the house and climbed the three cement steps. Vines trailed over the lintel, curled around window frames, and disappeared over the roof.

Callie knocked on the door.

There was no sound of footsteps approaching from the other side of the door, no flutter of curtains.

"Maybe he isn't home," EJ said in a near whisper. There wasn't fear in her voice—Callie had never seen EJ afraid of anything. More like wariness. "Ruth's cousin will be happy to help."

Callie ignored the suggestion and knocked again, a little louder. From what she knew of Neal Pasternik, he was quite old and not particularly keen on people.

She raised her hand to knock a third time. The vines overhead quaked.

"Shit," EJ said under her breath. She took Callie's upper arm, ready to pull her away from the house.

Callie resisted her tug. "It'll be all right." She glanced at the vines twitching above them. Pasternik was more than just a plant mage. "It . . . It'll be fine."

EJ didn't understand magic or mages, despite her use of both for personal and business endeavors. In a way, the magic community wasn't so different from the criminal circles EJ ran in. Flinch and you're seen as weak, potentially ripe for exploitation by certain individuals.

EJ stopped pulling on her arm, but didn't let go. Callie had to admit that knowing the other woman was there intending to protect her made her feel good. Though she had an inkling EJ might require protection from the plant mage if she wasn't careful.

The door opened a crack, enough to reveal a thin swath of light, but little else. "What?"

The person behind the voice wasn't visible.

Callie cleared her throat. "Mr. Pasternik? I'm Calliope Payne, daughter of Sophie and David, student of Jemma McAndrews. I'm here on a mission of good faith, swearing no harm."

It was an old-fashioned introduction, but Jemma had said Mr. Pasternik was an old-fashioned sort of man. And a bit of a grump about uninvited visitors. Hopefully, he'd be more amenable to her request if she followed tradition. Stating she was not seeking to do any harm meant in her use of his magic and influence as well as to him personally. Should Callie prove otherwise, the Tribunal would come down on her with a vengeance.

After a few moments of consideration, the mage opened the door wider, revealing himself. He was a short, wiry man of indeterminant age, the lines on his brown face suggesting he could be anywhere between sixty and one hundred years old. His neatly combed white hair and a slightly rumpled suit with a red, black, gray, and white Argyle sweater gave him the look of a boys' school headmaster.

"Jemma McAndrews? She's your mistress?"

Another term that had fallen out of use in recent years.

"My mentor, yes, sir." Callie hoped the gentle correction wouldn't irk Pasternik.

The man eyed her; then his gaze went to EJ. "And you?"

Callie felt tension ripple through EJ, but she showed nothing. "A friend."

That was all she'd give, though Callie figured Pasternik wouldn't admit them on that alone.

"EJ Jordan," Callie said. Another flicker of tension from EJ. Having a mage know your name was an old superstition that held no merit but still produced wariness in some. "My friend and associate. She's assisting me with the spell."

Close enough to the truth. EJ and the other Roses would be involved.

The vines over the door rustled.

Pasternik harrumphed and stepped aside. "Come in and be welcome," he said with archaic formality but little enthusiasm. "But don't touch anything, hear?"

Callie nodded, resisting the urge to grin at the mage. That last bit wasn't part of any formal exchange, just Pasternik's personality.

She and EJ crossed the threshold. Immediately, the damp earthiness of green and growing things enveloped them. The front room of the little house was filled with stands and tables covered with pots and containers that held all manner of plants in shades of green and other colors Callie didn't know existed. Overhead lights, floor lamps, table lamps, and strings of lights brightened the room, yet there was no overwhelming glare. It was, however, quite warm. Callie loosened the buttons of her coat, and she saw EJ do the same.

Pasternik closed the door. The vegetation quivered. "How's Jemma these days?"

"Doing well," Callie replied. "She sends her regards and asked me to return this to you along with her thanks."

She reached into her coat pocket for the small parcel Jemma had given her.

Pasternik gave a genuine smile as he gently took the package from her. "Ah, there's my pretty."

EJ and Callie exchanged looks. Callie had no idea what was inside the brown paper packet and had no intention of asking. What passed between two powerful mages was none of their concern.

His smile disappeared and his brow furrowed. "So what do you want?"

Jemma had warned her that the plant mage wasn't one to tolerate small talk.

"Grains of paradise, poke root berries, and bay leaves."

He quirked a bushy white eyebrow at her. "You didn't have to come all the way out here for those."

That was true, if she wanted run-of-the-mill ingredients. Ruth's cousin Henry was a very reliable plant mage who lived in the Y-J, but not one to grow components for others. Malmo's Nursery was popular and reliable; the mages Callie knew were happy with their products. Considering the object of the spell's focus, she figured it would be best to obtain the highest quality ingredients they could afford, away from any prying eyes that might rat them out to Underwood.

"We need the best."

The mage glanced at EJ. "I see. This way."

Pasternik turned on his heel and strutted toward the right-hand hall off the main room. He pocketed the parcel and took up a walking stick that had been leaning against the wall by the hall entrance.

They followed him through a small kitchen that smelled like coffee and bacon. The white and chrome fixtures sparkled in the sunlight coming through the single window. Vines crawled along the walls, their broad, deep green leaves standing out against the yellow patterned wallpaper. Out the back door, they stepped immediately into a spacious attached greenhouse.

The humidity hit Callie like a damp cloth plastered over her nose and mouth. The late autumn light coming through the glass walls and ceiling reflected off the dense foliage, giving everything a green tint. Green upon green upon green, with splashes of color from white to pink to orange to purple and nearly black. The perfume of hundreds of flowers and plants came to her. Sweet, spicy, musky, sharp, pungent. They should have overwhelmed, but each seemed to float in its own stream, taking its turn to entice, delight, or cause her nose to wrinkle.

They walked the right-side aisle between tables of planters, ponds carved into the earth that held immersed or floating vegetation, and large pots on the ground with trees and bushes brimming.

A rough-barked tree six feet tall stood in a colorful pot, separated from others. Deep orange flowers were nestled against hand-sized, thick, shiny leaves. Callie caught a whiff of a sweet aroma from the flowers. She stopped and leaned closer. Mmmm . . . vanilla . . . like the fresh baked cookies Gran made . . . The heady scent filled her. She closed her eyes, feeling as if she were floating on a cloud.

Lovely. Simply lovely. She could stay there all day, inhaling the perfume.

"Cal? Callie!" EJ's voice pulled her back to earth. She jostled Callie's arm. "You okay?"

Callie shook off the lingering daze. "Yeah. Sorry."

"Don't lag behind. Hard to say what will affect you," Pasternik warned.

He stood further along the aisle, holding the walking stick up into a giant ball of green and golden brown fluff.

A growling creak came from somewhere within the puffball.

"Come along," the mage called.

EJ took Callie's arm, and they hurried past man and tree. The canopy of fluff shook. The growl became a whine of what Callie swore was disappointment.

"Don't mind him," Pasternik said as he lowered the walking stick. "He's a bit grumpy today."

"Sounds hungry," EJ quipped, smirking at Callie.

"That too. This way." He led them deeper into the greenhouse.

Callie almost laughed at EJ's wide-eyed reaction to Pasternik's response. She wiped perspiration from her brow and pulled the collar of her blouse away from her throat, regretting not having removed her coat earlier.

"Here, now." Pasternik stopped at a set of tiered shelves. "Let's see what we've got."

Callie recognized a number of the plants growing with lush vitality. This particular area seemed to be a display of spell components, common and otherwise.

He selected two clay pots from among the many on the shelves. As far as Callie could tell, there were no labels or any sense of order. But then again, a plant mage wouldn't need labels.

"Bay leaf, poke root berries . . ." His hand hovered over a third pot. "Grains of paradise. Do you want fresh or dried? Something with more kick?"

Callie and EJ exchanged glances.

"What does that mean?" Callie asked.

"Depending on the plant, dried versus fresh changes the concentration and potency. Plants raised in their native soil are also more potent." He grinned. "And more expensive because I have to maintain the soil proper-like. But depending on what you're doing, could be worth it."

Of course, Callie wanted her spell to be as effective as possible. What mage wouldn't?

"How much more expensive?" EJ asked.

The mage studied her for a moment. "Twenty for a packet of grains."

Callie's mouth dropped open. She'd need three packets, one for each night. "How much for everything for three invocations?"

"One seventy-five," he said, not missing a beat. "But I'll knock off some, seeing you're Jemma's girl. One fifty."

Pasternik didn't part with his goods for bargain prices, that was certain. His time, experience, and expertise did not come cheaply. Another reason EJ was there.

Still, Callie's brain reeled. "One hundred and fifty dollars?"

Pasternik glared. "Well, I don't mean silk stockings."

"You guarantee your goods?" EJ asked.

The mage scoffed. "I guarantee the quality of my components. What I can't guarantee is that your spell will work as intended. That depends on the quality of your mage, not my 'goods' as you call them."

Callie felt heat rise from her chest to her cheeks as EJ's gaze flicked to her. Was she questioning the quality of "her" mage?"

EJ withdrew her leather wallet from her coat pocket. Opening it, she counted out several crisp bills and held them out to Pasternik.

He shook his head. "Needs to come from the mage. Direct line." He shrugged in response to EJ's cocked eyebrow. "I don't make the rules."

EJ handed Callie the cash. "I owe her for services. Legit wages."

She had offered Callie payment, but they hadn't performed the spell yet. Maybe she meant stealing Underwood's toothbrush. Callie took the bills, trying not to smile, and passed them to Pasternik.

He grunted with satisfaction, folded the money, and slid it into the front pocket of his trousers. He then went to work trimming leaves and berries from each plant and packaging three separate bundles of each in white cotton tied with red string. From another drawer, he pulled out three other bundles. "The grains of paradise," he said, setting them on the table with the six already there. "Anything else?"

Callie gathered the nine packets and put them in her coat pockets. "No, thank you. This should be fine."

Pasternik harrumphed again. He set the potted plants back where they belonged, then led the way to the house. Once again, he used his walking stick to keep whatever was in the fluffy tree-like plant at bay. Callie noticed EJ walked a little faster beneath the canopy.

Back outside, EJ opened the passenger door and Callie slid onto the seat. When her feet were in and she was settled, EJ shut the door, rounded the front, and got in the driver's seat.

Callie took a breath of the cool, fresh air and blew it out. "That went much better than I'd expected. More expensive, but it went well."

EJ glanced at her as she took Callie's arm. "I'm glad you thought so."

"You all right?" Callie asked. "I'll pay you back—"

EJ waved her off. "No. I asked you to do this, and of course I'll fund it."

She set the spark switch, gas, and key, then stomped the starter, all without looking at Callie. The Ford sputtered for a second then roared to life. The throaty engine sent vibrations throughout the vehicle.

Callie laid a hand on EJ's arm as she reached for the gear shift. "Then what is it?"

EJ didn't move for several moments, her eyes on Callie's hand. She sighed heavily and glanced at the vine-covered house before meeting Callie's gaze. "I've never really been around mages much except you and a few I've hired for small things here and there. The minute we stepped through that door, it was . . ."

Callie resisted the grin that threatened. "Disconcerting. Mages are like that. Well, some are. Pasternik, for sure, but I think he's more . . . off-putting than most."

"Yeah, I suppose." EJ seemed relieved that Callie understood. "It's never been a big deal before, you know? I hire mages, they do their thing, business as usual. But this felt different."

"It's business, but it's personal too," Callie said. "What we're after is more than a job done or a quick fix. You're involved in ways you hadn't been before."

Perhaps EJ had felt more of connection because of their connection. It was something to be aware of. To be wary of.

She realized she hadn't moved her hand from EJ's arm and quickly pulled away.

EJ looked at her. Was that—No, there was nothing in her dark brown eyes that meant anything.

"It is personal." EJ reached into the inside pocket of her coat and withdrew a cigarette case. From her side pocket, a silver lighter. She selected a long, thin cigarette and placed it between her lips, then offered the open case to Callie. Callie shook her head. EJ pocketed the case. She flicked open the lighter, and with a couple of turns of the wheel, a bright blue and yellow flame sprang up.

"I just never really thought about what they—you did," EJ said, lighting the end of the cigarette. Pungent smoke wafted through the car interior as she put the lighter away. "What goes into spells and stuff."

"It can get complicated."

"I think I see that now." EJ blew smoke out between her lips. "There's more than the cost of components, isn't there?"

Callie nodded slowly. "Energy, sometimes health. It depends on the spell."

EJ frowned. "Health? You didn't mention that. Are you going to get hurt by this? I don't want—"

She held up a hand to stop EJ. "Relax. It will take a lot out of me, but I should be okay with rest."

"You sure? Because your grandmother will kill me if anything happens to you."

Callie laughed. "True. But I'll be all right. Promise."

She could promise that the spell itself would likely be safe. But the aftermath? That depended on how Paul Underwood reacted once he realized what was happening.

EJ pursed her lips around her Chesterfield. "Is that why you all don't get together and take over this place, the government, ruling the world, that sort of thing—because it's too draining? You could do it, couldn't you?"

"Well, there is the Law to consider." Callie settled back against the car seat. "It would also require a lot of cooperation and coordination. Folks who don't use magic have a hell of a time working together to get something that enormous done. Mages aren't any different."

"I suppose not. People are people," EJ said as she put the car in gear. "We're basically only willing to cooperate as it suits us for the moment."

Did EJ mean the world in general or something more specific, closer to home?

They drove in silence for a few minutes, then EJ said, "Can

I ask you something?"

The closeness of the car interior suddenly seemed a little too close, but Callie was game for conversation. "In the spirit of cooperation, sure."

EJ grinned without taking her eyes from the road, but sobered quickly. "Why Nate? Why marry a guy you hardly knew? Someone who lived so far away?"

The unspoken question: Why did you leave all you knew, everyone who cared about you?

She couldn't give EJ the real answer. She was barely able to acknowledge it to her own self, for goodness sake. But she had to say something. EJ and the others deserved that much.

"I—I thought that was what I had to do. I wanted what Mom and Pop had. Nate offered that."

True enough. Not the entire truth, but enough of it.

EJ nodded slowly. "I get that. We didn't exactly grow up with silver spoons, did we? When we saw something we wanted or needed, we had to grab for it right then and there. Your folks were definitely something special."

Callie's throat tightened. She swallowed several times before being able to speak. "They were. Staying in the Y-J, I couldn't—" Her mouth dried. She couldn't say it, not yet. "I couldn't have found a guy like Nate there, yanno?"

That wasn't true and they both knew it. Marian had found her nice guy. There were others. But how could she tell EJ that she had to leave because it was EJ she'd thought about more than any guy she knew?

Still staring ahead, EJ's brow furrowed. "Yeah. Yeah, a rare breed, those nice guys. That makes sense."

Callie turned to gaze out the window, pretending to admire the passing scenery rather than let EJ see the lie on her face.

CHAPTER EIGHT

Callie hefted her suitcase up the back stairs of The Garden to EJ's office. She and EJ had spent the day before clearing out a space in the storeroom, preparing it for the next three evenings of spell incantation. The room itself didn't need any particular preparation, but the spell had to be performed on the premises and Callie was required to stay within its boundaries until the last night.

Hence the suitcase that contained her ritual garb, day clothes, pajamas, and toiletries.

EJ came out of the storeroom as Callie got to the top of the stairs and smiled. The sleeves of her crisp white shirt were rolled to the elbows, revealing the ink of a rose tattoo on her right forearm, the red tie at her throat loosened and the top button open. Her vest and trousers were dark gray with pale pinstriping. Though she wore a man's suit, it was tailored to her feminine form.

Callie bit the inside of her lip to stifle a moan of appreciation. The feelings that were responsible for her haring off to Spokane pushed out of their hidey-hole inside her. She shoved them back. Now was not the time, she told herself. Though she wasn't sure she'd ever be brave enough to allow the right time.

"Here, let me get that for you." EJ met her at the stairs and took the suitcase. She tilted her head, a bemused expression on her face. "You okay?"

"Fine." Callie moistened her lips and averted her gaze to keep from staring at EJ's ruby red mouth. "How are things here?"

EJ turned toward her office and went in. "Good. Almost ready. Mason brought a cot up for you. Hope the mattress is okay."

Callie stopped inside the door of the office. EJ had replaced the single chair with a narrow bed and a small side table with a lamp. Linens, blankets, a pillow, and a couple of towels rested on the mattress. "I don't want to be in the way."

"You won't be," EJ said. She set the suitcase near the bed and gestured to a closed door. "Besides, the bathroom is right there. Easier to access. Being stuck in a windowless storeroom ain't that appealing."

Callie smiled. "Can't argue that. Thank you."

"You're doing a lot here, Cal." EJ stepped closer and took Callie's coat and hat as she shed them to hang them on the wooden coatrack in a corner near the door. EJ's own coat and hat occupied one of the other two curlicues of wood. "I owe you a decent place to lay your head at the very least."

"You've done your part," Callie said. "Including agreeing to be part of the actual spell. When will the others be here?"

They needed to start after sundown, and all of the other Roses would contribute their energy to bolster its effect. It would be comforting and empowering to have her old friends around.

EJ moved back to the bed and set the linens on the desk. She picked up one of the sheets and unfolded it, handing one end to Callie. "Marian will be here after she gets her kids fed and in bed. The others about then, too. You said you have some things you need to do?"

Callie and EJ covered the mattress with the sheet and proceeded to fold and tuck corners. "Yes. Cleansing. Is there a tub in the bathroom?"

"Yep, and I made sure the hot water was running."

They finished making the bed.

"I'll bring up another blanket," EJ said, fluffing the pillow. "It can get chilly in here."

Callie reached for the pillow. "You're too good to me, EJ."

She started to laugh when EJ didn't let go, and their eyes met. EJ wasn't smiling.

"Anything to keep you safe and comfortable," she said, her voice a half register lower than usual, which hit Callie square in the libido.

"You're doing plenty." Callie tugged a little harder on the pillow. EJ released it. Callie turned her back on the other woman, placing the pillow carefully and avoiding looking at EJ. "I just hope this works."

"You don't think it will?"

Callie tried to keep the doubt at bay, but it bubbled to the surface.

She took a breath and faced EJ again. "I—to be honest, I don't know." EJ's brow furrowed. "It's like Pasternik said: nothing in magic is guaranteed. And I'm a bit rusty so, no, I'm not one hundred percent sure."

She hadn't really thought about how unsure she was until now.

EJ came closer and draped her arm around Callie's shoulders. She pulled her down to sit on the edge of the bed. "You'll do great. I have complete faith in you."

She had to shake off the doubt, because doubt and hesitation were surefire ways to muck up a spell.

"I've been going over everything Jemma gave me, all the steps and words."

EJ jostled her shoulder a little. "So what's the problem? You've got this, Callie. I know you do."

Callie felt EJ's confidence in her. Just like when they were kids. She smiled. "Thanks."

EJ patted her arm and stood. "I'll leave you to do your thing. I have to check in with the crew, make sure everyone knows to stay downstairs. I'll be back up in about an hour with some food. Do you need me to do anything else for you?"

"Only if you want to help me bathe."

EJ's eyebrows shot up, quickly followed by a wicked grin that shot heat through Callie's stomach. She'd meant it as a joke, but an image of her and EJ in a tub of sudsy water flashed through her brain. Heat became a near inferno. Callie jumped to her feet and hurried toward her suitcase. Sure that her face was as red as EJ's tie, she kept it averted while she popped open the clasps and randomly sorted through her things.

"A sandwich or something would be great. And a soda. No alcohol. Please."

"Sure." The bed springs creaked as EJ rose. Her footsteps headed toward the door. "Be back in a bit."

The office door clicked softly as EJ closed it behind her.

Callie sat back on her heels and blew out a slow breath. This was going to be a long, frustrating three days.

EJ balanced a plate of sandwiches in one hand and opened her office door with the other, taking care not to drop the bottle of soda pop under her arm. She pushed the door open and stopped dead in her tracks.

Callie straightened from a bent position over her suitcase where it lay on the bed, a double-edged dagger clutched in her hand. She wore a white robe that fell to her knees, cinched at the waist with a crimson sash. Her blond hair was damp, free from pins, and falling past her shoulders. The toes of her bare feet curled against the polished wood floor. As she turned, the robe gaped to reveal the swell of a pale breast.

"I—" EJ swallowed, attempting to relieve the sudden dryness

in her mouth. "I have food."

Callie smiled, and EJ would have thought her to be an angel, except for the blade. An avenging angel, perhaps. It suited her.

She sheathed the knife and set it on the desk. "So I see. Thank you."

EJ tore her gaze from Callie before she could fully appreciate how the light from the desk lamp cut through the robe, leaving little need for her imagination to fill in what lay beneath the silk. But, oh, how her imagination blossomed. She strode past Callie, accidentally on purpose brushing against her arm, feeling the delicate material feather across the back of her hand. A frisson of electricity skittered along her skin. EJ quickly set the plate and cola bottle on the desk before she dropped them.

"Just some chicken and a cola." She went around to the other side of the desk. "Got a bottle opener here somewhere."

She riffled through the top drawer and found it among the pen nibs and scraps of paper. A relatively clean tumbler was in a bottom drawer beside a bottle of bourbon. EJ put the glass and opener on the desk.

Callie stepped closer. EJ's gaze traveled up her body, hesitated at the deep V of the robe, and continued to her clear blue eyes. Free of makeup, the sprinkle of freckles across her nose and cheeks were just visible, giving her a girlish appearance. But she was definitely no longer a girl.

EJ couldn't help smiling.

Callie smiled back, and EJ's stomach fluttered.

"Can you help me with my hair?" Callie asked. "I need it out of the way, and it's better when someone else does it."

The Roses had often styled one another's hair, attempting to copy their favorite celebrities shown on the pages of movie magazines. Playing with Callie's when they were teenagers had always given EJ a secret delight.

EJ nodded, hoping she didn't show just how delighted she was now.

Callie found her tortoiseshell comb and a red ribbon and moved the suitcase off the bed. She sat, knees together, and turned so her back would face where EJ was to sit, holding the comb up near her shoulder.

EJ sat behind her on the edge of the bed. She gathered Callie's hair in both hands and brought it all together to fall down her back; she'd let it grow out these past ten years. The aroma of lilac and something sweet wafted to EJ's nose, and she resisted the urge to lean forward and inhale the enticing scent.

"Not too tight, but not too loose," Callie said as EJ took the comb. "I'd like it to last the three days, but not have a headache."

"Got it."

EJ ran the comb through her damp hair, then used her fingers to separate sections near the crown of her head. She began plaiting the sections, gathering additional hair from the sides as she went, making sure that, as requested, the braid was neither too tight nor too loose. As her fingers trailed through Callie's hair, skimming her scalp, EJ noticed Callie's shoulders relax. Yet her breathing seemed a little faster.

EJ focused on the rhythm, enjoying the sensation of the silky tresses sliding through her fingers. She gathered the last loose sections and continued braiding. The tip of her nail brushed the nape of Callie's neck. Callie shivered. EJ paused, her fingers entwined with the golden brown strands, her heart pattering against her sternum. Longing welled in her breast.

She shouldn't have these feelings for her friend, should she? But she did. Did Callie's reaction mean she felt the same?

Even if it did, this wasn't the time. Hell, no time was probably the time. Anything more than casual relationships could be used against her by Underwood or anyone else, and there was no way EJ would put Callie in the crosshairs of a target meant for herself.

"Here," Callie said, holding up the length of ribbon.

EJ finished off the braid. When she reached for the ribbon,

she wrapped her hand around Callie's and let it stay there for a moment too long. Another quiver. So she wasn't imagining things. The potential both thrilled and worried her.

They had so much to do over the next several days, and EJ desperately wanted to say something, do something, to let Callie know how she felt. But Callie shouldn't be distracted. Could EJ say something afterward? What would happen to their friendship, which had just started to feel right again after a decade apart? What kind of danger would Callie be in if she was in a relationship with EJ?

No, she couldn't risk that, for both their sakes.

EJ tied off the end and laid the braid over Callie's shoulder, letting her hand rest there. "How's that?"

Callie reached back to brush her palm over the plaiting. She turned her head to look at EJ. Her lips were parted, inches away, and so very kissable. Their gazes held.

Something passed between them, a connection that had started the night Callie had tended EJ's gunshot wound— maybe before that?—and had made itself known whenever they were together since then.

Just lean in . . .

Despite her head saying it was too risky, she eased forward. Callie's eyes fluttered closed. Their lips touched with the barest of contact.

"EJ . . ."

Her voice, low and throaty, vibrated through EJ, sending pings of want along nerves and bone and skin.

A rapid knock on the door sent them away from each other like the north poles of two magnets.

Shit. But maybe it was for the best. Maybe the universe was stopping them from doing something they'd regret later.

Callie abruptly rose. "Th-that must be the others."

Callie busied herself at her suitcase, putting clothes and toiletries away and moving the contents around.

EJ wiped her palms along her thighs and stood to answer the door. Bette, Marian, and Ruth waited on the other side.

Bette blew a bubble with the gum in her mouth, letting it pop. "Hiya."

EJ stepped aside to let them into the office.

Callie greeted each of them with smiles and thanks. "You all being here will add energy and stability to the spell," she told them.

"But it's not gonna be dangerous, right?" Bette chewed her gum faster, a nervous habit she'd had since they were kids.

"It shouldn't be," Callie said. "Just follow my directions. If you have questions, now's the time to ask. Once we get into the room, I have to ask you to not speak except to repeat certain phrases."

"No talking?" Ruth nudged Bette. "You're doomed."

Bette nudged back. "Shut it."

Marian's brow furrowed. "We'll do everything you need us to do. When do we start?"

Leave it to Marian to cut to the chase.

"There's special soap in the bathroom." Callie gestured in that direction. "Wash your hands, faces, and feet. Dry off with the white towel on the hook. When everyone's ready, I'll explain what to do, and we'll go into the storeroom. Anything else?" When no one spoke, Callie nodded. "Let's begin."

CHAPTER NINE

EJ padded barefoot from the bathroom to the office to join the others. She had her shirt sleeves and trouser legs rolled up, revealing smooth, lean limbs.

Callie smiled at her; then her eyes fell on the rose and thorns tattoo along EJ's inner right forearm. She'd caught a glimpse of it earlier, but now it was on full display. EJ had originally had it done when they were barely into their teens. That effort had been less detailed, so she must have found someone to clean it up. The red rose glistened as if actually dotted with dewdrops. The thorns looked as if they could pierce skin. Whoever had done the artwork was a master at the craft.

She forced her gaze from the luscious flower and skin and met EJ's eyes. There was something in those brown depths that told Callie she was thinking of their almost kiss. Regret and relief played tug-of-war within her. What if the other Roses hadn't shown up when they did? What would have happened?

More than a kiss maybe.

She moistened dried lips and handed EJ the last bundle of herbs for tonight's ritual. Ruth and Marian each had similar bundles, and Bette held a white candle. "Are we ready?"

The four exchanged glances and nodded.

"Let's do this," EJ said with a glint in her dark eyes.

Callie led them out into the hall, to the next room. The faint sound of music coming from downstairs leant a more festive air to what they were about to do than truly fit the occasion, but Callie appreciated the normalcy of it all. Perhaps the music would help reinforce the spell as the presence of the Roses was meant to.

"James flubbed his entrance again," Ruth said with a huff. "I'd better talk to him later."

Callie turned on the overhead light, and all of the Roses entered the musty storeroom. EJ shut the door behind them. The middle of the room had been cleared and swept, with crates and boxes stacked against the walls along with an old stage light and a few ladder-back chairs.

"Wait here," Callie said. "I'll call you over one by one. Be careful to step over the circle and hand me your offering."

She stood in the center of the cleared area, a space a good twenty feet on each side, and took a thick cylinder of white chalk from her satchel. She set the satchel down, then drew a continuous circle of protection from outside influence and counter-magic as she whispered words of strength and safety for those about to perform the spell. It was slow going, as she had to work the chalk into the crevices between floorboards to ensure there were no gaps.

When she was done, she returned the chalk to her bag. She then removed the small silver plate, one of three squares of white cloth, Paul Underwood's toothbrush, and her dagger. The carved wood handle fit her grip as if made for her, though the dagger was, according to Jemma, at least one hundred years old. She slid off the tooled leather sheath. The razor-sharp blade gleamed in the overhead light. She set it on the floor with care.

Callie faced the Roses. They all stared at her, wide-eyed with wonder or curiosity. Even Ruth, who practiced, seemed a little dazzled. Most spells didn't require such a formal setting or more than the caster. Few were made with more than one other person present. Fewer still were fortified with the intensity that went with blood magic.

These were her friends, her people. They had always been there for each other, even when time and distance and doubt separated them.

"Bette."

The petite blonde's body stiffened, and her eyes grew wider still.

"Enter this protective circle. Be welcome and safe."

Bette swallowed hard but didn't hesitate. She came forward, careful to step over the chalk, and handed Callie the candle.

"Bette, your loyalty toward the Roses is unfailing. The strength of your faith will boost the strength of our spell."

Bette smiled, a blush rising to her fair face.

Callie kissed each of her cheeks and directed her to stand at a specific point within the circle. Callie then squatted down and lit the candle with one of the matches from a small box she had brought. She let some wax drip into the center of the cloth-covered plate, then set the candle end in it.

She rose and called out, "Marian."

Marian came forward with the confidence she showed in everything she did.

"Enter this protective circle. Be welcome and safe." When Marian handed her the bundle of herbs, Callie smiled at her. "You have always been the solid rock on which we could rely. Your serenity and composure will keep us focused on the task ahead."

She bussed each of Marian's cheeks and had her stand at the point ninety degrees to Bette's right.

"Ruth."

Ruth smiled as she crossed the room, her excitement and anticipation clear. She understood more than anyone in the room what Callie was about to do.

"Enter this protective circle. Be welcome and safe. Your

knowledge and experience with the arts will help guide us through our task."

She kissed Ruth and set the bundle of herbs at her feet, then directed the other woman to stand to Bette's left.

Callie looked at EJ. The leader of the Roses stood near the door, eyes shining, clutching the white bundle. The rose and leaves on her forearm looked real enough that Callie almost swore that she could smell the perfume of the flower, that the thorn would prick her skin if she ran her finger over it. Her heart thudded hard in her chest.

"EJ. Enter this protective circle. Be welcome and safe."

EJ crossed the room and stepped over the chalk line, her gaze never leaving Callie's face. She held out the bundle. Callie took it, but then EJ's hands covered hers. Strength and confidence flowed from EJ, and when Callie kissed her cheeks, she felt the brush of EJ's lips and the warmth of her breath across her skin.

"You have always been the force behind the Roses, the light we all rallied toward when things got tough. Your leadership and dedication will see us through."

EJ smiled and squeezed her hands before moving to the spot in front of Callie.

They stood there silently for a few moments. Callie closed her eyes. The energy in the room shifted, gently swirling around her. Everything she needed was within the circle of crushed minerals, a circle so physically fragile yet pulsing with strength. Her strength. Their strength.

She opened her eyes. "Join hands."

The four Roses complied, reaching toward each other, completing the circle within the circle.

Callie knelt on the floor, the rough wood pressing into her skin through the thin layer of her robe. She took a calming breath and opened the herb packets.

"With faith and fire and blood, we protect this place from those who seek to harm." She nodded to the others and, as instructed earlier, they joined her in speaking the last phrase. "Turn away, turn away, turn away."

A little quiet and shaky, but Callie was sure of their commitment.

She sprinkled the herbs around the candle.

"With faith and fire and blood, we protect this place. Keep it safe for us to dwell within."

The Roses' voices came together again. "Turn away, turn away, turn away."

Next, Callie picked up the dagger. She opened her left hand and gently set the blade against her skin. She looked up into EJ's eyes, who stared at her, lips pressed together with apprehension. Callie almost smiled. *This was what blood mages do*, she wanted to say. *This is what we are.*

Callie drew the blade lightly across her palm. It didn't hurt in the least. She lifted the dagger; a thin line of crimson welled in her palm. She set the dagger down and picked up the toothbrush.

"With faith and fire and blood, we protect this place. Remove our enemies from this site."

The four of them spoke with more confidence now. "Turn away, turn away, turn away."

She squeezed her hand into a fist. Holding the toothbrush over the flame, she let her blood drip onto the bristles as she repeated the incantation three more times. Blood met the heated and magicked atmosphere, raising a burnt copper aroma to fill Callie's nostrils. Not an unpleasant scent. She inhaled again, deeper, magic now dancing along her limbs, seeping into her skin. Everything about this felt right, comfortable, necessary.

This is how it should be, always.

Her vision blurred.

Concentrate!

Gathering herself again, Callie turned her hand to end the flow of blood. Just a few drops were required, and she would be repeating the ritual twice more. She couldn't allow herself to get carried away. She laid the toothbrush beside the covered plate and rummaged in the satchel for a clean cloth to press to her left palm. Luckily, blood mages tended to clot and heal quickly.

Callie's head swam from the candle, from the herbs warmed by the melting wax, from the magic coursing through her and swirling around the room. She closed her eyes to maintain her bearings. Every nerve was alert, every sense finely tuned. She felt each small groove and splinter of the wood floor against her knees. She heard each of the Roses breathing, distinguishing the four of them. Bette's quick and shallow inhalations. Ruth's more normal rate, as she was excited but used to magic around her. Marian, steady and controlled, yet quivering slightly. And EJ . . . deeper, taking it all in, their connection vibrating between them like a plucked violin string. Callie inhaled, smelling each woman's body aroma and perfume, the combination reminding her of younger days, of the family they had made together when they all needed it most.

Callie opened her eyes, gazing up at EJ. The intensity of those dark eyes sent a shiver through her, and Callie fought to stay still rather than give in to the sudden base need that threatened to overtake her.

The moment passed. When she felt she could stand without her legs giving out or wanting to vault into EJ's arms, Callie got to her feet.

"The first of three is complete. Go as you came here tonight. Go with love. Go with peace."

One by one, starting with Bette, the Roses silently walked over the chalk line and to the door. Last to leave, EJ gave Callie a small smile, but the intensity of her gaze hadn't diminished.

Finally, assuring that the candle was secure and wouldn't burn anything it wasn't supposed to, Callie stepped out of the circle. She'd come back later to check on the candle, but for now she led the others out of the storeroom. EJ locked the door.

The five stood in the hall, silent, but with an air of energy around them.

"You can speak now," Callie said with a grin.

Ruth, Bette, and Marian started talking all at once as they returned to EJ's office and put their stockings and shoes on.

"Incredible. I feel so energetic."

"It's like I've had a pot of coffee all in one sitting."

"I never knew what really went on with magic, but wow!"

Callie laughed, ignoring a fleeting moment of lightheadedness. "It's not always like this, right, Ruth?"

The air mage nodded. "True. It's mostly routine sort of stuff. But *this*." She took Callie's hands. "This was amazing. And we get to do it two more times."

"Well," Marian said gathering her hat and coat, "I think I'm going home to put this burst of energy to use."

Bette winked at her. "I'm sure Ralph'll be grateful."

Marian grinned. "You bet he will. See y'all tomorrow."

Ruth and Bette said their good-byes as well, leaving Callie and EJ alone. With the excitement of their first session starting to wane, Callie couldn't stave off the weariness she felt. Her head swam again.

"Whoa!" EJ's voice held a note of alarm, and Callie felt EJ's arms go around her shoulders and waist. "You okay?"

Callie stood still for several moments, her head clearing as she once again felt EJ's strength seep into her. "I'll be all right. Just give me a sec."

"Come on, sit down." EJ guided her to the cot and had her sit. "Put your feet up, or your head between your knees. I never remember which to do."

Callie sat back on the bed and made sure her feet were up. "Me neither, but this is good."

EJ glanced at the desk. "You never ate your sandwich. I bet you're hungry."

Her stomach rumbled in agreement.

EJ passed her the sandwich and popped the cap off the soda bottle. She poured half of it in a glass and sat beside Callie on the cot. "Eat."

Suddenly ravenous, with hands shaking, Callie bit into the sandwich. She forced herself to take normal-sized bites and chew thoroughly. Half the sandwich was gone along with most of the soda in the glass before she spoke. "Thanks."

EJ refilled the glass and took the last swig from the bottle before setting it on the desk. "Thought you were gonna hit the floor there for a second. Scared the life outta me."

The heat of embarrassment rose on Callie's cheeks. "Sorry. It's been a while since I've done such an intense spell."

"Callie, if this is going to be too much . . ." There was concern in EJ's eyes, but something else. A hint of disappointment. EJ needed Underwood out of the way. Without the spell, she might resort to more drastic, permanent measures.

"I'll be fine." She patted EJ's hand. "Food and rest. I'll be right as rain. Promise."

Callie started to rise, but EJ pulled her back down onto the bed.

"Where do you think you're going?"

"I need to check the candle. It has to burn all the way down."

EJ rose. "I'll check on it. You will stay here, finish your sandwich, and get some sleep. I have to go down and check on things there anyway."

"Yes, but EJ—"

"But EJ nothing." She headed toward the door, rolling down her sleeves.

"Seriously, EJ."

EJ turned around, hands on her hips. "No arguments."

Callie held up her hands, but she couldn't help the grin on her face. "Not arguing, but you might want to put your shoes on first."

EJ looked down at her bare feet and wiggled her toes. When

her gaze met Callie's again, they both laughed.

EJ climbed the stairs to the second floor, weariness making her legs feel as if cement filled her shoes. Mason and Stella had agreed to finish locking up downstairs, thankfully. All EJ could think about was lying down. If she was this tired, she could only imagine how Callie felt.

Before heading to her office, EJ fished her key ring out of her trouser pocket and opened the storeroom door. All dark with a hint of wax and burnt herbs in the air. And something else, like a whisper of breeze across her skin, even under her clothing. Weird.

She turned on the overhead light. In the center of the white chalk circle, the candle had burned down to a puddle of wax. Satisfied that there would be no need to worry about a fire, she locked the door again and went to the office.

The emotions she'd felt during the incantation came back to her. Being there with her friends had filled her with joy and satisfaction. She hadn't felt a part of something like that since before the Roses mostly went their separate ways. It was easier to keep people at arms' length. Fewer complications. Safer. For everyone. The organization she had been building gave her a sense of accomplishment, sure, but this was different. This was personal and welcome, yet a bit unnerving. She didn't let attachments affect her, but ever since she'd walked into the butcher shop, things had been turned on their head.

You mean Callie turned you on your head.

Might as well admit that, to herself at least. Being with Callie these past couple of weeks as they prepared for tonight had been the happiest EJ had felt in a long while.

And tonight? Watching Callie, her white robe and the soft candlelight making her look more divine than human, had

119

definitely made EJ happy. She had bitten the inside of her lip to maintain her silence and composure. And the interrupted kiss, followed by the kiss Callie gave her during the ritual?

If only . . .

EJ shook off the bubble of need that formed low in her belly. Now was not the time. She couldn't let these thoughts distract herself or Callie from what she was so desperate to accomplish.

She slowly turned the knob of the office door and eased it open a crack. The overhead light wasn't on, but the desk lamp threw a bright enough pool to see by. EJ opened the door a little wider and peeked in.

Callie was on the cot, curled up on her side, facing into the room. Her brow was smooth, her expression relaxed in sleep. She had changed out of the white robe and wore a white flannel nightgown with pink roses, which her arm laying outside the wool blanket revealed.

EJ slipped out of her shoes and entered the office. She quietly closed the door behind her. Crossing the room, she set her shoes down by the chaise on the opposite wall from the cot. EJ looked over her shoulder to make sure she hadn't disturbed Callie, and her breath caught. In the soft light of the desk lamp, she looked serene and beautiful, a goddess in repose.

EJ pressed her fingertips against her eyes until white spots danced against black. How was she going to handle two more days of being this close to the woman without spilling her guts about her feelings? Though their almost kiss probably gave a lot away.

Better figure out what to do, and what's best for both of you.

With a sigh of resignation, she went around to the far side of the desk to her overnight bag. She pulled out a pair of striped flannel pajamas and her toothbrush before hanging up the clean shirt she'd wear the next day. She tossed the blanket Callie hadn't used onto the chaise.

After changing into her pajamas and brushing her teeth in

the bathroom, EJ returned to the office. She glanced at Callie, still sound asleep, and smiled. They hadn't slept in the same room since they were kids. After carefully draping her trousers, vest, and jacket on the chair, she turned off the desk lamp, leaving the meager streetlight outside the window to give her enough illumination not to run into the chaise. She lay down, adjusted the blanket over herself, and faced Callie.

Listening to the soft ins and outs of the other woman breathing helped EJ push the day's business and excitement aside. Tomorrow was another day likely to be filled with the same. That definitely wasn't a bad thing.

Callie woke slightly disoriented, staring at a strange wall, momentarily unsure of where she was but knowing it certainly wasn't her own bed. She rolled over. The room was configured wrong and the light strange. Right. At The Garden. Across from her, EJ snored softly, curled up on the chaise.

Callie smiled, pleased EJ had thought to stay with her overnight. Why hadn't she said anything to Callie?

Moving carefully so as to not wake EJ, Callie got out of bed. She padded quietly to the bathroom, the chill from the bare floor reminding her she'd forgotten her slippers. After washing her face, she returned to the office. EJ was pushing the blanket aside and sitting up.

Tousled hair and sleep-soft eyes sent a warm surge of pleasure lined with desire through Callie. EJ dressed to the nines was stunning. EJ sleepy in cotton flannel did something entirely different to Callie.

Seeing EJ at her most relaxed and vulnerable brought a hitch to Callie's chest. It had been a lifetime since they were free of bothersome things and could just be themselves.

"I didn't mean to wake you," Callie said, heading to her

suitcase. From the corner of her eye, she watched EJ stand and stretch, revealing a glimpse of the smooth brown skin of her stomach.

"You didn't," EJ assured her. When Callie rose, slippers in hand, EJ smiled. "Good morning."

Callie couldn't help but smile back. "Good morning."

"Valerie won't be in yet," EJ said, "but I make a mean pot of coffee and I'm a whizz at scrambled eggs."

"Breakfast sounds good. I need to gather last night's components first."

The incantation had a number of steps to be completed. Even after the third candle burned down to nothing at the end of the third night, there would still be final words and doings.

"Right." EJ crossed to the desk where her trousers lay over the back of the chair. She retrieved her key ring from the pocket.

The two of them exited the office and went into the storeroom.

"I'll be only a minute," Callie said as she turned on the overhead light.

The air in the room was chilly, laced with the faint aroma of the wax and herbs. The healed cut on her palm tingled with the remnants of power lingering in the room. That her magic had taken hold was a relief. Not that she doubted her abilities, exactly, but you never knew if it worked until it worked.

She stepped over the chalk line and crouched down in front of the silver plate. The white cloth beneath the melted candle and herbs had adhered to the plate. Carefully, she worked the cloth free and bundled everything together. She removed a white cloth sack from her satchel and put the bundle inside. Two more bundles would join it before being buried on the third night.

Callie took another square of cloth from her satchel, laying it out in preparation for tonight's portion of the ritual. The dagger and toothbrush waited there as well.

She stood and crossed the circle again, returning to where

EJ waited. An odd expression was on the other woman's face. "What is it?"

"I've never seen you like this."

Bemused, Callie glanced down at her nightgown. "What, in my pajamas?"

"So confident."

Callie brought her head up, the warmth of the comment growing as she noticed the intensity in EJ's gaze.

"It looks good on you," EJ said.

Callie opened her mouth, but no words came out. When EJ's eyes dropped to her lips, her throat dried.

EJ turned and opened the door. "I promised you breakfast."

Callie followed her out of the room, smiling and perked up as if she'd already had a couple of cups of coffee.

CHAPTER TEN

"The second of three is complete," Callie said to the Roses at the end of the second night. "Go as you came here tonight. Go with love. Go with peace."

The women filed out of the storeroom smiling. Tonight's incantation had been better than Callie could have asked for. All of the Roses knew their roles, knew what to expect. Their nervousness had been much lower than the night before, their enthusiasm as they'd entered the circle palpable. Confidence bolstered their responses to her words that would continue to infuse the spell within the walls of The Garden.

Callie was sure that after the final session, the spell would be a success, as would the reestablishment of the friendships she'd neglected for so long.

The relationships they'd had as kids were renewed and strengthened, adding to the power of the spell. No matter where any of them went, they would have each other. Bette, Ruth, and Marian were more than friends. They were family.

But Callie's bond to EJ had become even deeper than that.

She watched her as the Roses chatted and let their energy dissipate in the hall outside the storeroom. EJ smiled and laughed with them, a light in her eyes that drew Callie like a moth to a flame. And when their gazes met, Callie's magic danced inside her.

The blood bond they shared was growing stronger, there was no doubt about that. When she closed her eyes during the incantation, she could feel EJ there. Not because she knew the other woman was in the room, but she could literally feel her presence like a feather gliding across her skin and a whisper in her mind. *I am here.*

It was something she wouldn't dare tell EJ, or anyone else. Yes, she had warned EJ that there would be something between them, but even Callie hadn't anticipated its potency. Things like this were why blood mages in particular were viewed with suspicion if not outright fear. That sort of magic got witches burned in the past, and run out of some towns, at the least, in more modern times.

Callie understood, because it kind of scared the hell out of her as well.

It scared her yet made her want to expand on their connection at the same time, which was even more concerning. The stronger a bond through intimate contact, the greater the responsibility for the mage to keep the other person safe from the magic. Not that she would ever harm EJ with her magic, but spells could go awry.

As scary as that connection was, the excitement it sparked within Callie could not be denied.

"Good night," Bette called from the stairs, the last to leave the hall. "See you tomorrow."

One more night. They had one more night to finish the spell and get Paul Underwood out of their hair. And then what?

"Hungry?" EJ asked.

Callie turned around. EJ was rolling her sleeves down over her arms, the rose tattoo nearly out of sight. She strode over and slid the rich cotton back up. Her fingers glided over the smooth skin of EJ's forearm. Their contact sent a burst of need through Callie. EJ sucked in a breath.

Hungry? Yes, but not for food.

She met EJ's gaze, her dark eyes even darker with awareness and need. Yes, Callie felt that tickling in her lower belly as well.

"Yesterday," she said, her fingertips lingering on the petals of the tattooed rose, "before the others came up . . ."

The memory of her sitting in front of EJ replayed in Callie's mind: Deft fingers slipping through her damp hair, sending tingles from scalp to toes. The heat in EJ's eyes told Callie she recalled the moment as well.

"Yes?"

"Did I imagine it," Callie asked, the burble of her magic radiating from her belly, "or were you going to kiss me?"

EJ's mouth quirked into a half smile. "I think you were going to kiss me."

Callie laughed softly. "You may be right."

She closed the gap between them and touched her lips to EJ's. Something akin to a spark from rubbing feet on the carpet passed between them. EJ's grip on Callie's upper arms tightened, and she pressed her mouth firmly against Callie's.

Yes. This.

She had never kissed another woman before, but she knew *this* was what she wanted. This was *who* she wanted. The person she'd wanted for ages.

With a low moan, EJ pushed her tongue against the seam of Callie's mouth. One hand released her arm and EJ's fingers dug into her hip. Their magic-reinforced bond vibrated through Callie.

Just before Callie parted her lips to let EJ in, the conditions of the incantation blared in her head like a klaxon. *No alcohol! No sexual congress!*

She backed away, out of EJ's arms. "Damn it."

EJ blinked at her, hands still in the positions they had held on Callie's body. "What? What's wrong?"

Callie closed her eyes, willing away the need that came with using her magic. Such a cruel joke that magic fired up the libido, yet this spell required abstinence. Why couldn't she have found a spell that called for wantonness?

"I can't," she said, opening her eyes and conveying every bit of sorrow she felt. "The spell. It's not allowed."

EJ rubbed her hands up and down her cheeks. "Well, that's no fun."

Callie laid her hand on EJ's shoulder. What she would give to feel the woman's skin against hers. "I'm sorry. Are you . . . will you wait?"

The smile that curved her lips made Callie want to kiss her again. "For you? As long as it takes. I'll go get us some sandwiches."

EJ pecked her on the cheek and headed downstairs.

Callie sighed. One more night. She could manage one more night.

EJ walked through the door marked "Private" and into the main room of The Garden. The band was on fire tonight. It would have been nice to see a few more customers, but it was only Thursday. She smiled to herself. The weekend usually brought better crowds, so she wasn't too worried. Once Callie's spell was completed tonight, Underwood would be leaving her alone and things would pick up, sure enough.

And perhaps personal things would pick up as well.

She smiled to herself as she skirted the dance floor where two older couples were cutting a rug. Good on them. EJ liked to see folks of all ages, inclinations, and backgrounds in her place. They knew anyone of any stripe was welcome at The Garden as long as you respected others. Fridays and Saturdays were usually more boisterous, leaning toward younger patrons, but some of the older folks in the neighborhood kept up just fine. Hell, sometimes she was ushering them out at closing time.

Cigar and cigarette smoke hovered near the few occupied tables. People were talking, laughing, eating, and drinking. Exactly what she liked to see.

EJ straightened her tie, smiling as she made her way toward the lobby. She caught the eye of a blonde in a slinky black gown and winked. EJ recognized her but didn't know the woman's name. She came in fairly often with a man who was likely her husband. The woman grinned in response, giving EJ the up and down, ignoring the poor guy talking her ear off.

Not so long ago, EJ might have sent drinks to the couple, or sat down and flirted a little. No harm in flirting. It was good for business as long as it didn't go too far and irritate a jealous spouse. The women ate it up. Some of the guys did too, imagining who knew what with their girls and EJ if their hungry looks said what they seemed to say.

But now, thoughts of Callie put the brakes on flirting. As if sitting down with another woman even just for drinks and a few laughs would somehow damage their relationship.

What *was* their relationship, anyway?

The kissing was a clear sign that there could be more to their renewed friendship, but was that real or part of EJ's libido playing tricks on her? The night before last, with Callie nearly in her lap as she braided her hair, EJ had meant to do more than kiss her, and Callie looked like she was all too ready to respond. Until the knock on the door. And then last night, they'd both been willing but for the conditions of the spell. Damn their luck. The ritual was also tiring for Callie. She went to sleep not long after they finished, and EJ had a business to run.

But after tonight, after all was said and done?

Despite her head telling her it was a bad idea, that thought made EJ almost giddy.

Halfway across the dining room on her evening rounds, EJ's smile disappeared.

Wearing a black double-breasted suit and white fedora

with its charcoal band, Paul Underwood stood in the archway between the lobby and the main room, scanning the joint with a smirk that EJ wanted to punch off his face. On his arm, her red lips the same shade as her form-fitting dress, was Olive Lang. EJ had heard Olive was Underwood's side piece, even though she was young enough to be his daughter. Olive had even hung out with the Roses for a little while, ironically due to Janie's request to befriend the then-shy Olive and her little sister Rita. EJ and the others hadn't kept in touch with Olive. Rita, however . . . Well, best to forget all about her, her smoky voice, and her silky robe.

Seeing Olive clinging to Underwood's arm like a barnacle probably explained why she and the Roses had parted ways without a fuss.

Thomas Greer, Underwood's pin-striped lawyer, came up behind them, a fat stogie between his thin lips, followed by Bert Underwood, already bleary-eyed.

Great. Just fucking great.

Underwood grabbed the arm of a passing server and EJ's blood boiled. He spoke to her, gesturing toward a table. The young woman, Macie, nodded.

Before Macie moved off toward the bar, EJ reached them. She stared hard at Underwood, ignoring Olive, Bert, and Greer. "Take their orders, Macie, and bring the bill. They won't be staying."

Underwood stared back, dark eyes filled with derision. Macie hurried off.

"Evening, EJ," Olive said.

EJ glanced at the other woman and immediately wanted to slap the smirk off her porcelain doll face, too. Not bothering to return the greeting, EJ stepped closer to Underwood. His overdose of cologne assaulted her nose. "Touch any of my people like that again and I'll have you tossed out on your ass or arrested for assault."

He grinned. "Just trying to get her attention. Seeing how busy you are and all."

She ignored his crack about business being slow. She followed them to the table. Greer held a chair for Olive. She sat down, staring up at Underwood, batting her lashes. Greer lowered himself onto a chair. Bert grabbed a chair from an empty table and slouched into it. He fished a cigarette case from his coat pocket.

Underwood took his seat, opening the button of his suit jacket and placing his hat on the table. "I was just telling Tommy that we shouldn't expect too long a wait for service. How are your numbers, EJ? I heard you're in the red."

Her jaws tightened. Who the hell was feeding him information? "You heard wrong."

Underwood looked around the room again, calculating. "If I were running The Garden, I'd have this place packed every night."

"Well, you're not, and we're doing just fine."

He snorted, and EJ's vision went red.

Using every ounce of control she could muster, EJ spoke calmly and quietly. "Don't come into my place giving me attitude."

She saw Macie hovering nearby and waved her over.

Macie set the glasses down, her gaze jumping between EJ and Underwood. "Um, two dollars, please."

Underwood's gaze bore into EJ's, but no way would she flinch or look away. He reached into an inside jacket pocket. She tensed for a moment, wondering if he was carrying a piece. If he decided to shoot her, at least there would be witnesses.

He took out his wallet and handed three bills to Macie. "Keep the change, honey."

Macie took the cash, flashed him a brief, nervous smile and hurried away.

EJ set her hands on the table. "Drink your drinks and get

out. And if I ever see you or anyone associated with you in here again, you'll be leaving horizontally."

Olive's eyes widened. The lawyer sputtered.

Bert's beady eyes narrowed. "Who the fuck do you—"

Underwood raised a hand to shut him up, the other hand tightening around his glass. "Is that a threat?"

EJ leaned closer, keeping her gaze locked with his and her voice low. "You better fucking believe it is."

She straightened, gave him a final sneer, then turned to strut back toward the door marked "Private."

The other Roses, except for Callie, were waiting there, concern all over their faces.

Shit.

She had hoped they'd come in the back and go right upstairs.

When she reached them, Bette opened her mouth to say something, but EJ gestured for them all to stay quiet. She opened the door and ushered everyone through. Once they were in the narrow hall on the other side, and the door closed once again, they all began talking at the same time in hushed but urgent tones.

"What the hell is he doing here?"

"Does this mean the spell isn't working?"

"What do we do now?"

"What in the world does Olive see in that slimeball?"

EJ held up her hands to stave off more questions. She took a breath and blew it out slowly. Meeting each of their gazes, she made sure they knew she had everything under control. She hoped she did.

"Underwood is just being an ass," she said. "I don't know what his being here means. What it *doesn't* mean is that the magic isn't working, right, Ruth?"

"Is it working?" Marian asked. "Or is this wasting our time?"

"Magic isn't exact," Ruth said, frowning. "The ritual isn't going to be complete until tonight, so we can't expect results yet."

"See?" EJ said, trying to sound encouraged. "It ain't done yet. But listen up. Not a word to Callie about them being here. Confidence is crucial for her right now, and we don't want to worry her needlessly. Get yourselves settled and keep your lips zipped. Got it?"

They all nodded and made a visible effort to calm themselves. Ruth and Marian appeared to have it under control, but something in Bette's expression worried EJ.

"Bette?" She stared hard at the other woman. "Are you going to be able to keep your mouth shut?"

Undermining Callie's confidence on this last night could ruin everything. If Bette ran her mouth, Callie might balk, and then where would they be? In a nasty war with Underwood, that's where.

The shorter blonde drew herself up to her full height, defiance glinting in her eyes. "Let's go."

Ruth led them up the stairs.

As she climbed, with the music fading behind them, EJ replayed the encounter with Underwood in her head. The bastard. What nerve he had, coming around to her place. She didn't show her face in his restaurant or pool hall just to be an ass, did she?

Worry bit at her throat. If the spell didn't work, she'd have to figure out something else. Something more direct. Something more permanent.

Of course it'll work, she chided herself. Callie knew what she was doing. She needed to take her own advice and have faith in her friend.

Friend. More than a friend if they were to carry things past that amazing kiss last night.

But Underwood showing up here at The Garden brought home one important fact: anyone EJ cared about was vulnerable to the likes of Underwood or any other boss looking to scare her off. She couldn't and wouldn't put Callie in harm's way, no matter how painful it was to deny being with her.

EJ would rather die herself than risk Callie.

When the third and final night of the incantation had concluded, Callie dismissed the Roses from the circle. She joined them out in the hall, shutting the storage room door.

"When will we know if it's working?" Bette asked.

EJ shot her a glare that would have fried an egg.

What was that about?

"Hopefully soon," Callie said. "EJ, do you know anything about Underwood's activities or movements that we can use?"

EJ shifted her gaze to Callie, the look in her eyes much softer. "Yeah, he has some sort of meetings happening this week. Not sure of the details, but he's nervous about it."

Marian cocked an eyebrow. "And you know this how?"

"I have my sources," EJ said with a wink.

Marian rolled her eyes, smiling. "Of course you do. Okay, I gotta get home. Let me know if you need anything."

"And I have a set to do." Ruth gave EJ a mocking glare. "My boss is a bitch."

"Got that right," EJ said.

They all laughed, making their farewells and promises to meet up for coffee soon. Ruth, Bette, and Marian headed downstairs, chatting about kids and busy lives.

After spending so many of their younger years living day to day, unsure of what tomorrow would bring them, Callie was glad her friends were doing well. They had loves, lives, reasons to take the good with the bad and get up each day. This wasn't the vision she'd had for any of them fifteen years ago, which had prompted her leaving. Not after what had happened to Janie.

We need to get him. He needs to pay.

"Hey, you okay?"

EJ's touch to her upper arm opened Callie's eyes. She hadn't even realized they'd closed. Weariness hit her all at once, and her legs suddenly felt like jelly.

"Just tired. It's been a long few days."

EJ gently grasped her arm and tugged her toward the office. "Let's get your feet up and some food in you."

"As soon as the candle goes out, we need to complete the ritual," Callie reminded her.

"I know." EJ opened the office door and led her in. She guided Callie to the cot and had her sit down. "We have time. You need a break."

The concern in EJ's eyes created a well of emotion that knotted in Callie's throat.

You're just tired.

She sat back on the cot and put her feet up. EJ smiled, sending a different sort of feeling through her.

"Be right back," EJ said.

After they ate a couple of sandwiches and drank their colas, EJ insisted Callie nap for a while. They would collect the remnants of the spell components and head out after The Garden closed for the night.

Callie felt somewhat refreshed when EJ woke her just after midnight with a gentle shake of her shoulder. She changed into more appropriate out-at-night clothing, and packed everything else in her suitcase. While EJ took her bags downstairs, Callie went into the storeroom.

The scent of the burnt candle and herbs clung to the air, getting stronger as she approached the chalk circle. Careful to keep the line intact, she stepped over it and crouched by the remnants of the materials she'd used, still-warm wax and charred leaves, the white cloth adhered to the silver plate. She folded the fabric upon itself to contain all of the components and added it to the two bundles already in the bag within her satchel along with Underwood's toothbrush and the bloody clothes she'd used to stanch the shallow cuts on her palm. The sheathed dagger and chalk went into the satchel as well.

Taking a deep breath, Callie cleared her mind and began to brush away the chalk circle. As she scattered the dust, she whispered words of thanks to the Universe for wisdom and power. Once the entire circle was no more, she rose.

"All done?" EJ asked from the doorway.

Callie hadn't heard her return, intent on being as precise as she could with every aspect of the incantation from start to finish. And they weren't quite finished.

"With this part, yes," she said, picking up her satchel.

"The car's warming up down in the alley." EJ stood aside to let Callie precede her into the hall. She held up Callie's coat.

Callie thanked her and slipped her arms in. EJ's hands lingered on her shoulders for a heartbeat longer than necessary. They headed downstairs, and EJ opened the back door that led into the alley. Cool air tinged with the sour odor of garbage, exhaust, and rotting things wafted in. A covered light offered a dim pool of illumination over the black Model A.

They stepped into the alley and EJ locked the door behind them. She grasped Callie's hand, leading her around to the passenger side. Warmth surged up Callie's arm. She instinctively gave EJ's hand a squeeze. EJ opened the car door and helped Callie in.

"There's a blanket for you," she said, pointing to the quilt on the bench seat. "It's gonna be a bit of a trip and you might get cold."

Callie set her satchel at her feet and draped the quilt over her lap. "Thank you. That's very thoughtful."

EJ shrugged and grinned, then shut the door. She went around to the driver's side and got in. She glanced at Callie. "Ready?"

When Callie nodded, EJ put the car in gear and headed

down the narrow alley to the side street.

They drove for nearly an hour, initially through the quiet streets of Seattle, passing few other vehicles so late at night. As they left the city limits, heading southwest, only the headlamps of the car illuminated the narrow road. Beyond that moving pool of light, there was little to see in the darkness except when they passed the occasional lit window of a home in the distance.

As they drew closer to the secluded coastline, trees grew thicker and the road became narrower. Callie used EJ's flashlight to consult the map.

"I think this is as far as we can go," she said. "Pull over here somewhere."

"Yes, ma'am."

EJ maneuvered the car to the side of the road and cut the engine.

Callie pointed the flashlight into the woods. "We can walk in a bit, find a good spot."

"I'll get the shovel," EJ said, getting out. "Watch your step over there."

Callie left the blanket, but grabbed her satchel and got out of the car. EJ met her on that side. She dug into her coat pocket and took out a small brass compass. Callie chuckled. She had said they needed to go as far west as they could reasonably manage. EJ was taking no chances.

They moved away from the Model A and consulted the reading on the round face.

"Looks like that-a-way." EJ gestured in the general direction where the compass needle had pointed. "Want to lead or do you want me to?"

"I'll do it," Callie said. "Let's go. It's getting cold."

They walked into the woods, avoiding roots and other debris, and navigating around trees, though they managed to stay mainly on course. After they'd walked about one hundred yards from the road, Callie stopped.

"This'll do."

Without a word, EJ began digging.

"Deep enough that it won't be stumbled upon," Callie instructed, "but don't hurt yourself."

"Right," EJ grunted.

It didn't take her long to dig into the loamy soil. EJ stepped back and wiped her forearm across her brow.

Callie handed her the flashlight. She knelt by the hole and laid the sack of ritual remnants inside. The aroma of the candle wax, herbs, decaying leaves, rich soil, and sea air mixed and mingled as she covered the hole.

"Draw him away from that which we seek to protect." The incantation wasn't going to literally draw him to *that* spot, just away from The Garden in general. Though having Underwood stumble around the woods held petty appeal. She patted the soil down, then scattered loose debris over it. Satisfied, she rose, brushing her knees and hands clean. "Done."

EJ quirked a slender eyebrow at her. "That seemed rather . . . anticlimactic."

Callie laughed. "Magic is like that sometimes. Most times. Not always flashes and claps of thunder."

EJ nodded thoughtfully. "Maybe that's why more people don't do it. Not enough pizzazz."

Callie laughed again, then looped her arm through EJ's, taking the flashlight in her other hand. "Could be. Though I'm sure the studying and energy commitment has a little to do with it too."

They made their way back to the car. EJ returned the shovel to the backseat, and they both settled in for the return trip. Callie nodded off along the way. She sat up with a start, blinking herself awake. "Sorry about that."

"No worries," EJ said, taking her eyes off the road for a second to glance at her and smile. The city lights were close now. "Almost home."

Home.

Gran. The shop. Everything Callie had left then run back to. Yes, it was more comfortable, and now that she had started using her magic for real, she couldn't see herself putting it back under the bed with her spell book.

So now what?

"I dunno," EJ said. "Now what?"

Heat infused Callie's cheeks. She hadn't meant to say that part, or any of it, out loud.

"I-I suppose we go back to normal and see what happens."

"Normal for me isn't like everyone else's normal, Cal." EJ's attention returned to the road ahead. "Even with Underwood off my back and hopefully out of the Y-J, there's always someone out there looking to make a move. Hell, I do it too. Normal is maintain control and increase territory and revenue, and keep your ass alive."

Something knotted in Callie's chest. "Will you want me to do this again?"

Is that what EJ was doing, wooing her for future spells? Was that all she meant to EJ?

In the dim light of the interior of the car, Callie saw her frowning. "Not if I can help it."

That was . . . something.

"You know I'll do what I can to help."

EJ glanced at her, though not long enough for Callie to read her expression. "I appreciate that, but I don't want you in the middle of anything. It's not safe."

"I'm already in the middle of things, EJ."

Involved in the spell, involved with her, involved with the Roses again. Things that were potentially dangerous, but at the same time, where she wanted to be.

"Yeah, I know."

It wasn't disappointment in EJ's voice, exactly. More like resignation. Did she regret their kisses? It sure as heck hadn't seemed like it at the time.

EJ pulled up in front of Callie's building. Nothing moved on the quiet street. Other than the streetlights, all was dark except for the occasional light over a doorway or in an upper window.

While Callie got out of the car, EJ retrieved her suitcase. She came around to the sidewalk and gestured toward the door that led to Callie's apartment. "I'll walk you up."

"You don't have to," Callie said. She dug her keys out of her purse, half regretting she'd given EJ an out. "Unless you'd like to." Their gazes met. There was something in EJ's eyes that shot a bolt of excitement through her. She couldn't explain it, nor could she deny it existed. "I'd like you to."

EJ nodded.

Callie turned toward the door. Despite her shaking hands, she managed to get the lock open. EJ followed her into the dimly lit hall and stairwell. They passed the door that led to the rear of the butcher shop and went up. Another key opened the apartment door itself. Callie reached in and turned the switch to light the small dining area and kitchen.

The place still smelled faintly of the onions she'd fried four days ago, telling her she needed to air things out soon. The mantel clock in the living room chimed the half hour.

EJ put her suitcase down to the right of the doorway. "Get some rest. I'll see you soon."

Callie touched her arm before she turned to leave. EJ looked down at her hand, then up at her face, question in her dark eyes.

"Thank you," Callie said.

EJ covered her hand. "No, thank you. These past few days have been a lot for you. I appreciate all you've done."

"I hope it works."

"It will." EJ smiled, her own weariness showing in the lines at the corners of her eyes and mouth. "And it got us together again. Making mischief, just like old times."

Callie couldn't help but return the smile. "Yeah, old times."

Truth be told, she wanted new times with EJ.

EJ gently squeezed her fingers. "Come to The Garden tomorrow night. We'll have dinner and listen to Ruth sing. Just relax. Though you're probably sick of the place."

Callie laughed. "Never, as long as you don't make me sleep in your office."

"Only if you want to."

Recalling how EJ looked first thing in the morning the last few days, gorgeous in a sleep-tousled sort of way, sent a wave of heat through Callie. She could easily imagine waking up next to the other woman, or falling asleep beside her after doing things that made them drop from exhaustion onto their shared mattress.

"D-do you want a cup of tea or something?"

EJ's gaze dipped to Callie's mouth. She ran her pink tongue delicately across her lips, as if imagining tasting Callie's. *Yes, please.* Callie's fingers flexed slightly on EJ's arm.

EJ cleared her throat. "Thanks, but I'd better go. And you need real rest. See you tomorrow."

As she lowered her hand, Callie hoped she hid her disappointment. The spell was over. There were no more restrictions on what they could and couldn't do. She thought EJ was equally anxious to take things further. Had she done something to scare her off?

"Good night."

EJ leaned forward to kiss Callie's cheek. Callie turned her head, their lips barely brushing before EJ stepped back. "Good night."

Callie shut the door behind her, listening for EJ's footfalls. She heard nothing at first. Was EJ on the other side, reconsidering? Should she open the door and yank her back into the apartment?

Before she could act—if she were to be that bold—she heard the patter of EJ descending the stairs and the gentle slam of the outer door.

She let out a sigh, though whether it was of relief or frustration, she couldn't say. She wanted to spend more time with EJ. She wanted more, period. And she had thought EJ felt the same. No one kissed like they'd kissed the night before without feeling something, but then she'd throw up walls. For someone who was so forthright in her business decisions, EJ Jordan seemed to have a hard time sticking with a clear path when it came to Callie.

Maybe it was time to press the issue and find out what was going on in that woman's head. It was a risk; she didn't want to lose EJ as a friend. But now that Callie recognized what she herself wanted, if she didn't do *something* she'd burst.

CHAPTER ELEVEN

The following day seemed to drag on forever. Customers came and went in the shop, some openly curious about why it had been closed for several days and asking where Gran was. Callie gave them what she hoped to be vague but satisfactory answers, saying Gran was fine and visiting her sister, which was true. As for the closed shop, Callie either told them she'd been a little under the weather or steered them onto another topic, like which cut of beef they wanted for Sunday dinner.

No more than ten minutes before she was about to lock up, the front door banged open and the bell jangled wildly. Callie's head came up like a shot, expecting to see Mr. Madsen and about to ask him if he was all right. She'd lost count on the receipt she was tallying for his pick-up order and would need to start again.

But it wasn't Mr. Madsen.

Suit rumpled, tie askew, and graying hair out of its usual combed back neatness under his fedora, Paul Underwood stood in the middle of the shop breathing hard, his face red. He slammed the door closed, rattling the glass. "What the fuck do you think you're doing?"

Adrenaline roared in Callie's head. How dare he come in here like that?

She got to her feet, suppressing the urge to yell right back.

From the corner of her eye, she saw her cleaver on the cutting table. "I'll thank you not to tear in here like a madman, Mr. Underwood."

He stalked closer to the display cases. "You're doing something," he said through gritted teeth. "You and that bitch dyke."

She pressed her lips together, fighting to keep calm. How had he found out? "You watch your mouth and get out of my shop."

Underwood narrowed his gaze.

"Or what?" He stepped closer. If the counter hadn't been between them, Callie was sure he'd have been right in her face. "I'll find out exactly what you're doing and report you to the Tribunal. Back the fuck away."

The burden of years of being afraid of men like Underwood burst like an overinflated balloon. "Drop dead."

He slammed both hands on the low part of the counter and leaned forward. "I know you did something. My own people told me so. You're the only one strong enough to lay a spell like that. You're messing with my business, and if you don't fix it, you and your girlfriend will be sorry."

Fear and anger welled in Callie's gut. How did he know she was strong enough and what she was? What would he do? How did he know about her and EJ?

The next thing she knew, the cleaver was off the table and in her hand. "You're the one who better back off, Underwood. Get out of my shop."

His face turned scarlet as his lip curled into a snarl. "I'm not playing with you two bitches. Undo whatever you did or you're dead. Hear me? Dead."

He wasn't bluffing.

This was what EJ had meant by it being dangerous for her. For them. Callie didn't care. He could threaten. She would act.

"You are not and never will be welcome here, Paul

Underwood. Get out." Callie nicked her thumb with the tip of the blade. Underwood's eyes flashed with fear. Grim satisfaction joined the energy waking inside her. If he didn't know what, exactly, she was before, he did now. Good. Crimson trickled down her skin, hot and tingling. Magic swelled with each breath as she willed Underwood away. She pointed the head of the cleaver toward the door. "Get. Out."

Underwood paled. He stepped back, eyes wide.

In the opposite corner of the shop, Mr. Madsen stood with his back to the wall, eyes just as wide and face just as pale. Damn it. When had he come in?

Ignoring the poor man caught in the middle of her dealings with Underwood, Callie returned her attention to the crime boss. She slid her bloody thumb along the flat of the blade and pointed it at him again. Power surged through her. "Get out and don't come back."

Like a marionette being controlled by a drunk puppeteer, Underwood abruptly turned and stumbled to the door, yanking it open on the second fumbling try. The bell jangled and the door closed behind him with a thud.

The impromptu spell wouldn't keep Underwood away forever, despite the wording, or she would have used it at The Garden. Directing him to not come back was more power of suggestion than magical command. If his will was strong enough, and it probably was, he'd be able to counter it at some point. But it would work for now, and maybe Underwood would think twice before bothering her or EJ.

And likely she only made him madder.

Something else to consider. Damn him.

Callie stood frozen for another moment, waiting for her magic to dissipate and her heartbeat to return to normal. Calmness and relief came with lightheadedness. That surge of magic had come too soon after completing the three-day incantation. She squeezed her eyes shut and set the cleaver down. It would need to be properly washed.

I need to see EJ. Warn her that Underwood knows something. Somehow.

When she opened her eyes again, she met Mr. Madsen's still wary, wide-eyed gaze. Dabbing her cut thumb on her apron, she smiled at him and walked back to her receipt book on somewhat wobbly legs.

"Sorry about that. Got your order ready, Mr. Madsen. Let me just finish tallying it up."

The color started to return to the gentleman's face. "N-no hurry, Callie. No hurry at all."

EJ sat at her desk going over the books and raking her fingers through her hair. Her accountant swore everything was correct. Unfortunately, numbers didn't lie, he reminded her. They could be made to lie, but this wasn't the case.

She unscrewed the cap of the insulated flask and poured out a third cup of coffee. She had to focus, figure out where she could stop money from bleeding out of her business.

"No wonder they call it being in the red." Though she knew it was due to the red ink that seemed to dominate her ledger pages, it sure felt as if someone had opened a vein.

So where could she save a few bucks? Cut back on dining? They weren't making much off Valerie's dinners, but it kept her and the staff employed. Drinks? That wouldn't fly. And the supplier was giving her a decent discount already. Entertainment? Nah. Folks loved to dance. And if they weren't dancing, they were listening while eating and drinking. Besides, there was no way she'd give Ruth or the boys the sack.

She gulped a mouthful of hot coffee. There had to be something. If worse came to worse, she'd funnel a few thousand in from other endeavors. Her numbers game and unnamed, underground gambling room were doing well enough. As much as she wanted to keep The Garden legit on paper as well as in practice, she wanted to keep it open even more.

Someone knocked on the door. EJ glanced at the electric clock on the wall. Not much past six. Dinner was being served. This was usually a quiet part of the evening at The Garden.

"Please don't let it be anything serious," she muttered as she rose and went to the door.

Expecting Mason or one of the staff, EJ couldn't hide her surprise or pleasure when she saw Callie. But that good feeling ebbed when she saw the expression on Callie's face.

"What's wrong?"

Callie slipped past her and stopped in the middle of the room, hands clenched. EJ closed the door.

"What happened? Is Gran okay?"

"She's fine. Got a letter from her this morning." Callie's face was pale, but anger flashed in her blue eyes. "Underwood came to see me just now."

EJ's chest and fists tightened. "Are you all right? What did he want?"

"I'm fine." Callie started pacing the office, tossing her purse, then her hat, then her coat onto the chaise. "He said he knew I—we—were up to something."

"Shit."

"Exactly."

"How does he know?"

Callie stopped pacing and faced her. "He didn't say. Just said he had his own people, which makes sense, I suppose."

No one but the Roses, Callie's mentor, and the plant mage knew they were doing anything of a magical nature. And no one but the Roses knew who it was directed at.

"He was spitting nails, EJ. I thought he'd go off on me."

Anger edged toward rage throbbing in her temples. "Did he touch you?"

Anyone—especially Underwood—laying a hand on Callie wouldn't see the next day.

Callie shook her head. "I grabbed my cleaver and pricked my finger. Said a quick spell to push him out."

EJ chuckled. It wasn't a good idea to be on the wrong side of a blood mage even if they couldn't outright kill you.

"He left," Callie continued, "but not without saying we'd be sorry."

EJ rested her hands on Callie's shoulders. "Let him try something. We'll see who's sorry then."

She wouldn't bother Callie with the fact that Underwood had come in the other day, threatening her as well. He was a thorough bastard, she had to give him that.

"Poor Mr. Madsen saw at least the last bit. My hands were shaking so much I could barely write up the rest of his receipt."

EJ gave her shoulders a squeeze. "I'm glad Mr. Madsen was there." At Callie's indignant glare, she grinned and led her to the chaise to sit down. "Not because I think you needed him for protection." The hardware store owner was over sixty and had no mage skills that EJ knew of. "But at least he was there to witness Underwood threatening you."

Indignation became a sheepish lowering of her gaze. "And me threatening Underwood."

She slung her arm around Callie's shoulders and pulled her closer. Damn, she felt good in her arms. "Understandable, considering." She waited for Callie to respond. When she didn't, EJ gently jostled her. "Hey. What's wrong?"

"If Underwood knows what we did, he might be able to counter it."

EJ didn't understand enough about magic to know what that entailed, but Callie seemed worried. And if Callie was worried, EJ needed to pay attention. "How likely is that?"

Call's brow furrowed. "He'd need a mage as strong as, or stronger than, me. He'd need to know the spell we used, the components and incantation. They figured out something was done, so it's possible."

"Olive used to dabble when we were kids. Do you think she's strong enough?"

"I don't know. I don't think so."

Hope bubbled in EJ's chest. "Then what are the chances of a counter-spell? Pretty slim, I'd guess."

"Slim, but again, possible." Callie rose and started another round of pacing. "Maybe he has another mage working for him, someone other than Olive. Or it could have been someone slipping him information. I don't know."

EJ stood up and went to her desk. She slid the ledger into a drawer and locked it. "I don't know either, but if it's one of my people, there will be hell to pay."

She kept her hands busy to keep herself from clenching her fists.

Callie stopped pacing and faced her. "Do you think that's possible? Who?"

Who, indeed? No one at The Garden was privy to what, exactly, had been going on in the storeroom, and EJ would have sworn her life on the loyalty of her staff. But times were hard and people did things you wouldn't expect them to do for money. Or if they were threatened. The thought that one of her own was responsible for letting the cat out of the bag and for Underwood's visits felt like a kick in the gut.

"I don't know. No one, I hope." She went around the desk and took Callie's hands. "We'll figure it out. Let's get some dinner, and I think we can both use a drink."

EJ invited Callie to spend the evening at The Garden, but she still seemed agitated and wasn't enjoying herself by the time dessert arrived. Though it was Friday evening, and the atmosphere was revving up and gay, EJ could read the writing on the wall and on Callie's face.

She leaned closer, enjoying the floral scent of the woman beside her, and said, "You want to leave, don't you?"

Callie turned her head slightly, but EJ didn't back away much. They were within a scant few inches. Kissing distance. The look in Callie's eyes went from distracted to heated in a blink.

"I'm sorry, EJ, but yes, I'd like to leave." She did look sorry, and EJ's chest tightened. Underwood had shaken her, and EJ wanted to kill him for that. "I'll just head out. We can talk tomorrow."

They got up from the table. EJ helped her with her coat, letting her hands linger on Callie's shoulders. "I'll drive you. It's too cold and damp to walk."

Callie gestured toward the noisy, busy room. The band was hot tonight and people were already dancing up a storm. "You should stay. They should see you're here to take care of them."

That had always been part of EJ's MO. Let the customer know you're there for them and chances are they'd be there for you. But sometimes breaking routine was necessary.

"You need a little care right now." She reached down, grasped Callie's hand, and gave it a gentle squeeze. "They won't miss me for a bit. Come on."

Callie smiled at her. A tingle shot from the pit of EJ's stomach and radiated downward as well as along her limbs.

Hand in hand, they walked through the dining room. EJ nodded to Stella on the way to the front door where Mason kept watch. He assured EJ all would be well for however long she was gone. His smile said he approved of whatever was happening between her and Callie, and EJ felt her cheeks warm. Callie's blush turned that warmth to heat. Yeah, she definitely felt the way EJ did, that being alone together was going to do something to their friendship. Hopefully for the better.

The car sat in front of The Garden. EJ opened the passenger door for Callie and hurried around to the driver's side. The rain wasn't too heavy, but there was a chill that cut through her suit jacket. She didn't want to waste time running back up to her office for her coat.

She got the Model A running and headed down Jackson toward Callie's building. Neither spoke until she stopped at the curb.

"Come up," Callie said. "For tea or something."

She needed more than a tea companion. She needed company, reassurance that they would be safe. EJ could certainly provide that.

She smiled and killed the engine. "Love to."

EJ followed Callie through the outer door, as she had last night, and up the stairs. At the landing, Callie glanced over her shoulder as she unlocked the door. "The place is a bit of a mess."

"I'm not here to critique your housekeeping."

Callie's cheeks pinked prettily, and her smile grew under the overhead light. "Glad to hear that."

Inside, familiar scents brought EJ back to their early days together when she'd come by to pick up Callie and her Gran would push a plate in front of her while she waited. Coffee, floral perfume, bacon. EJ smiled at the memories.

"I'll get water boiling," Callie said as she hung up her coat. "Go make yourself comfortable."

EJ walked through the kitchen and past the open French doors that separated it from the front room. A couple of worn upholstered chairs, a couch, and a coffee table filled the small room. The knickknacks and photographs on shelves and other horizontal surfaces sent a pang of sadness through her. Mementos of travels, pictures of smiling family members—those hadn't existed for her. She remembered pretending they were hers when she was a kid. A silly fantasy that sometimes hit her hard when she went back to the apartment she shared with her father and whatever flavor of the week he was entertaining.

Her gaze fell on the portable Columbia Grafonola sitting on a corner table above a box of records. She remembered Gran being so tickled when she'd won it in a raffle from the Liberty Music Store several years before, saying how it reminded her of her late husband. The store owner had owed EJ for a short-term loan, and she happened to mention how great it would be if Gran were to win as she bought a dozen tickets in the woman's name the day before the drawing. Gran was thrilled, and the music store owner got a break on his final payment.

"How about some music?" EJ called out toward the kitchen. That would help lighten her mood. Something to keep their minds off of Underwood. EJ sure as hell needed it.

"Sounds great," Callie called back.

EJ knelt down and went through the selection. Gershwin. Dorsey. Armstrong. Ah, yes. Hoagy Carmichael. She stood and cranked the handle, making sure not to overwind. If she broke Gran's Grafonola she'd be in big trouble. After checking for a new needle, EJ placed the disc on the turn table and slid the release to start it spinning. When it got up to speed, she lowered the brass tone arm, careful not to let it drop on top of the record.

Scratches sounded through the arm's diaphragm before the strains of "Stardust" wafted into the living room.

"Oh, I love this one," Callie said from the doorway.

EJ turned around. God, she was so beautiful. From the day they'd met, when they were barely in their teens, EJ had been stunned by Callie's easy smile and bright eyes.

She held out her left hand. "Dance with me?"

Callie hesitated. Was she going to refuse? Laugh off EJ's invitation?

She stepped past EJ and shoved the coffee table out of the way, then turned, still smiling, and took the offered hand. EJ's breath hitched as they came together, not quite body to body, though her right arm went around Callie's back easily enough.

151

Callie laid her left hand on EJ's shoulder.

They started to dance, their bodies stiff at first, then quickly relaxing into a gentle sway. Callie closed her eyes and sighed as she laid her cheek on EJ's shoulder, facing away. The aroma of her shampoo and perfume filled EJ.

"You're a much better dancer now," Callie said as the circled the small space in the living room. "You used to step on my toes when we were first learning."

EJ smiled, remembering the dance parties the Roses had had among themselves. "I've had a little more practice since then."

Callie lifted her head and leaned back. One of her eyebrows arched. "Oh?"

"There's a lot of dancing at The Garden." EJ spun them around, guided Callie closer. She didn't resist. The sensation of their breasts pressing together almost threw EJ off. "I prefer this. A more intimate setting."

Callie stared at her for a moment, then leaned closer. Her breath brushed EJ's earlobe. "Me too."

They were quiet for a few bars, listening to the music, moving together. Callie's warm body, soft in all the right places, fit perfectly against EJ, like a missing piece of her was finally in place. The music, the swaying, the utter joy of being together, made everything else in the world fade away and pale by comparison.

"EJ?"

"Hmmm?"

"It's gonna be all right, right? With Underwood, I mean."

EJ felt the slight tremble of Callie's body. She tightened her hold. "I swear it."

One. Two. Another step and a gentle spin.

"EJ?"

"Yeah?"

"I would really like to kiss you right now. I mean, really kiss you. And then some."

EJ's eyes flew open, and she congratulated herself on not stumbling or stopping. They continued to dance as she moved her upper body slightly away from Callie so they could look at each other. The heat in the other woman's eyes was unmistakable.

"Would you?" The question came out in a whisper of wonder. Because who wouldn't be stunned by such a statement?

"I would, but I don't want to mess things up."

EJ grinned. "I'm sure you're a fine kisser and it wouldn't be messed up at all."

Callie rolled her eyes and gently slapped EJ on her shoulder. "No. I mean, yes, I *am* an amazing kisser." She offered a wicked smile that dried EJ's mouth. But then Callie's expression became serious. "But I don't want to mess up our friendship. That's too important to me."

EJ released Callie's hand and cupped her cheek. "It's important to me too."

"And I know . . . I know you're worried about what could happen to me."

EJ stiffened for a moment. Yeah, she'd said that more than a few times to warn Callie off. To warn herself off.

"I am worried." She stroked Callie's cheek with her thumb. "But with Underwood knowing about the spell, about us being together, we don't have to pretend nothing's going on. Now we can focus on countering whatever he has in mind."

Underwood could still do some serious damage, but at least he'd lost the element of surprise.

"Then maybe we can see where this can go."

EJ's stomach fluttered. "Maybe we should."

She leaned forward, head tilted, and closed her eyes as their lips met. She brushed her mouth across Callie's, kissed the corner, the middle, the opposite corner. Callie's lips parted slightly and their breath mingled, warmth swirling over sensitive skin. Hunger swelled in EJ. She met Callie's lips again and flicked her tongue against the seam of her mouth.

Callie let out a small whimper and let her in. Her arms went around EJ's neck. EJ wrapped her arms around Callie, pulling her in tight. Tongues and lips and teeth worked, gently touching and tasting. EJ's need grew as her heart raced.

"Don't stop," Callie said when they paused to take a breath.

EJ slid her hands along Callie's back. "I won't."

They kissed while the closing notes of "Stardust" became a faint tick-tick as the needle skimmed the inner ring of the record.

"Music stopped," Callie murmured against EJ's lips. She trailed kisses along EJ's jaw.

Tingles of delight danced across her skin. "D-do you want me to put another record on?"

"Mmmm . . . no."

Callie eased out of her arms, and EJ immediately felt the loss. She hid her disappointment as Callie crossed to the record player, returned the arm to its cradle, and shut it off. When Callie turned around, she smiled and crooked her finger. Anticipation soared, and EJ went toward her as if attached to a string. When she got close enough, Callie took her hand.

"This way."

Callie led her out of the living room, though the kitchen—pausing long enough to turn off the gas under the kettle as it was about to come to a boil—and down the short hallway. She brought them into her bedroom and stopped in the middle of the tidy room.

She released EJ's hand and turned around. Face to face, in the dim light from the window, Callie kicked off her shoes and started to unbutton her dress.

EJ swallowed hard, her hands clenching to keep from jumping in and helping. She watched Callie's deft fingers slide each button through its hole. At the last one, she slowly parted the garment and allowed it to drop to the floor. She stood in her bra, slip, and stockings, arms loose at her sides.

"Come here."

Powerless and unwilling to disobey, EJ stepped closer, close enough to feel Callie's breath feather across her lips, close enough that the silkiness of her slip brushed the lapels of EJ's suit jacket.

"You've been with women," Callie said softly, matter of fact.

It was no secret. Still, EJ pushed down the odd sensation of guilt. She had no reason to feel like she'd cheated on Callie. They'd been friends, not a couple. "Yes."

Callie took EJ's hands in both of hers and raised them to her lips. She kissed the back of each, then met EJ's gaze with a mixture of heat and boldness that shot to EJ's core. "Show me."

EJ slid her hands out of Callie's grasp and cupped her face between her palms. She kissed Callie slowly, gently, tasting her, telling herself not to cry, damn it, as emotions she couldn't explain flooded her. How many times had she imagined this moment? How many times had she shoved it out of her head, sure it would never happen in a million years, because Callie had never shown interest in girls? How many times had she used the excuse of not wanting to risk Callie's safety when really it was her own fears that kept EJ from acting?

Too many times, and too much time lost. But they were here now.

Callie moved her hands up EJ's body, and despite the layers of clothing covering her, EJ shivered as Callie's palms brushed over her breasts. She pushed EJ's jacket off her shoulders. EJ let it drop. Still kissing, they moved toward the bed, Callie stepping backward as EJ guided her, just like when they were dancing in the living room moments before.

Callie lowered herself to the mattress, hands still on EJ's shoulders, urging EJ to her knees. She ran her hands down Callie's hips and legs, enjoying the silkiness of the material over warm skin. As she trailed her fingers back up, she pushed the slip higher. Callie's legs clenched around her.

EJ broke the kiss. Staring into her eyes, she said, "We won't do anything you aren't ready for."

Callie nodded and leaned forward. "I want you to touch me," she whispered against EJ's lips. "I want . . . I want you."

A thrill shimmered through EJ. How long had she waited to hear those words? She kissed Callie, parting her lips and tangling their tongues. Determined not to move too quickly, EJ trailed her hands up from the other woman's thighs to lay them on her shoulders. She toyed with the bra and slips straps, running her fingers under the thin materials.

Callie moaned and covered one of EJ's hands. She helped EJ lower both straps on that side. EJ did the same on the other. She skimmed her palms over Callie's bare shoulders, then tugged the garments down, revealing the swells of her breasts.

EJ pressed her lips to the soft skin of one breast, flicked her tongue against it, then blew gently on the damp spot. She did the same with the other. Hooking a finger over the edge of the material, she drew both bra and slip down to uncover Callie's right nipple. She licked the tip and blew again.

Callie shivered. Her hands fisted in EJ's vest. "Again. Please."

EJ moved to the other breast and repeated the action.

Callie arched her back, pushing her nipple between EJ's lips. EJ took the invitation, enclosing her mouth around the taut skin and laving it with her tongue. She licked and sucked the nub of flesh, tasting the delicate saltiness of Callie's sweat, inhaling the heady, clean soap aroma of her skin.

"EJ . . ." Her name was a quiet cry of desperation.

EJ lifted her head and kissed Callie's lips, her cheek, her jaw. Callie tilted her head, and EJ took her earlobe between her teeth to give it a gentle nibble. She palmed Callie's breasts, grazing her nipples with the tips of her thumbs.

Callie raked her fingers through EJ's hair and turned her head. Their mouths met with a hungry need. EJ plunged her tongue past Callie's lips. Callie's fist tightened, pulling at the roots of EJ's hair with pinpoints of luscious pain. She shoved EJ away.

EJ landed on her ass, staring up as Callie stood. She unhooked her bra and quickly stripped it off. She stepped out of her underwear, revealing the dark triangle at the apex of her thighs. She reached for the snap on her garter holding up her stockings.

"Leave them," EJ said, stopping her.

Still bent slightly at the waist, Callie grinned at her.

EJ stood. She loosened the tie knotted at her throat, pulled it off and dropped it onto the floor. She unbuttoned her vest.

Callie's eyes glinted, and she hooked her finger in the waistband of EJ's trousers. EJ stepped closer, holding her gaze. Callie pushed the vest off her shoulders. She opened the two top buttons of EJ's shirt. Her fingers traced the triangle between her collarbones. She opened another button and leaned forward.

EJ's breath hitched as Callie's lips brushed against her skin. Her tongue flicked into the hollow. While she nuzzled EJ's neck, Callie worked on the line of buttons and moved the front of the shirt aside. Cool air prickled EJ's belly.

Taking hold of the suspenders, Callie walked backward to the bed and sat, pulling EJ down with her. They stretched out on the twin bed with Callie on her back and EJ on her side. One of Callie's arms was under EJ, her fingers swirling in EJ's hair as they kissed. Callie's other hand glided along EJ's arm.

EJ skimmed her palm over Callie's breasts, gently rolling each nipple between her fingers in turn. Every moan and whimper from her ticked EJ's desire up a notch. Their kisses grew deeper, more breathless. Callie covered EJ's hand and moved it lower. Her palm crossed Callie's abdomen. Her fingers brushed the curls at the top of Callie's mound.

Callie's hips twitched. She pushed EJ's hand lower. Together, their fingers parted her, and EJ's fingertip skimmed her lower lips. Her own arousal grew, a tightening bundle of need between her legs.

Callie pressed her fingers down, and EJ felt warm, silky wetness.

At the same time, she could imagine the sensation Callie was experiencing, of fingers sliding against her, of delicious pressure, the need building from her core. It was as if EJ was giving and getting at the same time.

"Inside me, EJ," Callie said between devouring kisses. "Now."

Never had she heard such demands from Callie's lips. They reminded her of when Callie was leading the Roses during the incantation, direct and in control. It made EJ smile as they kissed. She slid her fingers back and forth, gentle, teasing. Callie hissed a breath and bucked, spreading her legs. Her fingernails dug into the back of EJ's head and hand.

EJ drew her hand up again, swirled wet fingers over the firm nub there, then back down. Slowly, she increased speed and pressure. Callie's rhythmic thrusting met EJ's. EJ rubbed herself against Callie's hip, the friction of the clothing both enhancing the sensation and frustrating the hell out of her. She wanted Callie's hand to be there, or her mouth.

EJ considered going down on Callie, the desire to taste her nearly overwhelming. But she was loath to move. This first time, she wanted to watch Callie, knowing there would absolutely be a next time and as many times as they could manage.

EJ increased her pace. The bedsprings squeaked as Callie moved in rhythm, breathing hard. EJ slid two fingers inside her, loving the slickness, the tightness of the muscles as they clenched and released with each thrust. She bit-sucked the skin at the juncture of Callie's neck and shoulder, not caring if she left a mark. Callie was hers now.

A third finger caused Callie to arch her back and let out a breathless, "Oh!"

EJ's body reacted accordingly, and her teeth bit down a little harder than intended, Callie hissed at what had to be a jolt of pain.

EJ lifted her head. "Sorry! I'm so sorry."

Hurting Callie in any way, shape, or form was the last thing she ever wanted.

Callie grabbed EJ's hair and looked at her with such intensity EJ swore her eyes had gone completely black, though a trick of the light gave them a red glint. "Don't be. And don't stop."

Relieved, EJ grinned, then kissed her. Plunging tongues mimicked the action of her hand. Her fingers became slick, like silky dew off a morning rose.

Callie thrust faster, her breathing more shallow and her vagina gripping EJ's fingers.

"EJ, I . . . I . . ."

"Come for me," EJ said against her ear. "For me, Cal."

Callie arched her back. Her inner muscles grabbed and pulsed around EJ's fingers. EJ pressed herself into Callie's hip, imagining Callie's fingers were inside her, almost feeling them there. It gained her some relief, though not a full-on orgasm. She didn't care. Watching Callie lose herself in the pleasure EJ was able to give her was just as good. Well, almost as good, but she wasn't going to quibble.

She caressed Callie as she rode the wave to completeness, slowing, gently stroking her damp curls until Callie stilled her hand.

I love you, Calliope Payne.

The absolute truth of that hit EJ like a truck. Yeah, she loved Callie. Always had. And it would probably be the best, most difficult thing ever. For both of them.

She pressed her lips to Callie's mouth, trailed delicate pecks along her jaw and throat while they caught their breath. Her own libido was ready to go, but she was in no hurry to interrupt gazing at the gorgeous woman before her.

After a few moments, Callie's eyes fluttered open, and she

smiled. "You look like the cat that swallowed the canary."

EJ nuzzled her neck. "Maybe next time I'll be the canary eating the, ahem, kitty."

She stroked along Callie's sensitive flesh, making her jump and gasp. Callie laughed as she grabbed EJ's hand to keep it still. "You are terrible."

EJ nibbled her earlobe. "From your earlier reactions, I beg to differ."

They laughed and kissed.

Callie shifted to her side and had EJ lay on her back. When EJ was settled and firmly on the bed, Callie rolled on top of her, straddling one of her thighs. She leaned forward so her breasts were pressed against EJ's chest. EJ cupped Callie's ass, gently kneading the flesh.

"How about I show you how terrible *I* can be?" Callie asked.

EJ's simmering libido flared. "Please do."

Callie gave her a wicked grin and leaned down for a kiss.

A loud pounding sounded from the other room. Someone was furiously knocking on Callie's door.

That could not be good.

"Shit." Desire and anticipation evaporated. EJ eased Callie off of her. "Stay put. I'll see who it is."

As she walked out of the room, buttoning her shirt and cursing whoever was on the other side of the door, she realized she didn't have her gun with her. No gun and almost literally caught with her pants down. She didn't regret being with Callie like this, but she needed to keep her damn head or she'd lose it. Or worse, Callie would.

Get your shit together, Jordan.

Giving herself a mental shake, EJ entered the kitchen and scanned the room for something to use as a weapon. There. A block of knives. Drawing the largest one out of the holder, she went to the door and yanked it open.

One of her neighborhood boys stood on the other side, cap

in hand and panting as if he'd run a mile or two. "Sorry to bother you, Miss EJ, but Mr. Mason needs you at The Garden."

He glanced at the knife in EJ's hand, her untucked shirttails, and messy hair but wisely held his tongue.

"What's wrong?"

"Underwood men causin' trouble. Itchin' for a fight."

"Son of a bitch." EJ set the knife on the dining room table. She tucked her shirttails in. "Tell him I'm on my way."

The kid nodded, then hurried down the stairs.

EJ shut the door. She turned to go back to Callie, but Callie was standing in the hall entrance wearing a blue-and-white striped cotton robe. Worry creased the brow that EJ had so recently enjoyed seeing slick with orgasm-induced sweat.

"The spell was supposed to keep Underwood away from The Garden." Her disappointment was clear.

EJ walked over to her and wrapped her in a gentle embrace. "You said the magic isn't always what we want it to be. It's just a couple of his low-level goons, I'm sure. Or wannabes that are trying to get in his good graces. It'll be fine."

Callie returned the hug. EJ took a moment to again enjoy how they fit together. She leaned back, lifted Callie's chin with her fingers, and kissed her.

"I have to go."

"Will you come back? We haven't finished." Callie's smile was so very inviting, but when EJ looked at the clock on the dining room wall, she sighed.

"I don't think I'll be able to. I'll need to stick around until closing, maybe then some. It'll be late."

Callie finished buttoning her shirt for her, the brush of her fingers not intentionally erotic, but erotic nonetheless. "I don't mind waiting."

EJ kissed her again. "Get some sleep."

Callie fisted the front of the shirt and pulled EJ close. The kiss was long and deep and reminded EJ that her body wanted to finish what they'd started. But it wasn't meant to be. Not tonight at any rate.

"Be careful," Callie said when they parted.

Breathless, EJ nodded. "I will be. This thing with Underwood ends now."

She hurried to the bedroom for her jacket and shoes.

CHAPTER TWELVE

Callie woke the next morning as the sun poked through the gap in the blue Swiss dotted curtains covering her bedroom window. Saturday. Eddie was going to work a shift at the butcher shop this afternoon. No need to hurry to get up. She rolled onto her side, facing the room, and smiled when her gaze fell upon EJ's discarded tie on the floor.

Delicious memories of what they'd done the night before shimmered through her, heating her body all over again. There had been some moments where she'd felt like she was occupying both their minds, both their bodies. Had EJ felt it? She hadn't said anything. It was an aspect of their connection Callie hadn't considered, and one she hoped EJ had enjoyed as much as she had. She definitely looked forward to picking up where they'd left off. The sooner the better.

Recalling why EJ had to leave early, however, put a decided damper on her mood. Flipping back the covers, she got up to bathe and dress.

After fixing her hair and makeup, Callie draped EJ's tie over her wrist. Unsheathing her dagger, she pricked her left palm, then slowly rubbed her hands together. The blood was slick at first, but quickly turned tacky, as there wasn't much. She concentrated on EJ. Her magic, focused on EJ, came up with no more effort than it took to breathe.

"Where is she?" Callie said aloud, sending her request into the universe. "Where will I find her?"

Images of leaves and flowers surrounded EJ in her mind's eye. The Garden. Of course. EJ had either spent the night there or had gone home and returned early. Though she was a little disappointed if the latter was the case and EJ hadn't come back to Callie's, there was certainly a good reason for it. She wouldn't dwell. They'd have their time.

Callie washed her hands, noting the small cut had already healed, then got her coat and shoes. She folded the tie and slipped it into her pocket. Making sure doors were locked behind her, she headed to The Garden.

The October morning was bright and clear, promising a chilly but delightful afternoon. Perhaps she would try to convince EJ to take a drive along the coast, forget their troubles for a while.

Assuming the front door of The Garden was locked on a Sunday morning, Callie turned down the side street before the club then into the alley. There was EJ's car, parked just outside the rear door. She breathed through her mouth to keep the stink of garbage at bay. At least most of it was in bins and not strewn about.

She stopped at the back door and tried the knob. Locked. Not surprising. She knocked. After a few moments, she knocked again, harder. If anyone was working in the kitchen, or if EJ was up in her office, she needed to make herself heard. If no one answered, should she unlock the door and go in? The car and her magic told her EJ was here, but was she all right?

The door opened a crack, then wider. EJ stood there, hair mussed, smudges under her eyes. She slipped her right hand into her jacket pocket, but not before Callie caught the handgrip and hammer of a revolver. She wore the same suit, now rumpled, she'd been in last night.

Callie's skin prickled. Something was wrong.

EJ smiled, but Callie saw the weariness and wariness in her eyes. "Hey. Didn't expect you this early."

"I don't want to be in the way. You okay?"

EJ took both her hands and gently tugged her forward. Callie stepped through the doorway, into her arms. EJ kissed her. Callie's stomach fluttered.

"You will never ever be in my way," EJ said when she broke the kiss. "Got it?"

Callie noted the intensity in EJ's eyes. "Got it. But you didn't answer my question. Are you okay?"

EJ pecked her on the lips. "Better now. Come in. I was about to have some coffee."

Holding one of Callie's hands, EJ drew her inside, then closed and locked the door. She led Callie to the kitchen, a clean and organized space, as Valerie the cook would have it no other way.

"What happened last night?" Callie asked while they set up a tray with cups, spoons, cream, sugar, and a coffee carafe.

"Come see," EJ said nodding toward the door that led to the dining room.

Callie followed her and stopped dead in her tracks. Most of the tables were covered with dirty glasses, some knocked over, spilled contents staining the tablecloths. Chairs and broken glass were scattered across the dance floor.

Callie stared open-mouthed at the mess while EJ set the tray down on cleared table. She righted a couple of chairs and gestured for Callie to have a seat.

"A bit of a to-do." Her grim smile was meant to downplay the situation, but there was no downplaying this.

Callie found her voice as she strode over. "What happened?"

With almost unnerving calm, EJ held one of the chairs out for her. But as Callie got closer, she noticed the tension in the other woman's face. "Underwood's goons. Mason ended up with

165

a black eye and a nasty cut. Needed a few stitches, but he'll be okay."

Callie sank into the offered seat. EJ sat beside her and poured their coffees.

Guilt and anger warred in Callie's gut "I-I'm sorry. The spell was supposed to prevent things like this as well as keep Underwood himself off your back."

EJ sipped her coffee, holding up her other hand and waving Callie off. "This isn't on you. You said it yourself that magic can be particular. We were focused on Underwood, not his goons. From his attitude when he went to your shop, the spell seemed to have worked, right? This is on him. All of it."

"I'll help clean up." She had to do something.

EJ laid her hand on Callie's arm. "Later. The others will be here soon to pitch in. Let's have a couple of minutes, okay?"

By the time they were finished with their second cups and started to right chairs, several others had arrived to help, acknowledging Callie as part of EJ's crew with quiet greetings and nods. Callie, Ruth, Macie the server, one of the bus boys, and the cook's assistant grabbed mops, rags, and brooms and got to work. They chose tasks using the standard "Rock, Paper, Scissors" method to determine first pick, garnering a bit of much needed laughter. Mason came in with his left arm in a sling and a swollen eye. Stella, still glamorous even in her plain blouse and skirt, stood at his side frowning up at him. Taking the hint, EJ sent them home.

While they cleaned, EJ took inventory of the glasses, plates, silver, and table coverings that would need to be replaced. Some of the chairs were no good as anything other than firewood, but most were fine or would need only minor repairs.

Ruth claimed the piano and sound equipment were in working order and even provided them with a little relief, playing a Chopin piece then a bit of Gershwin. When she was finished, everyone applauded. Had she used a bit of her magic to ease their worries? Maybe, but mostly Callie and the others enjoyed listening to their talented friend.

The last of the broken glasses and dishes had been swept up, the last chair set back in place, and the bus boy and cook's assistant were washing dishes and silverware when Seattle Police Department Lieutenant Lorne Bradford strolled in from the lobby through the arched doorway. Had there been any music playing, Callie would have expected a sour note to be struck.

Bradford was from the neighborhood, known to almost everyone from when he was a beat cop chasing loiterers off corners and giving the Roses the hairy eyeball whenever he passed by. Rumor had it that he was willing to turn his back on certain activities while extending a hand for some extra cash. The Roses were never part of that economic exchange, of course— hence the harassment. Callie was pretty sure his practices hadn't stopped with his rise in the ranks. Chances were, he was making even more from heavier hitters in the city.

Three uniformed officers followed him in, spreading out a few paces from each other and stopping when Bradford hesitated near the first table. Callie's nerves jangled. Cops were not a welcome sight during her youth, and more than a few had harassed EJ for her particular friendliness with girls. Despite the cooperation between the police and local covens, the regular PD weren't necessarily keen on mages either.

Among the three uniformed cops, Callie recognized Ruth's suitor, Joe, from a picture the singer had shared at EJ's. He kept his expression neutral, though he looked over at Ruth several times. If he was dating Ruth, Callie was sure he, at least, could be trusted.

Bradford unbuttoned his tan overcoat and scanned the room, hands on hips and thin moustache twitching. Everyone stopped what they were doing, looking first at the lieutenant then at EJ.

EJ glared at him from the table where she sat keeping track

of inventory. "We're closed."

Bradford grinned and came forward. The uniformed cops stayed put. "Not for me you aren't. The door was unlocked."

EJ sighed and rose. "What do you want, Bradford? We're busy here."

"We need to chat, Miss Jordan." He glanced at Callie. "You too, Miss Payne."

EJ came around the table, toward Callie. She made eye contact with Macie and Ruth, cocking her head toward the back area of the club. Macie hurried out. Ruth took her time, glaring at Bradford, but softening her gaze slightly when it fell on Joe. She sauntered after Macie.

When both were gone, Callie and EJ joined Bradford. They all sat in silence for a few moments until Bradford leaned back in the chair.

Callie noticed one of the uniformed men mumbling and moving his hands in small gestures in front of his waist. One of the Tribunal's seekers, mages used to liaison magical and non-magical legal situations. Why? What was he looking for? From what EJ and the others had said as they recounted the brawl, there had been no magic used.

Would he be able to detect her spell from the past few nights? If he was a strong enough mage he could, though it would be unlikely for him to suss out what it was meant to do and toward whom it was directed. Unlikely, but not impossible.

"What happened last night?"

EJ shrugged. "Things got a little wild."

"A little too wild." Bradford frowned. "Heard your man Mason got cut pretty bad."

"He'll be fine." EJ shook her head. "Is that why you're here? Seeing if Mason's okay? Ain't you sweet. Or are you here to take my statement on the assault or a disturbing the peace call since they came into my place looking for trouble?"

His lip curled up in a smirk. "You wish." He looked at Callie.

"How about you? You here last night?"

"She wasn't," EJ said.

Without taking his eyes off Callie, Bradford said, "I wasn't talking to you, Miss Jordan. Miss Payne? Where were you last night?"

"I was here until about seven, then went home."

"Alone?"

Before she could reply, EJ spoke for her again. "I brought her home."

Bradford eyed the two of them. Did he know about their relationship? Did it matter to him? Would he say or do anything? Callie's face warmed. The lieutenant offered nothing but his scowl. "And you turned right around and came back here?"

EJ didn't hesitate. "Got back here around eight-thirty. Maybe nine." At his cocked eyebrow of query, she added, "We had tea and listened to some music. Shot the breeze. You know how we women get."

Bradford glanced between them. "Sure. And no one was with you after that, Miss Payne?"

Callie held his gaze. "No."

He nodded, then turned to EJ. "How did the evening start?"

EJ gestured toward the room. "Dining, dancing, the usual Friday night action."

"Except for the brawl." Branford crossed his arms. "Who did what?"

EJ mimicked his posture. "I got called back here from Callie's. Some mooks were causing trouble for my servers. It got heated, then out of hand. Eventually my guys threw them out and we closed for the night."

"What time?"

"Nine-thirty. Ten. I wasn't exactly checking the clock." She shrugged. "Took Mason to the hospital to get stitched up. Dropped him home. Got back at eleven, maybe a little later, to keep an eye out in case someone got some sort of

169

smart idea to return."

"Who else was here?" Bradford looked around the room. Though the others had left, they were probably listening at the door in the back.

"When I returned from dropping Mason off?" EJ rubbed her jaw, making a thinking expression Callie suspected was a ruse. EJ knew exactly who had been here last night and when. "The band, a couple of the kitchen crew, a few servers. They'd started to clean up. I told them to call it a night and we'd finish today. They left before midnight."

Callie watched the uniformed cop who was casting. His hands had been still for the past few minutes. His face was impassive and he hadn't jumped in to call either of them liars. That had to be points in their favor.

"You stayed here?" Bradford asked with a note of incredulity in his voice. "Alone?"

EJ's expression darkened. "Yeah, alone. It's my place. What did you expect me to do, hide under the covers at home?"

He ignored her question. "So no one to vouch for you—for either of you—from midnight to this morning."

Callie and EJ exchanged glances. What was he getting at?

"You'll just have to take our word for it I guess," EJ said.

Bradford snorted. "Not likely."

"Why?" Callie asked. "What happened between midnight and this morning?"

He didn't say anything for a moment, merely looked at each of them in turn, frowning. "Paul Underwood died."

CHAPTER THIRTEEN

"Died?" EJ couldn't have hidden her shock if she tried. At least she managed to hold back a laugh that wanted to burst out. "How?"

Bradford narrowed his gaze. "Not for public knowledge at this time. But I'm more interested in who at the moment. Starting with the two of you."

Callie's eyes widened. "Us? Why us?"

The lieutenant pointed at each of them in turn. "Because you, Miss Payne, threatened him in your shop yesterday. And you, Miss Jordan, did the same here in this very room," he stabbed the table with his finger, accenting each syllable, "not three days ago."

EJ stiffened.

"*He* came to *our* places of business first, Bradford. *He* threatened *us* with harm. And while threats ain't action, maybe put that little fact in your notebook." She kept her temper in check, but it wasn't easy when you were being accused of murder. Even if the guy deserved it. "I'm not gonna mourn the man, but you can't pin this on either of us because we had words."

"More than words. Motivation, opportunity, and means, Miss Jordan," Bradford growled as he ticked off the cornerstones of crime on tobacco-stained fingers. He stood and buttoned his coat, his gaze flicking to Callie. "We got a Tribunal witch on the case."

Callie's face went white. "You suspect magic is involved?"

Despite having side-stepped EJ's question about how Underwood had bought it, Bradford now nodded slowly. "There's some indication, yes. Since you just happen to be friendly with one of Underwood's rivals and a mage, Miss Payne, we thought it prudent to talk to you first." He looked at both of them pointedly. "Don't leave town. I'll have more questions for you."

He turned and strode toward the door. Two of the uniformed cops fell in behind him. Joe offered EJ and Callie a nearly imperceptible nod, then hurried to catch up. They all disappeared into the lobby. The front door closed hard behind them.

"Son of a bitch." EJ rose and began pacing, running her hands through her hair. "Son of a fucking bitch."

She wasn't upset that Underwood was dead. Far from it. The bastard deserved what he got. Hell, however it had happened probably wasn't nearly as painful as EJ would have preferred. But how had she and Callie been eyed as suspects?

"We need to find out what happened," Callie said.

EJ whirled to face her, her knee-jerk "no shit" tempered to silence by Callie's expression. The woman was scared. EJ sat down beside her. "It wasn't either of us."

Uncertainty clouded Callie's eyes.

"Wait. Do you think I did this?" EJ asked. "I don't use magic."

Uncertainty became indignation. "You think it was me?" Callie asked. "I specifically told you I wouldn't harm anyone like that, not on purpose. If my spell went awry, I'll take responsibility for that, but if that liaison cop was able to sense my spell here and they think it had anything to do with Underwood's death, I could be in real trouble. Or do you think I hated him enough, wanted to please you enough, to jeopardize my vow? The Laws?"

Callie's color was high in her cheeks and her breathing had

kicked up a notch.

Shit.

"I didn't say that."

"Didn't you?" Callie crossed her arms. "Who else do you know who uses magic like that? Who else, other than us, had a beef with him?"

Her words, laden with hurt though they were, struck EJ. There was supposed to be trust between them now, wasn't there? "I can name half a dozen people off the top of my head."

Callie opened her mouth to say something, but abruptly snapped it closed. The furrow across her brow deepened. "I didn't say it was you either. It's possible the incantation went so completely awry it caused harm. A small possibility, but still a possibility. If a Tribunal is called and that turns out to be what it is, I'll pay that price. But harm never was the intent."

What sort of price would they mete out?

EJ shuddered to consider it.

"Cal, I swear—"

She caught a flutter of movement at the edge of her vision. Macie and the others stood near the door leading to the kitchen and office, eyes riveted to the two of them. She and Callie had gotten loud. Too loud. Their emotions had gotten the better of them.

She took Callie's hand. "Okay, let's stop this."

Callie's lips were pressed into a thin line, the tension practically making her vibrate under EJ's touch.

"I'm sorry," EJ said. "I don't think you did anything to hurt him. I know you take your vow seriously."

"I do. Even if he deserved it, I wouldn't kill him unless it was in self-defense or to save another."

EJ skimmed her thumb over the back of the other woman's hand. Callie hadn't said she didn't believe EJ had killed him. She gave Callie a crooked grin. "For the record, I didn't do it either."

Callie's cheeks darkened. She squeezed EJ's hands, then

held on. "I believe you. Really I do."

EJ nodded. "Thanks."

"Why didn't you tell me Underwood was here the other night?"

Damn, she had hoped Callie hadn't caught that bit from Bradford.

"It was in the middle of the spell. I didn't want you distracted." She raised her hand as Callie started to say something, likely about being square with her. "I know. But he was just being a prick and you didn't need the aggravation. We exchanged words, and yeah some threats, nothing more."

Mostly nothing more, but she didn't need to know that. If every questionable conversation ended in actual violence, there would need to be a lot more cemeteries in Seattle.

"Bradford doesn't believe either of us," Callie said, thankfully letting it go. "And neither of us has an alibi. How do we prove it wasn't us?"

EJ kissed her fingers. "First, we need to get details about his death. Joe might be able to help."

Ruth's suitor was usually a good source of information on happenings within the police force. He wasn't a dirty cop by any definition, but he was loyal to his girl.

"I'll have Ruth get word to him," EJ said. "Though he may not have much for us."

"Every little bit would help." Callie eased her hands from EJ's and stood to continue cleaning up. "Who else would want him dead?"

EJ voiced her first thought. "Rivals. Aside from me, I heard Mickey Crandell was sniffing around Underwood's warehouse not so long ago."

"The wife," Callie offered. "The night of the party, Kay either ignored him or looked like she was about to puke when she laid eyes on him."

"Didn't we all? What about his girlfriend?" EJ suggested. "I wouldn't be surprised if Underwood was looking for a new skirt. Olive is getting a bit long in the tooth for him."

Callie looked appalled. "She's our age."

"Like I said . . ." EJ couldn't help but chuckle at the disgust on her lovely face. "But seriously, he was a bastard to pretty much everyone. Always had been."

Something in Callie's expression shifted, and EJ knew she was thinking about Janie. "Yeah, he was."

She walked over to Callie and enveloped her in a gentle hug. "Someone did us a huge favor even if we are being looked at for it." She pressed her lips to Callie's temple. "We didn't do anything. We'll be all right."

"But we *did* do something, EJ." Callie eased out of her arms. "If that spell had anything to do with his death, the Tribunal will come down hard. We need to figure out whose magic is involved."

EJ blinked surprise. "Can you do that?"

"I would think the Tribunal witch is already working on it. Some mages leave particular markers or do spells a certain way or with certain components all the time. They can be quite individual, like a signature or finger marks. Looking for a mage like that isn't something I've done. We'd need to know what to look for, know what to compare it to."

EJ remained cautiously optimistic at finding the actual killer. No matter what, they had to prove themselves innocent. Then she would thank whoever had knocked off Underwood with a case of the finest Canadian whiskey.

She kissed Callie on the cheek. "We'll figure it out."

Officer Joe Kribniak looked nervous as hell when he came into The Garden later that afternoon. He had changed out of his uniform and wore a brown suit with a patterned tie. He removed his fedora and palmed his wavy brown hair back off his forehead, eyes darting around as if he expected Lieutenant Bradford to emerge from under a table.

Sitting at EJ's favorite corner table with her and Ruth, Callie nudged Ruth's shoulder and gestured toward the man. Ruth raised her head from the sheet music she was making notes on. Black bob swinging, she turned and smiled at Joe, waving him over. He visibly relaxed and came through.

"Hello, Joe," Ruth said as she stood. When he was close enough, she reached for his hands and offered her cheek. Very prim and proper.

Joe's face pinked, but he dutifully took her hands and pecked her on the cheek. "Hiya, Ruthie." Nodding to EJ and Callie, he said, "Ladies."

EJ gestured to the chair beside Ruth's. "Take a load off, Joe. Can I get you a drink?"

"Whiskey and soda, thanks." He took another look around the room where some chairs were up on tables and the lights on the stage were dark. "Not opening tonight?"

EJ rose, her smile tight. "Nah. Taking a few days off. I'll be right back with your drink. Make yourself comfortable."

Callie watched EJ head to the bar, noting her casual, cat-like movements. She didn't just walk; she strode, she glided. It wasn't a strut like some put on, but a natural gait that was all power and sex appeal. Her moves in the bedroom had been the same, and Callie couldn't wait for more.

". . . Callie?"

Ruth calling her name snagged Callie from entering an extremely naughty daydream.

"I'm sorry," she said. "Lost in thought for a second."

Ruth glanced over to where EJ was pouring drinks. Her smirk said she knew exactly what Callie had been thinking. "I asked if you wanted me to hang around or not."

"Oh, sure. Stay." She and EJ had figured Joe might be more

comfortable with Ruth around. Besides, there was nothing they were going to discuss that Ruth couldn't know as well.

The two of them smiled at each other and Joe's arm moved, as if he was now holding Ruth's hand under the table. "That's swell," he said, grinning.

EJ returned with the tray of drinks. Along with Joe's whiskey, there was a gin and tonic for Ruth, seltzer and lime for Callie, and a shot of bourbon for EJ.

"Not working tonight, are you, Joe?" EJ asked as she set the drink in front of him and sat again.

"Nah. And I have tomorrow off."

Ruth smiled. "I have tonight and tomorrow off too."

Joe's cheeks darkened again. "Maybe we can . . . do something."

"I'd like that."

The two stared at each other without speaking. Callie grinned, practically seeing the little hearts circling their heads and filling their eyes.

EJ cleared her throat. "So, Joe." He blinked a couple of times before looking her way. "What can you tell us about the Underwood situation?"

Joe took a healthy swig of his drink, then wiped his mouth with one finger. He held the glass with both hands, eyes on EJ. Gone was the love-struck young copper. In his place, a confident young man, who knew his way around the seamier side of the neighborhood and who held her gaze. "Underwood died sometime late last night or early this morning. Street sweeper found his car over on Belforth. Brains blown into the back seat."

Callie winced. She hated Underwood, had no problem with him being dead, but the situation was not good on a number of levels.

"Murder?" EJ asked.

Joe took another sip. "Maybe. Maybe suicide. But there's something Bradford doesn't want out there yet."

"Spit it out, Joe." EJ's patience was close to nothing today, with good reason.

"There was a dame in the car too."

Callie's heart stopped. "Who?"

Joe shrugged and shook his head. "No idea. Took a slug under her chin. Blew her face off, pretty much."

"Oh, good god." Ruth looked green around the gills. Even as a blood mage, Callie sympathized with her. It was a gruesome image.

"Olive, maybe?" Callie suggested.

Olive and her sister Rita had run with the Roses for a bit, but Olive had been more interested in status and power than in hanging out with a bunch of half wild girls. Rita followed her sister wherever she went and whatever she did. Both had moved on to other prospects before they were out of their teens. Callie hadn't thought much about them until she'd learned Olive was Underwood's mistress.

"Underwood offed her then himself?" EJ asked. She didn't seem nearly as disturbed.

"Or vice versa. Coroner's still looking at angles and stuff. Found a silver cigarette case on the seat between them with O.L. engraved on it."

"Olive Lang." Ruth shuddered.

A pang of sadness went through Callie. She hadn't been close to the Langs, but the way this situation seemed to be shaping up, it was a terrible way for her to go.

"Or it was left there to make it look like Olive." EJ tapped an unlit cigarette in the table.

"Until we figure out who the other body is, yeah, who knows." Joe glanced at Callie. "Some dame from the Tribunal's been poking around, too."

Callie's gut tightened. It was standard procedure to check for magic association with most crime scenes, particularly ones that resulted in bodily harm or death. Making a magic-influenced crime look run-of-the-mill wasn't a new thing. Apparently, the Tribunal mage had found something at the scene if they had a PD liaison officer accompanying Bradford on his visits to question people. "Anything from them yet?"

"Nothing specific. Definitely some magic residue or whatever it is, but that's all the rest of us know."

The "residue" was something like a fingerprint left behind by the mage. Perceptible, but not always easy to pinpoint. Narrowing down the elemental affinity would be a good start, as the population of mages was small and their affinity a matter of record. If the Tribunal mage was on the trail of a specific mage, they wouldn't necessarily inform the city police until they were sure. Even that depended on the standing of the suspect mage. The Tribunal could insist on taking care of the situation themselves. Jurisdiction for magic violations was theirs alone.

"Suspects?" EJ held her glass but hadn't drunk from it yet. "Other than me and Callie, I mean."

Joe shrugged. "Bradford's questioning the missus. Or will when she's able. Doctor had to give her some sort of nerve-calming stuff."

Callie barely suppressed a snort. A little over the top on the devastated widow front, even for Kay Underwood. At their anniversary party, it was obvious she loathed the man.

"Has he questioned Bert or Rita Lang, being Olive's only relative and all?" EJ asked.

"Bert was with Kay, so Bradford may have asked a few things when he gave notice. Nothing on Rita, as far as I know, since Olive hasn't been officially identified as the other victim. But he may question her to figure out Olive's whereabouts." Joe turned the now empty glass in his hand. "He did go see Underwood's partner, the lawyer."

EJ's eyes widened. "Partner? When did Greer become his partner?"

"Recently, according to Greer. Which sounds a little fishy."

"Yeah it does." EJ sipped her drink. "What did he have to say?"

"That he hadn't seen Underwood since Friday. Had some sort of meeting before Bert Underwood went to dinner with the wife and son. Bradford'll check it out."

"Who benefits most by Underwood being gone?" Ruth asked. "Other than everyone."

EJ grinned at her, but quickly sobered. "Kay Underwood likely gets a nice insurance settlement, I'd wager. Bert won't be hurting either. I'd imagine his new partner gets at least half control of the business."

Joe gave a low whistle. "Underwood had his hands in a lot of things. That business is no small potatoes."

"What about Olive?" Callie asked. "If she isn't the other body, I mean."

"I'd guess her loyalty is price dependent," EJ said. "If she wanted more from him and Underwood said no, would Olive have had to off him to move on to her next sugar daddy? Maybe so."

So three or four others aside from them. Callie was relieved that there were more names on Bradford's list.

"There's also the businesspeople he pissed off," Joe reminded them. "Rumor had it he was into Crispin Lerner for a chunk of cash."

EJ had mentioned as much at the meeting with the Roses before they enacted the spell.

"Not a man you want to stiff," EJ said.

"Nope."

Callie didn't recognize the name, but from their reactions she didn't need to know more about Crispin Lerner. He was a dangerous man to cross, period.

"But if he owed Lerner money," she ventured, "why would Lerner have him killed? Dead men don't pay up."

"True," EJ said. "Though if Underwood had gone on too

long, Lerner might decide to get rid of the thorn in his side and lean on the new partner, or even Kay. He's not above squeezing all he can out of family or making an example of welchers. Neither was Underwood."

"That's quite a number of folks with motive." Ruth rested her chin in her hand, elbow on the table. "Who had means and opportunity?"

Joe grinned. "You sound like Bradford. But aside from EJ and Callie, for sure, I don't know." He glanced at them with a sheepish expression. "Sorry, ladies."

Callie ran her finger around the rim of her glass. "It's the magic residue I wonder about. I'm assuming Olive was registered."

EJ touched her arm, gaining her attention. "And if she's registered, maybe they'd be able to figure out if it was her magic that did Underwood in."

"That's the way I understand it, though being magic it can be fiddly. Maybe, like you said, EJ, Olive had had enough of him," Callie said.

"Or maybe he got tired of her," EJ suggested. "One tries to break it off. The other gets upset. Bam! Then sees what they did, feels bad. Bam!"

Callie winced at each Bam! Did Paul and Olive love each other that much to take the other's life then their own? She wouldn't have given Underwood that much emotional credit.

"If they found residual magic, it could have been Olive's attempt to defend herself, or to hurt Underwood first." Callie considered Olive's potential spell options, if she had the ability. "If she wasn't strong enough to hold him off, he gets mad, shoots her, and takes his own life. Or she gets his gun and vice versa."

A tidy explanation if that's how it actually happened. There were lots of "maybes" and "ifs."

"Any idea what Underwood had been up to last night?" EJ asked.

"Yeah. Bradford checked in at El Fuego," Joe said. "That's been his and Olive's latest hangout. They'd been there until closing, supposedly. According to the bartender, Olive's sister Rita was there too, but he didn't see them give each other so much as a glance."

The Cuban bar rarely closed before 3 a.m. And the beat cop hadn't seen Underwood's car there at midnight when he'd gone down Belforth Street on his rounds.

"Still gives Olive time." EJ rubbed her eyes with her fingertips. "Three hours at least."

"Gives a lot of people time," Callie said, silently adding themselves, at least as far as Bradford was concerned.

EJ rested her arms on the table and leaned forward. "Listen, Joe, we need to know everything Bradford learns. Me and Callie are innocent, but he sounded damn sure we had something to do with this."

"I'll tell you what I can, EJ, you know that." He glanced at Ruth and gave her a fleeting smile. "Thing is, it was a messy scene with no clear way of knowing who might have been there."

"Except for magic being detected," Callie added. "Do you know the seeker, the TLO?"

If they could connect with the Tribunal Liaison Officer, they might get a heads-up on that aspect of it.

"Charlie Raymond," Joe said. "He was here this morning. Green, but a decent guy. Seems to know his stuff."

From what Callie remembered of the muttering, gesturing officer, he was young but serious. This might be his first case. That he hadn't found anything here at The Garden was a good sign. Tribunal enforcers would have come by now.

"What about the Tribunal investigator?" Callie asked.

"Tall, scary dame," Joe said. "Frances something. Eddings? Elmont?"

"Eccles." Callie remembered the stern Covenant Investigation Office agent from Tribunals she'd sat in on as a teen learning the Laws. Frances Eccles was a no-nonsense sort. "Taking a life is a serious crime. If magic was involved, she'll be anxious to get to the bottom of it and punish the mage. Severely."

"I'll talk to Raymond," Joe offered. "I just don't want him getting suspicious of my motives."

Joe walked a fine line at times. If they wanted to keep him as a source, they'd have to let him do things in a manner that worked for him.

"We appreciate anything you can tell us," EJ stood and fished inside her jacket pocket for her leather wallet. She dropped a couple of twenties on the table. Joe's and Ruth's eyes widened and went to her. "We're not gonna be open for a few days. Why don't you get yourselves a nice meal somewhere."

Joe gave her a tight smile. "You're not paying me off or anything, are you, EJ?"

EJ laughed. "Nah. It's Ruth's wages. I don't know when we'll be back to full operation, and she was supposed to do a couple of shows. Not fair to her not to get paid, right?"

Ruth scooped up the cash. "Right. Thanks, EJ."

EJ held a hand out to Callie. Callie took it and rose. They bade the couple good night.

"Make sure the front door locks on the way out, will you, Ruth?" EJ said while leading Callie to the back.

"Will do," the singer called out. "Good night."

Without turning around, EJ waved to them and opened the door marked "Private." She led Callie past the dark kitchen, checked that the rear door was locked, and took her upstairs.

Anticipation fluttered in Callie's belly, growing with each hurried footstep on the wooden steps. When they arrived at the office door, EJ threw it open and tugged her inside. Callie felt as if they were dancing again. She allowed herself to sweep into the room, using the energy of EJ's tug to whirl around and curl into her embrace. Laughing, she kissed EJ soundly.

EJ pushed the door shut and wrapped her arms around

Callie, deepening the kiss. Hands stroked and explored. Lips and tongues and teeth teased and nipped. Callie slid her palms over the fashionable vest covering EJ's torso, her hands and fingers briefly pausing on the other woman's breasts before she started to unbutton the garment.

EJ groaned as she stilled Callie's hands. "Wait," she said, breathlessly interrupting their kisses. "There's something I need to do."

"Lock the door?" Callie traced EJ's lips with the tip of her tongue. EJ moaned. "Get naked?"

EJ squeezed her fingers gently. "Definitely that last part at some point, but I need to talk to Rita Lang. She probably knows more than Bradford would get out of her."

Callie sighed and took a half step back. "I'm sure, but you hurried up here for a reason, and I didn't think that was it."

EJ grinned, lowered their clasped hands, and pecked Callie on the lips. "We will continue, I promise, but this can't wait."

Callie didn't let her disappointment show, at least she hoped not. "I know."

Releasing her hands, EJ crossed the room to her desk. She opened a drawer and pulled out a black address book. "I don't have Olive's address . . ." She flipped through a few pages and ran her finger down listings. "Here. I'll drop in on Rita and see what she knows."

Striding back, EJ framed Callie's face between her palms and kissed her. "This won't take long."

"Good," Callie said, moistening her lips. She grinned at the heat in EJ's gaze as she followed the path Callie's tongue took. "But you aren't going alone."

Something darkened EJ's eyes. "Cal, I—"

Callie kissed her, hard and long and deep, then grabbed EJ's hand. "Let's go."

CHAPTER FOURTEEN

As she and Callie climbed the stairs to Rita's second-floor walkup, EJ kicked herself again for not telling Callie about her connection to the younger Lang sister. All the way over to the building, she had had ample time, but little in the way of easing it into conversation. What could she say? "Here's Rita's block. Oh, by the way, I've slept with her"? The truth would be out soon enough.

The hallway carpeting was worn but clean, the lighting softened by dusty fixtures. Four apartments on each floor were labeled A through D. Rita's was A, the first on the right.

Callie stood beside EJ, tugging off her gloves and shaking her hands out. Not because of the cold, EJ realized. The blood mage was preparing a spell.

"Is that necessary?" It wasn't a criticism, and luckily Callie didn't seem to take it that way.

Callie glanced at her. "Hope not. Go ahead and knock."

Did she sense something EJ couldn't, or was Callie playing it safe?

EJ was suddenly reassured by the gun in her pocket.

She knocked three times, paused, then twice more with a beat in between. It wasn't until she heard the lock being thrown that she realized she'd used the signal she and Rita had worked

185

out years ago.

"Shit."

Callie tensed beside her. "What's wrong?"

"Nothing. I—"

The door swung open, cutting off the rest of EJ's response, such as it was.

Rita grinned when she saw EJ. Smirked was more accurate. She was barefoot, with red-painted toenails. Her sleek, black bob swayed slightly as she tilted her head. The red and white silk robe with gold thread accents that barely reached mid-thigh was as buttery soft as it looked, something EJ knew as fact.

"Well, well, well. Look who's at my door." She glanced at Callie, her smile more predator than pleased. Rita said something in Mandarin to the effect of "You have some fucking nerve." Or at least EJ assumed that was what she said. Her limited language skills were rusty, though the expression on Rita's face translated the words clear enough. "Come to apologize, EJ?"

From the corner of her eye, EJ saw Callie's gaze narrow at the other woman.

Rita was purposely stirring shit, even if she didn't know EJ's relationship with Callie. But she had the right of it, damn her.

"I've already apologized to you. Twice."

Rita pouted, her reddened lower lip sticking out prettily. "Never hurts to hear such things more than once or twice. What do you and your . . . friend . . . want? I'm busy."

As far as EJ knew, Rita had no regular job, so busy was relative.

"We won't be long. This is Callie."

Rita gave Callie the up and down. "Yeah, I remember. The butcher's kid."

Callie nodded. "That's right."

"Can we come in, Rita?"

Rita quirked a slender black eyebrow. "Somehow I doubt you're looking for a threesome, but sure." She turned around and

186

walked back into the apartment. "Excuse the clutter."

EJ gestured for Callie to precede her. The searing glare Callie gave her meant EJ would be doing some feather-smoothing once they were alone. Not that she could blame Callie for being ruffled.

She closed the door and followed Callie and Rita into the small sitting area. The kitchen was no more than a sink, stove, and icebox along one wall. Two doors led from the room, both closed. A number of magazines and a heavy green-glass ashtray containing several butts and a small pile of ashes were on the low table between two chairs and a floral divan. The air had a cigarette smoke and light rose perfume to it. Rita's scent. Where it used to stoke EJ's desires, it now made her nostalgic and a little wary.

Rita dropped herself on a wing-backed chair. A novel lay open, face down, on the floor alongside a cup of what looked like coffee. EJ remembered she liked hers light and sweet.

"Have a seat," she said gesturing to the divan. "I'd offer you something, but I'm fresh out."

EJ was pretty sure that was also bullshit, but they weren't there on a social call.

Callie opened her coat and perched on the edge of the divan. "We won't take up much of your time."

Rita gave her a look EJ could only describe as amused, but there was more to it. "My time is yours, honey. What do you want?"

"We're wondering where Olive is," Callie said.

Good job not tipping our hand, EJ thought.

She chose to stand beside Callie rather than sit. Would Rita see that as anything more than a need to access her gun should the need arise? EJ really couldn't care less if she did.

Rita took her time, shifting her gaze from Callie to EJ. "Haven't seen her. She was here for a while but moved out months ago."

Olive Lang had been Paul Underwood's moll for well over a year, so that wasn't a surprise. "Where'd she go?"

Rita shrugged. "Somewhere north of the Y-J. Nice digs. Closer to Underwood."

"You haven't seen your own sister in months?" Callie asked.

According to Joe, Rita and Olive had been at El Fuego last night. How could they have missed each other?

Rita looked unaffected, but EJ knew Olive's relationship with Underwood had put some strain on the sisters' relationship. It wasn't jealousy exactly, at least not for Paul Underwood himself. More for the prestige and perks that came with being on his arm. That was something EJ couldn't provide Rita, according to Rita. EJ's screwing around hadn't helped, nor had Rita's sniping.

She shook off the remnants of that disaster, grateful they'd gotten out of it alive, if not as friends.

"We aren't exactly close these days." Rita reached into the pocket of her robe.

EJ tensed for a moment, then saw she'd retrieved a silver cigarette case with R.L. engraved on it, similar to the one found in Underwood's car. Some wannabe big shot had been trying to see which sister he could impress first, according to Rita. The big shot ended up losing his shirt, his freedom, and both sisters in a deal gone wrong that sent him to McNeil Island.

Rita slipped a thin cigarette between her lips, lit the end with a silver lighter, and snapped the lid closed to extinguish the flame. She blew a stream of smoke from the corner of her mouth, her gaze on EJ.

"Can you give us her address?" Callie pressed her hands together in what EJ first took as a gesture of frustration. Then she caught a glimpse of a blood-red spot on Callie's thumb.

Shit.

She was casting a spell of some sort. If Rita had any magic sense—EJ was pretty sure she didn't, but who could say for sure?—she might pick up on what was happening.

"I could," Rita said with her typical smirk. "What's in it for me?"

EJ let out a huff of frustration. "Come on, Rita. Olive might need some help."

Getting into the other woman's face never worked well. Push, and Rita threw up walls higher than Smith Tower.

Rita took a long drag on her cigarette and blew smoke over her head. "Why should I help her? What has she ever done for me?"

Of course. In the Lang sisters' world, it was all about who did what for who, what sort of advantage you could get, even over your own flesh and blood.

And that's different from you how?

EJ glanced down at Callie. Their current relationship might have started as gaining something from her, but it had changed. Hadn't it?

"I don't know," Callie said, "but Paul Underwood is dead and Olive might know something."

Rita's eyebrows shot up and her body stiffened. "Dead? When?"

Her shock seemed genuine. Olive might be the woman in the passenger seat, but if Rita knew anything about that, she was a hell of an actress. EJ wasn't going to assume anything. But she wasn't going to be the one to tell Rita her sister might also be dead, especially without confirmation of the identity of the dame.

"Last night. You hadn't heard?"

"No."

"You were with Paul and Olive last night." Callie sure as hell didn't believe her.

"No, we happened to be at El Fuego at the same time. That was all I saw of them."

"When was this?"

Rita gave Callie a look of derision that could have peeled

paint. "You ain't a cop or my mother."

EJ crossed her arms. "I thought you said you hadn't seen Olive for months?"

Rita knew she'd been caught in the lie, but played it off as EJ expected her to, rolling her eyes. "I saw her across the club. That isn't the same as seeing her seeing her. We didn't acknowledge each other, let alone speak. When I left at eleven, they were still there."

EJ had a hard time not pressing Rita about what had happened between her and Olive. The sisters had been close up until the last year or two. Up until Paul Underwood. But she knew it was best to let it lie.

"And after eleven?" Callie asked. "Were you with anyone?"

Shit. Callie was seeing if Rita had an alibi for the time Underwood and maybe Olive had been killed. EJ wouldn't have considered Rita as a killer, despite her sour grapes with Underwood and her sister. That was all it had been, hadn't it?

Rita scowled at Callie. If she shut them out now, they'd never find Olive, if she was still alive. "You want a blow-by-blow, honey? Well, let's see. We came back here, and first he put his hand up my dress, then she put her tongue—"

"Fine," EJ said, taking Rita's attention from Callie. "We'll go talk to Olive. Could you please give us the address?"

Rita may have feigned not knowing her sister's whereabouts, but EJ knew that was as much bullshit as anything. She sat silently for a few moments then sighed.

"North Bank apartments. I don't know which one. Underwood has her set up real nice and sweet, the bastard."

So there was jealousy. Enough for Rita to be a suspect? Maybe.

"Thank you," Callie said, standing. "You want us to tell Olive anything if we catch up to her?"

Rita's left eyebrow quirked. "Nothing polite."

Callie nodded once, her right hand out. "Thank you, Rita."

Rita rose, hesitated for a moment, then took Callie's hand in a barely passable handshake. "Good luck if you meet her. You'll need it."

Callie responded with her own wry smile. She glanced at EJ and headed to the door.

"Next time you pop by," Rita said for EJ's ears only, "leave the current girl at home. I don't think she likes me."

"I'd say the feelings mutual." EJ buttoned her coat.

Rita laughed. "I'm sure we could be bosom buddies under other circumstances."

"Sure. Thanks, Rita. Take care of yourself." EJ was surprised that she actually meant it.

And more surprisingly, Rita took it that way too. The teasing sarcasm left her eyes. "Yeah, you too."

EJ followed Callie into the hall and gave Rita a nod as she shut the door and threw the locks. Turning to Callie, she started to say how that had gone better than expected.

Mouth pressed into a tight line, Callie turned away from her and strode to the staircase.

Well, shit.

Callie didn't hurry down the stairs, but she didn't dally either. EJ's footfalls came behind her. It didn't seem like she was in a hurry to catch up. Smart of her to give Callie space.

Callie shoved the door open and went outside. Cold wind slapped her in the face, cooling the heat that had risen along her neck and cheeks.

What did you expect? For EJ to mention having had a thing with Rita while you were reminiscing about running with the Roses that first night at dinner? When you were enacting the incantation? When you were in bed together?

She unclenched her fists and brought her left hand to her

mouth to soothe the sting of the small cut along the edge of her thumbnail. The tang of blood on her tongue wasn't quite enough to initiate another heady rush of magic. The few drops she'd needed while with Rita Lang gave the means to determine the woman was hiding something but not necessarily lying.

EJ finally came up behind her.

Callie drew a deep breath. Rita wasn't the only one not on the up and up.

"I can explain," EJ said.

Callie pulled her gloves out of her coat pocket and concentrated on tugging them on. "You and Rita were lovers. You had some sort of falling out. Do I have it right?"

"Well, yes."

"Then there's nothing really to explain, is there?"

There wasn't, but that didn't mean she wouldn't be open to hearing an explanation.

She headed down the cement stairs to the sidewalk. EJ caught her upper arm and turned her so they were face to face. Her dark eyes were hooded, her brow furrowed.

"I should have said something before we set out here. I don't know why I didn't." Callie started to make suggestions, but EJ held up her free hand. "No, you're right. I was a coward. I should have warned you, talked to you about it, and I didn't. I apologize."

Callie pressed her lips together. She could count on one hand the number of times EJ ever apologized for anything. EJ watched her as if waiting for a bomb to go off. Anger ebbing, Callie shook her head. "How am I supposed to be mad when you admit you're wrong?"

EJ gave her that dazzling smile. "You can still be mad. Hoping you'll forgive me sooner."

Callie grabbed her by the lapels and jerked her closer, kissing her quick and hard. Such public displays weren't smart, but she didn't care. She *did* hope Rita was looking out her window.

When she stepped back, EJ dazed, blinked rapidly.

"Look, I know I have no right to be jealous," Callie said. "You're gorgeous and any woman would be an idiot to pass you by."

EJ's eyebrows rose. "Oh, really?"

The implication that Callie had been such an idiot didn't miss its mark.

She rolled her eyes. "Yes, I was an idiot back then. Kept my feelings buried so deep, I didn't even know what they were." She met EJ's gaze, noting her own sudden seriousness was reflected there. "I married Nate because I thought I wanted what my parents had. He was nice. A good man. I imagined a normal life—whatever that meant—with him. But it wasn't what I truly wanted or needed."

"If he hadn't died, what would you have done?" There was a rare trace of uncertainty in EJ's face.

Callie shook her head. "I don't know. I don't think it would have lasted much longer, to be honest. Ten years of fooling ourselves was enough."

"And now?"

She smiled as she smoothed the other woman's coat. "And now I have you. But no more keeping things from me."

EJ's expression darkened. "There are some things that might be safer for you not to know, Cal."

Considering EJ's business, that was probably true.

"We'll have to trust each other, I suppose," Callie said.

There it was, the understanding that each of them walked in worlds the other might not understand or be safe within.

"I'll be square with you where I can," EJ said.

Callie raised an eyebrow. "Like with ex-girlfriends?"

"Like with ex-girlfriends." EJ drew an X across her chest. "Cross my heart."

"Okay." Callie looped her arm through EJ's. "Are there anymore I should know about?"

As they walked toward the car, EJ made a show of appearing

to think about it and count on the fingers of her free hand. Callie laughed and swatted her arm.

EJ chuckled. "I never took you for the jealous type."

"Oh, yes. Jealous and vindictive."

EJ's brows shot up, her eyes wide. "And vindictive. Dangerous combination for a blood mage."

Callie winked at her. "Keep that in mind."

Olive Lang's apartment building was in one of the nicer sections of Seattle, north of the Y-J, not far from Smith Tower. EJ figured it behooved Underwood to keep his mistress as far from his wife as he could manage, and apparently Olive's company was worth a short drive. It was also worth a few bucks in rent.

EJ pulled up across the street from the address Rita had given them. Olive's building was a newer brick structure, sleek and modern. There wasn't a doorman, but it looked like an enclosed entry housed an intercom system across from mailboxes.

"If she's dead," Callie said, "I can't imagine ringing her apartment will be much help."

"Not likely, but maybe we can find a nosy neighbor." EJ got out and came around to the passenger side as Callie stepped onto the sidewalk. "I would've gotten that for you."

Callie smiled and chucked her gently under the chin. "I know. Come on."

They crossed the street and went up the few stairs to the outer doors of the building. EJ pulled the door open, letting Callie precede her into the spacious foyer. The bank of brass mailboxes on the left were numbered, but the panel of buzzers to the apartments had slips with first initials and last names. EJ and Callie scanned the list.

"I don't see her name," Callie said. "Did she go by anything else?"

EJ looked over the names again, but nothing jumped out as a pseudonym for Underwood's mistress. Then the tag for E. Olling caught her eye. "Here."

Callie looked at the slip of paper behind the glass. "Really? How can you be sure?"

"When we were kids, we killed some time messing with the arrangement of the letters of our names, in case we needed a fake name to give the cops. Olive thought up Eva Olling."

Callie grinned. "What about you?"

"Jane D'Oriele. Dad was French, apparently." Callie laughed, and it made EJ smile. She loved hearing Callie laugh. She picked up the handset and dialed the apartment number under Olive's alias. "Not expecting anything, but what the hell."

She let the ring go on for a minute before hanging up.

"Now what?" Callie asked. "Should we go up?"

As EJ considered it, a well-dressed woman of about fifty came into the lobby from the interior of the building. Her going-gray black hair was perfectly coifed beneath her hat. Her dark green wool coat was the same length as her rose-print day dress. She eyed Callie and EJ with curiosity.

"Are you looking for someone?" she asked.

EJ gave her a brilliant smile. "Yes, ma'am. Miss Eva Olling. She doesn't seem to be in. Do you know her?"

"I haven't seen Miss Olling for a couple of days," the woman said.

The way she said it made EJ think the woman knew Olive, a.k.a Eva, to some extent. "I see. Could you tell us if she was coming or going?"

"Going." She stepped closer and lowered her voice. "Got into a fancy car."

Was that the last time Olive drove off with Underwood?

"A black Ford coupe?" EJ asked, describing Underwood's car.

The woman's eyes glinted. "No, a dark green Plymouth. I

happend to be looking out my window. It faces the street."

They'd scored their Nosy Nellie.

"Have you seen that car before?" Callie asked.

The woman's expression turned thoughtful. "A few times. And the black one too." She gave them a knowing look. "Miss Olling is quite popular."

If there were several cars retrieving Olive, EJ wondered if Underwood had finally had it up to his beady eyes with her "popularity."

"Why are you so interested in Miss Olling and who she's with?"

EJ resisted asking why she was such a busybody herself and instead smiled again. "We're friends of hers. We were supposed to meet up, but she didn't show."

Suspicion narrowed Nosy Nellie's eyes. "If you're her friends, you should know who she pals around with, shouldn't you?"

Callie reached out and patted the woman's arm. "Oh, you know how it is when one set of friends doesn't associate with another set of friends and you have to go back and forth between them." She gave her own dazzling smile. "I'm sure we'll catch up with Ol—Miss Olling soon enough. Thank you. Come on, Jane."

Callie took EJ's arm and led her out the front door, pausing only to turn back and wave to the older woman. They didn't speak again until they got into EJ's car.

"I know who came for Olive," Callie said.

EJ stared at her for a moment, counting her blessings for having this woman on her side. "Other than Underwood."

"Other than *Paul* Underwood."

The way she said his first name told EJ all she needed to know. "Bert?"

No. Olive never paid much attention to that pipsqueak.

"The Plymouth is Kay's car," Callie said. "One of the servers had to ask to have it moved so they could park the catering truck before the party."

"Kay Underwood was sleeping with Olive?" She gave a prolonged whistle of surprise. "Will wonders never cease?"

What didn't surprise her was Kay stepping out on Paul, or that Olive swung both ways. But Olive and Kay? That was unexpected. She was never one to show appreciation for other women. Or anyone, actually.

"Holy shit." EJ sat back in the driver's seat, imagining what sort of tap dance Olive and Kay had to do to keep Paul in the dark. Unless. . . "You don't think they were all into it together?"

"I shudder at the idea of Paul Underwood in any sexual situation," Callie said, giving a visible shake of disgust. "Maybe they were. Maybe Kay and Olive were doing their own thing on the side. There's only one of the three available to talk to."

"We'll have a chat with Kay Underwood as soon as Joe lets us know Bradford is finished with her."

CHAPTER FIFTEEN

Callie was about to turn over the closed sign and lock up early as was usual on a Sunday when someone started through the door. Setting aside thoughts of how much she wanted to have the day done and soak in a hot bath, she smiled at the matronly woman in a stylish dark brown suit.

The woman strode up to the gap between the two display cases, not once looking at the selection of meats. Perhaps she had a specific order in mind or wanted to arrange for a larger delivery at a later date. That would be a boon for sure. Well worth staying open a little longer.

"Good afternoon," Callie said. "What can I—"

Her smile faltered. Recognition pinged in Callie's brain. This was no customer.

"Calliope Payne?"

"Yes?"

"My name is Frances Eccles. I'm with the Covenant Investigations Office." She opened a leather wallet that showed Callie an identification card with her photo and embossed with the Coven insignia——stylized images of the five elements, earth, air, water, fire, and blood, encircled by the name of the office and "1695," the year of the CIO's inception. In those years after the last of the Salem Trials, mages had retaliated against injustice and a truce of sorts had been born. "Is there somewhere we can speak privately?"

Covering her discomfort, Callie squared her shoulders. "Am I under arrest?"

Eccles smiled thinly as she returned the wallet to her coat pocket. "That's not how we work, so no, but I do have questions. My purpose is to gather information and report to the Council. There have been no charges filed against you."

The word "yet" hung silently between them. The implication that something was indeed going to be formalized felt similar to SPD Lieutenant Bradford's visit. Callie had nothing to hide, at least nothing associated with Paul Underwood's death, which was certainly the reason for Frances Eccles's appearance here. Still, she would tread carefully.

"Let me lock up and we can go upstairs to my place."

The older woman stood patiently while Callie went through her end-of-the-day routine. Not only would Callie never shirk the duties of keeping a clean shop, but it also gave her time to settle herself.

When she finished, she had Eccles come through the back room and follow her up the stairs. The door to the street was already locked, ensuring no one would walk in on them. Callie led the other woman into the apartment and gestured for her to have a seat at the kitchen table.

"Can I get you tea or coffee?" This wasn't a social call, but politeness never hurt.

"Just some water, thank you," Eccles said as she sat down. "You are permitted to have an advocate or adviser with you if you wish."

Callie turned on the cold water tap and took two glasses from the cupboard. "Do you think I need an advocate?"

Eccles smiled benignly. "That isn't my decision to make. I just want to let you know what your options are, Miss Payne."

Callie set their glasses down then took a seat on the other

side of the table. She felt a little better having the polished wood and lace tablecloth between them. "If I understand the procedure correctly, I can refuse to answer certain questions since this isn't a testimony."

Eccles's smile turned brittle. "Of course. As I said, I'm simply gathering information. If the Council feels the need, you will be called before them and put under oath."

A Tribunal. Not a pleasant event for the accused from what Callie had seen from the observers' gallery years ago. The Council of Five had presided over what amounted to a trial where they were judge and jury.

"All right. What do you want to know?"

Eccles took a notebook and pen from her bag. "A verification of your identity first. You are Calliope Ann Payne, daughter of Sophie and David?"

"Yes."

"You reside here with your paternal grandmother, Fiona Morley Payne, a water witch registered with the Coven."

"Yes."

"You yourself have been registered since you were fifteen as required by law."

"Yes."

Callie suspected the questions were purposely meant to relax her, to make her think the investigation was going to be easy. But she had been a Rose. Still was, at heart, and interrogative techniques didn't vary much, whether cops or covens.

Eccles looked up from the page of her notebook, her gray eyes still holding a hint of warmth. "You were away from the area for a dozen years, Miss Payne. I take it you checked in with the local coven wherever you resided?"

Callie swallowed some water. "No. I was in Spokane for all that time, but never practiced."

The older woman tilted her head. "Never? Not once?"

The minor spells she performed to move a heavy sideboard

or couch didn't count, did they?

"My late husband and his family weren't particularly keen on it."

True, though Nate's parents didn't know Callie was a witch until after Nate had died. Once her in-laws learned she was a blood witch, the relationship had gone from cordial to borderline hostile.

"Interesting. Though you should have registered with them."

She held Eccles's gaze and channeled her inner EJ, refusing to be intimidated by the woman. "I understand that if I'm not actively practicing, registration is optional if I'm already registered elsewhere."

The Covenant that witches were to follow, which included registration overseen by local covens, had so far been held together by honor and honesty. There were Covenant breakers and Oath breakers, rogues not registered at all, but the repercussions of truly harmful magic often took care of them before a Tribunal was convened.

Eccles didn't concede. "It is, but better safe than sorry." She flipped a page of her book. "We understand you performed a spell at Eileen Jordan's establishment, The Garden. Which one and what was the purpose?"

How did she know that? Then again, how had Paul Underwood known, bringing him to her shop the day before he'd died? Had Paul told the CIO?

Callie cleared her throat. "EJ came to me asking for a spell that would keep Paul Underwood away from her business interests, specifically her club, The Garden. It was understood, by sworn verbal agreement, that I would not enact any spell intending physical harm to Paul Underwood or anyone else. I consulted with Jemma McAndrews and determined Repel would be the best incantation to enact."

Eccles made notes. "That requires particular plant materials."

"We went to Neil Pasternik for supplies."

"We?"

"EJ and I."

More jotting.

"And who did you have assist you with the incantation itself?"

Damn, this woman knew her spells.

"EJ, Ruth Cheng, and two other friends who don't practice."

Ruth would be registered with the Coven, which would protect her to a degree, as long as the investigation didn't find the spell itself a violation.

That brought Eccles's head up again. "You entrusted the power of magic with three uninitiated?"

Callie bristled. For some, "uninitiated" implied ignorance or being lesser for not practicing. Bette, Marian, and EJ were far from that. "The spell requires established relationships between participants. It doesn't specify practitioners, only strong positive connections."

Eccles pressed her lips together and made a small sound of concession, then returned to writing. "You completed the spell requirements without issue? You didn't change anything?"

"No, of course not." What was she getting at? "Because we were specifically focusing on Paul Underwood, I wanted to make sure the spell came off as cleanly as I could. Preventing unintentional outcome is crucial with any spell."

It was a key lesson for all witches. Granted, it didn't always work that way, but you had to do your damnedest to focus spells. Sloppy witchcraft was dangerous or even deadly.

"So you included a personal item from Underwood."

Callie considered the best way to answer. Spell components were best acquired with consent, but that wasn't always possible.

"Miss Payne?"

"I did."

"Without his knowledge?"

Callie couldn't help the laugh that came out. "Of course

without his knowledge. But I replaced the item itself."

Eccles's lips pressed together. "Still, theft isn't condoned by the Coven."

Neither was what Underwood had been doing to Janie, but if Callie brought that up it would do more harm to her case than good. Revenge magic, and the spell could be taken as such, treaded too close to intended harm.

"I'll accept whatever punishment the Tribunal metes out over a toothbrush."

The investigator made more notes. "And the spell performed in the Underwood bathroom?"

Callie's heart stuttered. She'd almost forgotten about that. She hadn't thought the spell to be enough to leave her mark, but they'd found it. Or found something. Eccles didn't specifically say they'd found *her* signature. Though considering she'd admitted to taking the toothbrush, it made sense to conclude it was her.

"Petty and childish. And also more of an annoyance to him than dangerous. Again, if the Coven sees fit to censure me over potential razor burn, I understand."

"Why the animosity toward Paul Underwood, Miss Payne?" Eccles fixed her with a steady stare. "What did you have against him?"

Everything.

"He was an ass and a bully. Always had been. He was trying to cause trouble for my friend. We merely wanted him to leave things alone."

"You've known the Underwoods for a while, haven't you?" It wasn't a question despite the way Frances Eccles stated it.

"Yes, we used to—" Janie's face floated in her mind's eye. She was the real reason Callie had agreed to go after Underwood. Would it hurt or help to admit that?

"Used to what, Miss Payne?" Eccles' gaze was both curious and intense. What did she already know?

"His niece, Janie, was a very dear friend. She was part of our group."

"The Roses."

It wasn't a surprise that Eccles knew about their gang. They weren't particularly secretive.

"Yes. Janie was one of ours, and when she died, we . . . We never got a straight story about how it happened."

Eccles didn't say anything for a few moments; then she asked, "And you suspected something wasn't right?"

Here we go.

Callie cleared her throat. "She told us about Paul and Kay Underwood being strict, and more than hinted that they were abusive. We saw the marks, but Janie wouldn't give us details. I think she was afraid of what they'd do if she told. Then one day, she didn't meet with us. Within a couple of days, she was gone."

Frances Eccles's gaze hardened. Her lips pressed together.

"You think the Underwoods had something to do with her death." Before Callie could respond, she asked, "What did he come to see you about the day before he died?"

Underwood's rage when he'd entered the butcher shop played in her head. And her own reaction. "Somehow, he had found out about the spell to keep him away from The Garden, though he didn't seem to know exactly what I'd done. He insulted and threatened me and EJ."

"What did you do?"

"Used another repel spell to get him out."

"While a bystander, a non-practitioner, was there."

How did she learn these things? Though Callie supposed it was part of her job.

"Yes. You can ask Mr. Madsen what happened. He likely saw Underwood come in yelling and witnessed me casting the spell. Nothing I said or did intended harm to Underwood, though it would have been within my right to defend myself."

"Absolutely." Eccles nodded, but that didn't soften her

stance. "Just as he had a right to defend himself against attack."

Heat rose on Callie's neck. "We didn't attack him. He was angry because we were doing something against his wishes. We dared to stand up to him."

She held Frances Eccles's gaze for a number of racing heartbeats before the other woman looked down at her notes. "And the death of Jocko Perry?"

EJ's man who had been shot by Underwood men. Men who subsequently died, who had injured EJ.

"Terrible. Not through magic, though."

Eccles narrowed her eyes slightly. "But related to your friend's request for help."

Callie shrugged. "I have no idea. Up until that point, I hadn't agreed to anything. EJ was afraid things would escalate. She didn't want more bloodshed. Doesn't want it."

"Yet there has been." The woman seemed almost sad about it. "Do you know Olive Lang?"

Callie had the strange feeling that Eccles knew she and EJ had been looking for Olive and had spoken to Rita. But Rita wouldn't have said anything to anyone of authority, let alone a CIO investigator.

"I knew her a little when we were younger, but we never really ran in the same circles after she moved to another neighborhood."

"How about Tessa Blake or Millie St. John?"

Callie shook her head. Neither name was familiar. "Why?"

Eccles closed her notebook and slid it into her bag. Rising, she said, "Thank you for your time, Miss Payne. I'll contact you if I need more information."

That she wouldn't tell Callie why those folks were significant spoke volumes. Were they witches? Associated with Paul Underwood?

"If you know I performed the spell in the Underwoods' bathroom," Callie said, "then you know I wasn't involved in Paul

Underwood's murder."

Eccles stared at her for a few seconds, her expression unreadable. "There are ways to conceal magic, Miss Payne, especially for a blood mage such as yourself. I'll be in touch."

The older woman let herself out. Callie watched her go down the stairs and out the other door. She closed the apartment door, running their conversation through her head. Had she said the right things? Would Eccles make some sort of recommendation to the Council that would result in a Tribunal?

It was hard to say what was going on in the woman's head, which made her ideal for investigating Coven business.

And unfortunately, Callie was now Coven business.

Later that afternoon, EJ parked down a side street three blocks from the alley where the street sweeper had found Underwood and the mystery woman. They were taking a chance heading to the crime scene, but that's what Callie needed to get them more information. The cops weren't looking terribly hard for other suspects, and Frances Eccles's visit had made it clear the Tribunal was interested in them as well. It was up to her and EJ to clear themselves.

They strode down the nearly empty street, footfalls echoing off the brick and stone buildings. Despite their casual demeanor, Callie's heart was racing. What if the cops were still hanging around? What if someone noticed them? They were both wearing nondescript clothing, and EJ had her fedora pulled low over her eyes, but there was always the chance of being recognized.

"Down this way," EJ said, guiding her onto another street. An even more backway route than Callie had considered, with fewer eyes on them but more obstacles. It was slow going as they had to avoid things strewn in their path and questionable puddles. Rodents scurried in the shadows. The smell wasn't all that pleasant, either. Not the most genteel area. What had Underwood and his lady friend been doing here? "Just a few more blocks. You okay?"

"Peachy," Callie muttered, just managing to miss stepping in ... something.

EJ patted her hand where it lay on her arm and gave Callie's fingers a gentle squeeze. "We'll grab a bite and a drink after this."

"We'll need both." Callie's stomach rumbled in agreement.

After another block, EJ said, "Up here."

They rounded the corner. The stretch of alley looked and smelled like any other, with a few trash cans and boxes added for good measure. The brick buildings flanking the narrow thoroughfare had their curtains drawn, and nothing was lit up on the first three floors. Commercial buildings, closed for the weekend, with apartments above, like many others in the city.

Within half a dozen steps along the road, Callie felt a tickle across the back of her neck as if someone was brushing their fingers along her skin. Five or six more steps and the fingers pinched. It was a sensation she'd never experienced before and, truth be told, didn't necessarily want to experience again. But somehow she knew what it meant.

"Here," she said, stopping in her tracks. She disengaged herself from EJ's arm and rubbed the nape of her neck as she scanned the dank alley. "They were found right here. Keep a lookout. We can't afford interruptions."

The request was met with an agreeing grunt from EJ, who was already scanning up and down the alley, hand inside her coat pocket, likely over her gun.

It should have made Callie nervous, but instead she felt protected.

What does that say about you, Callie-girl?

More than she wanted to go into at the moment.

Callie reached into her satchel for her supplies. Without a

personal item from Olive Lang, the spell would require more concentration and, of course, more blood. Necromancy wasn't something she had much experience or interest in, but in this case it might be their only hope in determining what had happened.

She laid the white handkerchief on the damp ground and placed the fat white candle upon it. She lit the wick with her favorite silver lighter. The flame flickered then steadied as she retrieved her dagger from the satchel. If someone from the CIO checked, they'd likely be able to determine it was her magic. Eccles had commented about being able to hide magic. Callie had no idea how to do that. She hoped the CIO had finished their testing of the scene and wouldn't be back. If they did trace something back to her, the timing of the magic cast should be sufficient to prove it came after Underwood had been killed.

"Here goes," she said, and pricked her palm with the sharp tip of the blade. Droplets fell upon the wick, sending a smoky hiss into the night. "We mean you no harm, Olive Lang. We wish you peace. We want to know what happened. We want to find whoever's responsible for your death. We wish you peace."

She repeated the spell twice more, watching her blood sizzle and drip down the sides of the candle.

Nothing.

Not a peep from Olive.

Opening her mind and awareness, she repeated the words yet again.

More blood. Drip. Hiss.

"Olive Lang, we mean you no harm. We—"

The air seemed to be sucked away from Callie, leaving her gasping for a moment, and returned with hurricane-force speed. Grit and debris swirled around her, threatening to extinguish the candle. Something—no, someone—roared in her ears. Its rage vibrated through her body.

Callie's heart burst into a gallop. She slammed her hand

over the candle, ignoring the burn to extinguish the flame. *Go away go away go away!*

Breathing hard, she remained still, waiting for the anger to fade out.

"What happened?" EJ asked, crouched down beside her.

Callie steadied her breath and wiped grime from her eyes. "You didn't feel it?"

EJ shook her head. "Got a little chill, but then heard you make a noise before you slammed your hand over the candle." She turned Callie's palm face up. There was no mark. "You okay?"

"Olive's not here."

EJ blinked at her. "Not here? Or not responding to the spell?"

"Not here." Though there was a chance Olive's spirit would have tried to ignore them, the incantation compelled response. Callie suspected Olive would want to tell everyone and anyone who had killed her. Without a personal item to focus on, however, the door was opened for others. "But someone else was."

Understanding furrowed EJ's brow. "Underwood."

Callie nodded. "I think so. It could have been the woman, but this felt more like him. He's still here and understandably angry. Very angry. I suppose I should have asked who killed him, but he didn't seem in the mood for conversation."

"You can do that? Talk to the dead?"

"Me? No. I was aiming to get an idea of who might be here. Some can get impressions, and from what I understand, it's notoriously vague. A necromancer's interpretation isn't admissible at a Tribunal, but it can point them in certain directions."

"I wonder what the Tribunal investigators may have gotten out of Underwood." EJ helped her gather her things, and they started walking back to the car. Callie shivered despite the warmth of her coat and the closeness to EJ. "If you believe it wasn't Olive here, the CIO might know that as well. Did you get

209

any sense of who the other person could be?"

"No. Why did someone want us and the police to think it was Olive? Did they think they could fool the Tribunal?"

EJ let out a humorless laugh. "You are asking the wrong person that last question. But I think we can get something out of the evening. Come on. I chatted with Joe earlier. We have another stop to make."

CHAPTER SIXTEEN

They turned onto the street where the Underwoods lived and immediately saw the green Plymouth parked in front of the building. EJ gave Callie a smirk.

"We might suspect Kay and Olive were sneaking around behind Paul's back," Callie said, "but that doesn't mean one of them killed him and whoever the other woman was."

"Oh, one or both of them are involved," EJ said with surety. "Why else have a dame in the car with him?"

EJ parked a block away from the Underwoods' building. She came around to the passenger door as Callie got out.

"You keep beating me to it," she said with a grin. "When are you gonna let me hold a door for you?"

Callie laughed. "Not any time soon. Speaking of, they have a doorman at their building."

She had noted that the night of the anniversary party.

The amusement left EJ's face. "That could be a problem. How are we going to get up to see Kay? The element of surprise sure would help."

"There's a back door," Callie said. "I went out through it when I came to nab Underwood's toothbrush. I may be able to get it open."

The smile that curved EJ's lips made Callie consider tugging the other woman into the backseat of the car. Unfortunately, they had a lot to do and little time for canoodling at the moment.

"You are brilliant." EJ darted forward and pecked her on the cheek. "Lead on."

Callie took her around the building to a side street and along the narrow alley in the back. There were the standard garbage bins and questionable stench, but not as bad as other alleys they had traversed of late. The rear door of the building had no handle on the outside, only a keyhole. She touched her fingertips to the cold metal lock and visualized a key.

"Don't you need—"

Callie held up her hand to stop the question EJ was about to raise. "Not if I can concentrate."

To her credit, EJ stayed silent as Callie invoked a telekinetic spell to align the tumblers correctly. Using blood magic would have been easier than mental magic. Too easy. The draw of that pleasant tingling sensation throughout her body was addictive. It was an endless and growing loop: the more she used blood magic, the more she craved using it. Enacting simple spells like this without using blood would help reduce that desire. If she was careful, she'd be able to use blood for more involved incantations without becoming reliant upon it for all incantations.

Some mages got to the point that only blood magic would work for them no matter what simple magic was performed. Jemma had warned her of the dangers from the beginning of her apprenticeship. Callie hadn't used her magic as much in the last ten years as she had this past week and needed to be careful.

A few metallic clicks, then Callie pulled on the door using an invisible "handle." Inside, the rear stairwell was lit by plain light fixtures. A door marked "basement" and another marked "hallway" stood on either side of the stairs.

EJ held the outer door while Callie went in and gently shut it behind them. Callie started up the stairs. EJ followed, their footsteps tapping on the linoleum treads. At the fourth-floor access, Callie opened the door a crack and peered along the well-lit hallway. No one was about. She stepped in, and EJ closed the door.

"Down the hall on the left," she said quietly, though there was no reason to think anyone in the neighboring apartments would hear them if she spoke in normal tones. It felt right to speak softly for some reason. Nerves, she supposed.

They stopped in front of the Underwoods' apartment. By silent agreement Callie was the one to ring the bell. Within a few moments the door opened. Kay Underwood, perfectly coiffed and dressed in charcoal black from head to toe, stood in the doorway with a quizzical expression on her wan face as she gazed at Callie. The older woman didn't seem to recognize her. No surprise. It had been years since they'd been face to face.

But when she glanced up at EJ standing behind Callie and to the right, her blue eyes narrowed. "What the hell are you doing here?"

Apparently, Kay knew EJ well enough.

"We have a few questions, Mrs. Underwood." Though she was an adult now, Callie wouldn't call Kay Underwood by her given name. Even if she was a bitch who'd made Janie's life miserable. Renewed anger at the woman bubbled in Callie's gut.

Kay looked back at her. "And you are—" Recognition dawned in her eyes. "Callie Payne. Right. Well, I have nothing to talk to either of you about. Leave or I'm calling the cops."

She started to shut the door in their faces, but EJ moved forward and slid her foot in the gap. Kay Underwood glared.

"We had nothing to do with Paul's death. We only want to know about Olive," EJ said. Kay's eyes widened slightly before she quickly school her expression into one of irritation. "Or you can call the cops and we can bring her up with them."

If looks could kill, EJ would have been shot full of holes by Kay Underwood's glower. EJ pushed the door open. Callie got a feeling of déjà vu from when they had gone to visit Rita Lang.

Their appearance on certain doorsteps certainly seemed to be rubbing folks the wrong way. The question was why.

Callie followed EJ into the apartment, pretending she'd never been there before by looking around as EJ was doing. She supposed some polite remark on the décor would have been appropriate under other circumstances.

Kay stood in the doorway that led to the living room and crossed her arms. It didn't look like they'd be invited to sit and have refreshments. "What do you want to know?"

"Paul was keeping Olive on the side." EJ didn't make it a question, as it wasn't. Everyone knew Underwood and Olive were a thing. "What about you?"

Kay tilted her head. "What about me? Are you asking if I had a man on the side?"

"No," Callie said, "we're asking if you and Olive were seeing each other, and whether or not Paul knew."

The older woman lifted her chin, defiance hardening her eyes into shards of ice. Indignant about being asked if she was a Sapphic or for being accused of infidelity at all?

"We don't give a damn if you were," EJ said. "We're trying to figure out why someone put another dame's body in the car with Paul and made it look like Olive was there. Because we know she wasn't. And why'd they make it look like we were involved? Did you and Olive cook up that scheme?"

Callie winced a little at EJ showing Bradford's hand regarding the other body, and their own by acknowledging Olive's spirit wasn't at the site of Underwood's death, but if it helped clear them, it had to be done.

"She was using both of us."

The admission came out with both anger and heartbreak, the latter of which Callie never expected to hear from Kay Underwood. Her sympathies wavered for a moment, but Callie immediately regrouped, remembering who they were dealing with.

"So it was Olive's idea to have another woman killed in her place?" EJ didn't sound convinced. "That gets the cops looking away from the real killer and drags us into it as fall guys. I don't know if I'm willing to give her that much credit."

Callie didn't know adult Olive all that well, but if she was the mastermind of Paul Underwood's demise and laid out enough doubt to have her and EJ questioned by the police, she wasn't stupid. Or she was doing someone else's bidding.

"She's cleverer than you think." Kay gave a humorless laugh. "More than I realized. We were able to keep Paul in the dark, but she was damn good at playing us off each other."

There was something in Kay's voice, in the sag of her shoulders, that told Callie she was more affected than mere anger by Olive's betrayal. This was a woman who grieved, though not necessarily due to the death of her husband.

"Olive got the best of both of you. You got tired of dancing around Paul and decided to off him." Again, EJ wasn't asking. She'd have made a decent detective interrogating suspects.

Kay shook her head. "Neither one of us is that stupid. First off, Paul kept a tight fist on the money he made. His will left me some cash, but it's Bert who'll take over the majority of the financials."

Bert? Was Underwood's son experienced enough to step into his father's shoes? Callie wasn't so sure. And what about Paul's new partner, Thomas Greer? What was his new role if not handling the financials?

"Second," the other woman continued, "Paul and I had our differences, but I wouldn't have killed someone else if I was mad at *him*. He, however, was very good at extending threats to scare folks. I'm more direct."

"Were you direct with Janie?" The question popped out of Callie and hung between them before she truly registered what she'd said.

The three of them stared at each other in silence for a few

thudding heartbeats. Finally, Kay Underwood's fierce expression softened.

"Janie was . . . I made a terrible mistake. I didn't stand up to Paul as I should have when it came to her. And she suffered for it. I wish I'd had the guts then. I'm sorry I didn't. She deserved better."

Now was their chance to learn the truth. Paul Underwood was dead. They'd never get him to confess. But Kay Underwood knew what had happened. Callie swallowed hard. She wanted to know, yet wasn't sure she was ready for the answer.

"What did he do to her?"

Kay paled. "You saw the marks. He was rough with her, like he was with me and Bert. I tried to keep Bert from being like his father, but that was pointless. Then Paul . . ."

Her jaw tightened and her lips pressed together.

"Paul what?" Myriad horrible images ran through Callie's mind.

Kay took a slow breath. "He . . . he touched her."

Callie's head swam. Not just beaten. Worse. Much worse.

"She threatened to go to the cops. He got mad, like he does—did. He pushed her, and she fell down the stairs. He claimed it was an accident. We called the doctor but . . ."

Callie's lungs seemed to stop working. Paul Underwood had pushed Janie down the stairs in anger to shut her up. He had killed her, just like EJ said.

"She was never sick." The quiet of EJ's voice drew Callie's gaze to her. Rage. She had never really seen rage like that on EJ's face. "He fucking killed her and you covered it up."

"I didn't—"

EJ stepped closer, her finger raised and pointing into Kay's face. Callie thought she was going to punch the woman. She wouldn't interfere. "Don't you dare. Don't you fucking dare say a word. She was brutalized, injured, and you didn't do shit."

"H-he was a monster," Kay stammered. "You know that."

"She was a kid!" Spittle flew from EJ's lips. Kay closed her eyes but didn't move.

Callie hoped the walls were thick or that the neighbors weren't home. They didn't need to hear her and EJ railing at Kay.

"She was a fucking kid." EJ spoke softly and stepped back, gathering herself, regaining control. "I get that you were abused by him as well, Kay, but for fuck's sake."

"I-I know. I'm sorry. I'm so sorry."

The admission and apology hit Callie in the gut. It was not what she'd expected from Kay Underwood. Not at all. It didn't change the fact that the Underwoods were responsible for Janie's death and misery, but it was more of an apology than they would ever have gotten out of Paul.

They stood in the entry, anger and grief thickening the silence between them. The truth was out, but Callie felt as impotent as the day they'd learned Janie had died.

"Where's Olive now?" EJ asked shifting away from the painful topic. There was nothing to be done now. They couldn't get revenge on Paul, and though she deserved their wrath, Kay had suffered as well. "She hasn't been to her apartment for a few days."

Callie pressed her fingertips against her eyes until white and red starbursts flared. *Focus on what we need to do now to get out of trouble.*

Kay turned brittle again. "I wish I knew."

Her tone implied Olive Lang was no longer appreciated, that if she caught up with her lover it might not go well. That could work to their advantage. If Kay was done with Olive, maybe she'd help them.

"How powerful is she, really?" Callie needed to know what they'd be up against because confronting Olive over the murder of Paul Underwood and the unidentified woman would not be a walk in the park.

Kay shook her head. "She isn't. I mean, not very. She talks

a good game, but isn't disciplined enough from what I've been able to tell."

As an uninitiated, Kay might not have been able to gauge Olive's true strength.

"Paul didn't use her for his dealings?" EJ cocked an eyebrow of skepticism.

"Not that I'm aware of." She gave Callie a significant glance, like she was the only reason EJ was in business. Hardly.

Callie and EJ exchanged looks, silent questions passing between them. Was Olive keeping her talents from Kay as a precaution, or was she truly not powerful enough to have pulled off a double murder and cover it up? If Olive was as clever as Kay said, she could have kept the full extent of her power close to her chest. Callie knew from experience you could be close to someone and not have them know who and what you really were.

But if Olive wasn't powerful enough to have helped Paul and then kill him, who was?

"We didn't do this," EJ said again. "And if you want to know who did, you'd best either help us or stay out of our way. That includes running to the cops or the Tribunal."

The threat in EJ's voice seemed to penetrate Kay Underwood's inclination to make things difficult. Perhaps it was guilt over Janie. Whatever her reasoning, she gave a curt nod.

"We weren't here." EJ turned, taking Callie gently by the upper arm, and escorted her out of the apartment.

The lock clicked in place behind them.

"Now what?" Callie asked.

"Now we get dinner and a stiff drink and figure out where the hell Olive is."

They headed down the rear stairwell, out the back door, and through the alley. At the entrance on the main street, EJ glanced up and down to make sure they weren't going to be observed, and suddenly drew Callie against the building.

"Shit."

"What?" Callie whispered. Cops? Tribunal?

"Greer." She took off her fedora and leaned forward enough to see the street without being seen. "Son of a bitch."

"Is he coming this way?" Callie leaned past her. Thomas Greer was heading to the front door of the Underwoods' building, briefcase swinging at his side. That was not a surprise. He likely had a slew of legal papers for Kay and Bert to sign.

When he was inside, EJ stepped onto the sidewalk. "Look at the car he came in."

She gestured across the street with her chin as she set her hat on her head.

A green Plymouth glinted in the late day sun. Its near twin—Kay Underwood's car—was almost directly across from it.

CHAPTER SEVENTEEN

Son of a bitch. Son of a gods-damned bitch.

The words kept running through EJ's head.

Nosy Nellie at Olive's apartment building had seen a green Plymouth. One, as far as she knew. Could it have been two different cars?

EJ wondered who copied from whom and whether it was intentional somehow.

But that was neither here nor there. The important thing was that, at least circumstantially, they may have found Olive's third lover. Jesus, the woman must have some stamina.

"That's a hell of a coincidence," Callie said beside her.

"I was thinking the same thing." EJ looped her arm through Callie's and walked to her car.

"What do we do about it?"

She opened the passenger door for Callie and got her settled. "We follow him. If Olive isn't at her place or with Kay Underwood, I'm thinking she's maybe with the driver of the other green Plymouth."

"Makes as much sense as anything." Callie frowned. "Olive sure liked to live dangerously, sleeping with both Underwoods *and* possibly their lawyer? The girl has guts."

"But not brains. She was playing with fire." EJ slumped in

the driver's seat. "Though it looks like Paul was the dim bulb here. Olive might have been cheating on him with two people he supposedly trusted."

Callie snorted. "Good. He deserved whatever he got."

EJ couldn't argue with her. Underwood was scum and got what was coming to him. They only had to prove it wasn't them who did it.

They sat in silence for a minute or two, staring at the front door of the apartment, each lost in thought. EJ kept running Kay Underwood's words through her head.

She knew he hurt her, but didn't do shit.

Anger, disgust, and sadness thickened into a cold ball in her gut.

You tried to tell us, Janie. Why didn't we listen better?

Suddenly her throat tightened and her eyes burned. EJ tried to hold down the sob, but it leaked out.

Turning to her, Callie reached for her hand. Her own face was blotchy with suppressed emotion, her eyes shiny.

"I should have killed him a long time ago," EJ rasped.

Callie squeezed her fingers. When she spoke, her voice was soft, as if she were afraid to speak of it. "We didn't know everything, EJ. She didn't tell us how bad it was."

"She should have. We should have asked her." There was a hint of anger in her voice from the lump in her chest. She wasn't mad at Janie. She was mad—enraged—about what she'd gone through. About her own inability to do anything about it.

"You never told us everything that happened to you, did you?" Callie asked.

The question startled EJ, and she swiveled her head to look at Callie. "He never did *that*."

Her father had been an abusive bastard, no doubt about it. EJ had sported plenty of bruises and a busted finger more than once. She'd stayed out of their apartment for a couple of days after her father had kicked her in the ribs, luckily a glancing blow that only bruised and hadn't broken anything. Never, ever had he touched her in any other way.

"No, but he hurt you more than you let on."

True. Because weakness got exploited. Weakness got you hurt more, or even dead.

"Because you were angry and embarrassed," Callie continued, getting to the real heart of it. "You didn't want anyone to feel sorry for you, so you kept it to yourself. I suspect Janie did the same thing and was threatened by Paul and Bert to keep her mouth shut."

Old pain swirled with the anger. Callie flinched as if feeling it as well. "You knew. About my dad."

"I didn't know all of it," Callie said. "And I didn't know how to talk to you about it without making you feel worse. I'm sorry about that." She took EJ's hand in both of hers. "I'm sorry you went through that alone. I'm sorry Janie did too. I wish we could have been better about that for both of you."

Tears slid down EJ's cheeks. No one had ever wanted to do anything like that for her. Ever. Except Callie. And Gran. And maybe a few of the Roses if they had known.

Her throat burned with the effort of keeping it in after all this time, after hearing Kay Underwood admit the terrible things that had happened to Janie. "I wanted to protect her, Cal. I wanted to protect all of you, and I failed. I failed, and she died, and you left, and—and—"

A sob burst from her chest, then another. The pain of losing Janie, of her own troubles as a kid, of her inability to do what needed to be done to keep all the Roses safe, squeezed her like a vise. Her vision blurred.

She felt Callie's arms wrap around her and pull her into a tight hug. EJ buried her face in the side of Callie's neck, her floral perfume filling her.

"Oh, honey, oh EJ," Callie whispered. Her hand cupped the back of EJ's head, her body absorbing EJ's shaking sobs. "You did so much for us. All of us. Still do. You didn't fail anyone. We were kids. Just kids."

They were just kids, but kids who had had to grow up pretty damn fast, whether they wanted to or not. And some hadn't gotten a chance to grow up at all.

Callie held her until EJ's tears stopped and her breathing returned to normal. It would be oh so nice to stay like this forever, wrapped in the arms of the woman she loved, but fantasies like that didn't happen to real people.

EJ eased out of Callie's arms and swiped beneath her eyes with the heels of her hands. Surely the kohl liner she used had smeared into a mess.

"Here, let me." Callie took a handkerchief from her purse and gently swiped around EJ's eyes, then dabbed at her own. She wasn't wearing any makeup that would make her look like a raccoon, but she'd been crying along with EJ.

"Thanks," EJ said. She pecked Callie on the cheek.

Callie cupped her face between her palms. "You won't blame yourself anymore, right? This was on them."

EJ nodded and leaned forward. Her lips brushed Callie's. Something passed between them, something more than mutual grief and comfort. Something more than the connection they'd made the night EJ had sought out the mage for healing her physical hurts. Something more that she couldn't name but knew she wanted oh so much.

Movement at the corner of her eye stopped her from deepening the kiss.

Greer.

As much as she wanted to be with Callie, they had to act. With a wince of an apology, she gestured out the window. "There he is."

Callie straightened in her seat. "Let's go."

EJ started the car and followed the green Plymouth.

EJ stayed well behind Greer, but not so far that she lost him. Callie was impressed with her ability to trail him in fairly light traffic. When Greer pulled over, EJ moved past him. Callie ducked down so he wouldn't catch sight of her.

EJ swung into a spot in front of an apartment building.

"He must live or work in one of these." EJ turned in her seat. A feral grin curved her mouth. She seemed to have recovered from the earlier emotional bout, but Callie knew EJ well enough to understand that anger was part of the grieving process for her. "There."

Callie peered back over the seat. Pinstripe-suited Greer sauntered toward them, briefcase in hand. He tipped his hat at a woman walking by. After she passed, he turned to watch her over his shoulder. When he faced them again, he was grinning. Within a few steps he entered an office building.

"He doesn't seem all that broken up over Underwood being dead," Callie said straightening in her seat.

"Can't fault him for that."

EJ was right. There wouldn't be too many mourning the loss.

"Kay wasn't too heartbroken either," Callie reminded her.

She couldn't imagine living in a situation where no one had any emotional connection, where it was all about how much someone could squeeze out of another person until they were empty. "How does a human being function like that?"

EJ stared out the windscreen, and when she spoke, her voice was soft, contemplative. "Everything becomes a prize to win. Money, power, influence. You can't have those and be emotional or sentimental. It's all about who is better at manipulating others, better at putting up walls no one can get past. The first to crack is seen as weak, caring about the wrong things. Vulnerability can get you hurt or worse."

Callie studied EJ's profile, noting the furrow of her brow. "Do you care about the wrong things, EJ?"

The words sounded pathetic in her own ears, but she had to know. Since leaving Kay Underwood's apartment, she felt like they were on a different level of trust and candidness now.

EJ turned to meet Callie's gaze. She reached out, covering Callie's hand, and smiled. "Not the wrong thing, Cal. Never. Though, to be honest, what we have is a vulnerability for both of us. Any relationship in this world has it. But it's also our strength, eh? You and me, we can be unstoppable."

It was a nice thought, but was it something real? She was part of EJ's world now. Was that something Callie actually wanted? What risk might it be for her or Gran or the shop?

EJ started to lean forward, her dark eyes soft and inviting, lips parted. Callie closed her eyes. Yes, maybe this was what she wanted. Where was the harm in wishing for something better than what you had? And EJ would protect her. Hell, now that Callie was practicing her magic, she could protect both of them, couldn't she?

Instead of the anticipated touch of EJ's mouth to hers, Callie felt the distinct lack of contact as a not-so-stunned "Well, look at that" came from EJ.

Her eyes flew open. "What?"

"Look who's coming up the street." EJ's nodded toward the sidewalk, her previously soft and inviting gaze now hard as steel.

Strolling toward them, Olive Lang swung two large shopping bags at her sides like she didn't have a care in the world. Her red coat buttoned to her throat and her sunglasses did little to disguise who she was, but perhaps no one was expecting her to be walking around.

"Looking good for a supposedly dead woman," Callie quipped.

"Right?"

EJ started to get out of the car, but Callie stopped her with a hand on her arm.

"Wait. We know where she's going."

As if on cue, Olive entered the same building Greer had disappeared into.

"Ten'll get you twenty he's got her stashed in a room or apartment up there," EJ said.

"I'm not taking that sucker bet."

EJ chuckled.

"So Olive and Greer. But did they kill Underwood and the other woman?"

"It would make sense," EJ said, nodding. "Let's follow her up."

"No, wait."

EJ was out of the car before Callie could stop her. She came around to the passenger side and opened the door.

"Come on. I just want to get the layout of where they are."

"Why?" Only one reason made sense to Callie. EJ wanted to know exactly where they were so she could have eyes on them in case more than eyes might be necessary. "It's probably Greer's office and a little love nest apartment."

"Won't know until we go in." EJ smiled and held her hand out.

Callie heaved a sigh and got out of the car.

EJ shut the door, then looped Callie's hand under her arm to rest on her forearm. "We'll just take a quick look."

They strolled to the building. There was no indication on the heavy metal and glass doors as to what went on inside, no signs for businesses or intercom buttons. Random people didn't enter this building by happenstance.

EJ pulled the door open and held it for Callie, who immediately felt a frisson of energy shimmer through her. At first she thought it had come from the carpeted floor, a jolt of static electricity, but then queasiness swirled in her stomach.

"EJ."

EJ came up beside her. "What? What's wrong? You look like you're about to spew."

Callie swallowed down the tickle of discomfort crawling up her throat. "There's a ward."

She scanned the lobby as if the protective runes might be evident. Of course they were not. Nothing glowed or shimmered. There was no neon sign pointing to where in the lobby a mage had traced lines of magic. Yet she knew they were there. That powerful or meant to be detected?

The elevator a dozen feet away dinged, and the doors slid open. A man and a woman stepped out, chatting. They wore evening clothes, as if headed out to some sort of swanky club or event. With barely a glance they passed EJ and Callie.

Concern lined EJ's face. "Are you okay? Is it dangerous?"

Callie shook her head. "I don't think so. I think it's just an alert to whoever laid it. Or it could be a deterrent for folks coming in."

"Wouldn't that have to be specific to a person? Like the spell you did against Underwood?"

Despite the unpleasant gurgling in her gut, Callie smiled. EJ might not have been too keen on magic, but she was learning some of the ins and outs of it.

"Yes and no. It's likely a general security spell for the entire building, letting a guard know who's coming and going."

A very strong security spell, though not one to outright harm someone. Still, Callie wouldn't want to upset the mage who set it.

EJ glanced up at the ceiling and around the lobby as if looking for some sort of sign herself. "A general alarm would go off every time someone came or went."

"A person or two or a particular energy could be detected if the mage was strong enough. Others would be noted, perhaps counting who came in and went out to make sure the building was clear." Callie wiped a thin film of sweat off her upper lip.

"Can we go back outside? I need some air."

EJ took her arm again and guided her through the front doors. The cool, fresh air and distance from the ward cleared her head and calmed her stomach. They returned to EJ's car. EJ opened the passenger door and got Callie settled before going around to the driver's side. Enclosed within the vehicle, EJ gazed at Callie with naked concern.

"Feeling better?"

"Much. Thank you." Callie tilted her head back against the seat and closed her eyes. "I didn't think Olive was strong enough for that sort of spell."

"Are you sure it was her? Maybe she had help."

"Possibly."

EJ started the car. "However they're doing it, we won't have you going back in there."

Callie nodded in agreement, then realized what EJ hadn't said. She sat up and shot EJ a glare. "You're thinking of going back in."

EJ avoided looking at her, watching the traffic as she maneuvered back onto the street. "It will be to our advantage to know where they are and what we might have to deal with."

"You didn't feel the ward or anything."

"Nope."

Callie appreciated EJ's new interest in magic, but there was a lot she didn't understand.

"You may not have felt anything because *you* are the target, EJ."

EJ showed no reaction to that, merely staring ahead as she drove. "Not a surprise."

Callie had learned to recognize her mask of stubborn determination. "Dammit, EJ, you can't go in there."

"No, *you* can't." EJ glanced at her. "Which tells me I absolutely should. I'm not going to sit back and wait for them to come to me on this. Fuck that. I will not hide from the likes of

Thomas Greer and Olive Lang."

Callie shook her head, staring out the side window. *Damn her. Damn her stubbornness. Damn her foolhardy idea of being bulletproof, even though the new scar on her arm proved otherwise. Damn her need to prove she wasn't to be trifled with.*

"You go in there and you will die."

"Thanks for the vote of confidence."

"That's not what I'm saying, EJ, and you know it."

"That doesn't make it any less important that we find out what Greer and Olive are up to. You can't go up. Someone has to."

Callie turned to look at her. EJ continued to stare ahead. "And if they know you're coming?"

She shrugged. "Even mages aren't immune to bullets, right?"

Anger welled in Callie's gut. Anger and worry and disappointment. "So that's your answer? Shoot them?"

EJ threw her a look. "What else am I supposed to do, Cal? Reason with them? There is no reasoning with them. Underwood wanted what I have. I'm not going to wait around to see if the new management is going to back off. Not if they're pinning the murders on us. I'd wager they didn't kill Underwood because they felt he was going too far with harassing me and my people. And I'm not going to wait around for Bradford to decide to cuff us for something we didn't do."

"Better he cuffs us for killing Greer and Olive?"

"If I'm going to go to prison, I'd rather it was for something I actually did."

Callie pressed her fingers to her temples and rubbed at the oncoming headache. "There has to be another way."

"If you come up with something, let me know."

"Another spell might work." Truth be told, Callie wasn't sure which one or if they had time. To focus it on Greer or Olive, to make it strong enough to actually be effective, they'd need personal items, time, a particular incantation of some sort, and possibly more blood than a mere dribble.

"We tried it that way. I truly appreciate what you did, but sometimes magic is no replacement for a good old-fashioned punch in the mouth."

Or a bullet in the head.

EJ hadn't said it, but that's where this was leading.

The thought that occurred to her left her mouth before Callie could stop it. "You were counting on the spell to fail from the beginning, weren't you? You never expected me to succeed, and now you can justify going after Underwood's people to show how tough you are."

"What?" EJ's head whipped toward her, then back to focus on traffic. "Don't be ridiculous." She sounded sincere, but could Callie believe her? "I have had every ounce of faith in you, but yeah, I also make backup plans for everything I do."

"And since I did fail, you have your contingency plan. Kill whoever gets in your way."

She couldn't believe she had played right into EJ's hands.

Color rose on EJ's face. "Stop saying that. You didn't fail. And I never planned on killing anyone."

"You certainly aren't shying away from it."

The look on her face told Callie everything. Killing might not have been EJ's first choice—if it had been, she wouldn't have sought out Callie and her magic—but it was never completely off the table.

Callie had deluded herself if she assumed EJ might have changed, that being part of her life would temper those tendencies.

Of course EJ's criminal past had "matured" into darker and more dangerous activities and methods. *We're not kids anymore.* No, and grown-up gang leaders didn't balk at such violence.

EJ slammed her palms on the steering wheel. The Model A swerved. Callie grabbed the door and braced her other hand on the dashboard. EJ quickly regained control, but Callie saw her hands were shaking. She angled the car to the side of the road and stopped at the curb. Shifting to neutral, she set the brake and stared out through the windscreen, chest heaving.

"I don't know what you think I am, Callie, but I'll tell you what I'm not." She turned her head, hands gripping the wheel hard enough to turn her knuckles nearly white. "I'm not a coward. I will not back down from Greer or Olive or anyone else. I won't live in fear. I won't let anyone take what's mine, what I've earned, what I've built. Never again."

The air between them seemed to pulse with emotion. Fear, anger, worry. And something else. Callie knew how EJ had lived as a kid, barely getting by, her mother gone, her father inattentive when he wasn't smacking her around. EJ had to fend for herself. She'd had to fight tooth and nail to get whatever she had wanted and needed herself. She guarded what was precious to her like a starving dog with a bone.

Her throat tight, Callie had to swallow twice before her words made it out. "I understand, but I can't be part of whatever you plan to do to Greer and Olive."

"I'm not asking you to."

A dry, humorless bark of a laugh scraped her throat. "No, you're asking me to stand by as you go get yourself killed." She levered the door open. "Sorry, EJ, but I can't do that either."

She got out and slammed the door shut behind her. As she started down the walk, Callie heard EJ get out of the car.

"Callie, wait!"

Callie turned. EJ came toward her. Callie spotted a half-full trash can on the walk. She flicked her wrist and rolled the metal can in front of EJ with a screech of metal on cement, fast enough to block her way but slow enough that EJ had time to stop before being bowled over.

People on the sidewalk hesitated for a moment, then hurried along, giving them a wide berth, heads down, gazes averted.

EJ stared at Callie, dark eyes wide.

"No, EJ." Her voice was thick with tears. "No. I thought I could be part of this, be with you, but I was wrong. You're not the coward. I am."

EJ's shoulders dropped. Sorrow filled her face. Callie hadn't seen her look like that since she'd spotted EJ standing at the back of the church the day she'd married Nate.

She turned her back on EJ and walked home.

CHAPTER EIGHTEEN

EJ parked half a block away from Greer's building. Light from the setting sun trickled through slate clouds, making it feel later than it was. Pedestrians and vehicles passed, as lost in their own worlds as EJ was focused on hers. After about half an hour, she didn't see many coming or going through the main doors, even though it was the end of the workday and people should have been heading home. What sort of business building didn't have employees or do business?

One that was hiding something.

She got out of the car. Callie had said the magic she felt might be an alarm of some sort, or an identifier. Maybe if she went inside with others around, whoever might be monitoring the—ward, was it?—wouldn't notice. And if she was noticed, so what? It was a public building.

The argument with Callie the day before ate at her, churning the little she'd been able to eat today into a roiling mess. She got Callie's point, but something had to be done. Waiting for the other shoe to drop had never been EJ's thing. If it needed doing, get it done. She'd smooth things over with Callie later, remind her she was the bravest, best person EJ knew. And if she couldn't fix it? No, she would. Had to. Because she couldn't lose Callie. Not again.

But she couldn't think about that now. She had to focus on the task at hand. Distractions got you dead.

So do dumb stunts.

EJ had to agree with the Callie-voice in her head, but here she was.

Sure, she could have gone to the cops, but why would they care? They were probably rooting for rival gangs to off each other. That made their jobs easier. Bradford might be interested in Olive Lang being alive, and that would maybe take some of the heat off her and Callie, but would it be enough? She couldn't make that bet and was too distrustful of the police to rely on them.

She waited near the door, but not so near as to be in the way or, hopefully, noticeable. The newspaper she held up kept her face partially hidden, in case there were any non-magic eyes on the entrance. After fifteen or twenty minutes, a pair of men headed toward the glass and metal doors. EJ fell in step behind them, but not too close.

The men strode toward the elevators. EJ passed them, head turned away as if looking at the boring artwork on the walls and made for the stairwell. The heavy door shut behind her, and she looked up at the concrete and metal. Six stories to check for anything associated with Thomas Greer. She started up the stairs.

At the first landing, EJ cautiously opened the door to that floor. No one was present. She entered the hallway, quietly closing the door behind her. All the office doors along the hall had numbers and placards telling who or what was behind them, individual and company names that she didn't care about or recognize. There had been no directory in the lobby. Apparently, you only came to this building if you knew who you needed to see.

Pretentious asses. A description that fit Greer like a glove.

The second and third floors were also not occupied by

Thomas Greer. EJ eased open the door to the fourth floor. A man and a woman each in business attire stood with their backs to EJ, perusing some papers in the woman's hand. She pointed something out to the man. He nodded, said something too low for EJ to hear, and turned toward the elevators. The woman strode to a nearby office and shut the door firmly behind her.

EJ slipped into the hall. At the far end, one of the doors had a plaque with "Thomas Greer, Esquire."

Finally.

EJ pressed her ear against the smooth wood. No muffled conversation, no ringing telephone. She wrapped one hand around the brass knob, half expecting to be shocked or burned. Only cool metal. With the other hand, she eased her revolver out of her pocket. She turned the knob, feeling more than hearing the soft click of the latch.

The office beyond was dark, silent.

Something wasn't ri—Bright light. Then nothing.

Standing in the cool room, Callie held the meaty pig leg steady and swung the cleaver, aiming for the narrow gap between the hock joints. Mrs. Henderson was fond of smoked hocks to use in her pea soup, and Mr. Kramer enjoyed pickled pigs feet, so she'd be sure to set some aside for them for their regular shopping visits.

The blade should have separated the foot from the lower leg with one swift, clean whack. Should have. Instead, the sharp edge cut through the thick skin and embedded itself in the leg bone.

"Dammit."

She hadn't missed such an easy cut in years.

That she'd screwed up was a testament to how mad she was at EJ.

"You'd better concentrate before you lose a finger," Gran said from the doorway.

It was good to have her home now that the danger from Paul Underwood had passed. Callie had updated Gran on what had happened, particularly the accusations from Bradford and the interview with Frances Eccles. She'd noticed Gran thumbing through her own spell book the other night. This wasn't her fight, but try telling Gran that.

Callie levered the cleaver out of the bone. "I'm fine."

"Mmhmm."

She didn't have to see Gran's face to note the disbelief. She didn't believe it either.

The day had been hell. She hadn't heard from EJ, and her own ego hadn't let her be the first to break. Callie wasn't in the wrong here, though she wasn't completely sure EJ was either.

Out in the shop, the bell over the front door tinkled. Gran's sensible shoes clicked against the linoleum as she went to help the new customer. Callie hoped it would be an easy order as it was nearly closing time.

EJ was a grown woman, she reminded herself as she separated another leg. A businesswoman. A woman who'd had to be tough and resilient for years. She'd taken risks and ignored laws since she was a kid. What made Callie think she'd be able to influence her? Because they'd renewed their friendship? Because they'd gone beyond that? She and EJ would never agree on things like laws because EJ had little problem with breaking most of them.

Tension vibrated up her arm as she held the cleaver handle in a vise-like grip. That certainly wouldn't help her butcher this hog. She dried her damp palms on her apron and hefted the cleaver again. Closing her eyes, she took a deep breath. Her head cleared as she exhaled.

The satisfying thump of steel separating flesh and bone as it hit the butcher block shimmied up her arm. She opened her eyes.

There. That was better.

"Callie!"

The edge in Gran's voice stopped Callie from calling out that she'd be right there. Had someone come in who shouldn't be there? Were her new wards not working? Cleaver still in hand, Callie hurried to the shop, a protection spell ready on her tongue.

Gran stood on the customer side of the counter, her back to Callie. There was no one else in the shop. Callie took in the space, the same warm smell of pine shaving, the same tang of meat chilling in the cases. Nothing out of the ordinary.

No. Something was off. Something that prodded her magic. "Gran? What is it?"

Gran turned, her face pale but eyes blazing. She held up a parcel. "Addressed to you."

The packet was wrapped in brown paper and tied with white string. It looked pliable, as if it contained fabric or an item of clothing.

Callie passed behind the counter. As she drew closer, the sense of something wrong increased. Tingles danced along her skin, something like it felt when she did magic, but in a disconcerting way.

Gran held up the parcel so Callie could read the thick, black ink spelling out her name in block letters. No address.

She wrapped her hands along the edges to take it. The sense of "wrongness" hurtled up her arms. She almost dropped the package, but something familiar swirled through the distasteful sensation.

"EJ."

Callie swallowed the boulder of fear that suddenly lodged in her throat and tore at the paper and string with trembling hands. Her head swam with the sudden assault of the scent of EJ's blood, of magic, of their connection. What was once a white hand towel was now stained and stiff with drying splotches and smears of dark red. A folded piece of paper was pinned to it with EJ's carved rose brooch.

"Don't touch it," Gran said, her voice distorted by the flood of fear and magic in Callie's head.

She looked up, blinking slowly as she erected a mental barrier against the magic to keep from being overwhelmed. "They have her."

Callie eased the ivory pin out of the cloth. The familiarity of EJ warmed her palm as she lifted the edge of the paper with a fingertip. In the same thick, black block lettering was "TONIGHT 8PM."

There was no need for any other details. She knew exactly where to go.

"Callie."

In that single word, Callie heard all of Gran's concern, understanding, and an attempt to persuade her not to go out tonight.

Their eyes met.

"It's too dangerous, Callie. We should call the police or—"

Callie shook her head and crumpled the note. Her other hand itched beneath the bloodstained cloth. "No. They can't help with this. They won't. Not to help the likes of EJ Jordan. The people who have her know that too."

They also knew less than three hours wasn't much time for Callie.

Or thought they knew her.

She walked through the back of the shop and up the stairs to their apartment.

She had spells to prepare.

CHAPTER NINETEEN

Awareness came to EJ as if she was surfacing from a deep dive within the ocean. The salty burn of an accidental swallow of water seared her nostrils and bit at her throat. She had never been submerged so fully in open water, or even in a pool, just in the bathtub. The same distortion of sound wobbled into her ears.

Once the burn was gone, it was rather soothing, actually, this sensation of floating in depthless, dark water, like she could drift and sleep forever . . .

Pain at the back of her head and the dizzying disorientation of being pulled upright jolted her back to reality. There was no water. No pool or ocean. Anger and fear roared through her like a tidal wave.

"Wakey wakey." Olive Lang's smirking red lipsticked mouth swam into view. "Time to play your part, EJ."

"Fuck you." EJ wasn't sure she had actually enunciated the words, but by the disapproving look on Olive's face, she got the gist across. EJ grinned. Her lower lip stung, and she tasted blood.

Right. Punched in the face. That explained why Olive was sort of blurry.

"You're not my type, EJ."

"Not sleazy lawyer enough for you?" EJ didn't know if Greer was within earshot. She didn't care.

Olive leaned closer. "Not rich or powerful enough."

She moved away, releasing EJ's hair. At least that pain eased some.

EJ fought to keep her head up and assess her surroundings. She faced an open doorway, which led into another office. Greer's reception area? Had to be. The room in which she sat—tied to a hard chair, arms behind her back—had a more luxurious feel. The floor was rich maroon carpeting, with landscape paintings on the walls above a leather-covered couch. On the other side of the room a sideboard displayed decanters of liquor and glasses. That meant Greer's desk was behind her.

EJ gently licked her swollen lower lip, then her upper. More blood. Her nose throbbed. Shit. Had they broken her nose? The lower part of her face felt stiff. She looked down. Blood splattered on her previously white shirt and blue vest.

"Damn it. Another ruined shirt."

"Clothing bills are the least of your problems, Miss Jordan." Greer's voice came from behind her. She hadn't heard him speak often; his high tenor didn't fit his larger frame.

EJ tried to look back over her shoulder, but she could only see the edge of the desk. Also, it hurt like hell to twist her body that way. Not that she was going to let Greer and Olive see that.

"I suppose you're my biggest problem now, is that it, Greer?"

"You don't think so?" He sounded amused.

"Problems imply solutions." EJ shrugged as best she could with her arms bound. "There's no way I'm giving you what you want, whatever it is, so I have to accept what you plan to do to me."

Maybe if he thought she'd given up he'd drop his guard and she could do something. Though she didn't know what that might be exactly. Perhaps she should accept that he was going to kill her. At least it would give her no reason to hesitate when it was time to act.

"*You* might not give me what I want," Greer said.

A heavy thud sounded beyond the outer office, then a gunshot.

EJ's entire body went stiff and cold.

There was a cry and a second thud as if a large body had been thrown against the wall beside the door.

"But she can."

Greer's two henchmen lay crumpled against the wall. Callie didn't think they were dead. She hoped not, but she wasn't going to concern herself about it. They had EJ. Anything she did was now fair game.

EJ was behind the door. Greer would be there too, and probably Olive. They'd use EJ as bait, a bargaining chip, a shield. But for what? What could Callie give them? Or what did they think she could give them?

She paused in front of Greer's office door, eyes closed, and stroked the ivory rose pin at her throat. Beyond the smooth wood she felt EJ as she had when she'd located her at The Garden using her tie. As far as she could tell, EJ was alive, and likely would be at least until Greer told Callie what he wanted. He could easily have killed her at any time but hadn't.

The very thought grabbed Callie by the throat, took her breath.

She shook it off, for the moment at least. EJ wasn't dead. She knew that, felt it. They were both alive, and Callie was going to do her damnedest to keep it that way.

Callie listened for any indication of how many might be beyond the door. Greer and Olive. Anyone else? The spells she had prepared weren't number specific, but it would be nice to know what she was up against.

Silence throbbed around her. The building seemed to be holding its breath. She hadn't felt the ward when she came in the front door. The shield she'd erected before leaving home was hopefully doing its job. Though they were expecting her, any element of surprise would be to her advantage.

EJ's words about them being each other's vulnerability echoed in her head. She'd been right. It was what it was. They would be better prepared next time, assuming there was a next time.

From one of her coat pockets, Callie withdrew her dagger and made a short slit on her palm. Hands trembling with the thrill of her magic coursing through her, she drew bloody symbols along the sleeves of her coat, reinforcing the spell of protection.

When the henchman had fired his gun at her, the bullet had glanced off her side, slightly weakening the integrity of the spell. It wasn't an incantation she'd used before tonight, but it was simple and made more powerful by her particular affinity. The magic settled over her like a second skin, its presence bolstered by the new blood. She wondered if a point-blank shot would have been deflected, but had no desire to test that hypothesis if she could avoid it.

Gathering blood onto her forefinger, Callie made the required marks and gestures on the office door and over the knob and lock. "Open."

She "pushed" the door hard, keeping it held against the wall, and let the force of her magic swirl into the room like a tornado. If anyone was waiting inside, they'd be thrown off their feet, or at least be disoriented by the magic and debris swirling about. Papers, a stapler, coffee cups, and pens whipped around the outer office as Callie entered.

No one was there.

She let the magic settle, though kept at the ready, and office paraphernalia clattered to the floor. Greer's secretary's office was in disarray. The overhead light swung back and forth, dislodged from its ceiling fixture, creating dancing shadows. A desk, chairs, a couch, a filing cabinet, all askew.

Diagonal from the outer door, another door to Greer's inner office stood open. Callie couldn't see inside, but she knew EJ was there.

The whirlwind spell still at her command, she cautiously stepped in and maneuvered herself to see through the doorway. Inside, EJ sat in a straight-backed chair, arms secured behind her. She was coatless, her hair mussed, her right eye swollen. Blood was smeared under her nose and over her mouth and chin. Dried blood stained her shirt and vest.

Callie's heart stuttered as EJ grinned.

"Hey," she croaked. "Sorry I'm such a mess."

Callie laughed, but clamped her mouth shut and swallowed hard when it was about to become a sob of relief.

Behind EJ, Thomas Greer sat at his large walnut desk, hand and arm steadied atop it to better aim the .357 pointed at the back of EJ's head. Olive sat on the corner of the desk, smirking, with her legs crossed, like some secretary about to take dictation. Callie wanted to punch them both in their faces.

"Glad you could make it, Miss Payne," Greer said. "Please, have a seat."

"I'd rather stand, thanks."

Greer shrugged. "Suit yourself. With Miss Jordan between us, I'd imagine it's easier for both of us to see what might happen to her if you try something." He waggled the revolver back and forth a little, as if she hadn't seen it. "As you may be aware, Miss Payne—"

"What do you want, Greer?"

He seemed disappointed that she wanted to get to the crux of the matter. Probably because he was accustomed to hearing himself argue ad nauseam.

"Miss Jordan is to sign over all her holdings to the Underwood organization, all nice and legal, then leave town. Clean break. Start over somewhere else far from Seattle."

EJ laughed. "Right. Drop dead."

Greer's features clouded, though Olive looked somewhat amused. She'd better hope he never saw her laughing at him. Men didn't respond well to that sort of reaction.

"Honestly, Miss Jordan, do you think you're in any position to deny me?" He turned his glare onto Callie. "If she doesn't agree to it, you'll need to convince her."

Callie almost laughed at him herself. "How do you propose I do that? EJ would rather die than give you anything."

Greer's grin sent chills through her. "You're a blood mage, Miss Payne. You have talents and skills that can easily counter the strongest of wills."

What he was suggesting was terribly immoral and against the Laws. Not a shock really.

"You seem to know a lot about magic, Greer." Callie glanced at Olive. "Or did you give him some lessons?"

Olive shrugged. "I may have let a few trade secrets out of the bag."

"I make it my business to understand the people I'm dealing with," Greer said.

If he needed to learn "trade secrets," Greer wasn't the mage. And Olive hadn't been given the credit to be powerful enough to enact the magic necessary to put up the building ward or detect Callie's spell at The Garden. So who *was* their mage?

Whoever it was, Callie needed to be strong enough to counter them. But first things first. She needed to get EJ and herself out.

"Now," Greer continued, "do whatever bit of woo-woo magic you need to do in order to get Miss Jordan to sign."

"If I do, you'll let us go?" Even as she asked, Callie knew there was no way in hell that was going to happen. EJ's eyebrows twitched with wariness.

Another chilling Greer grin. "Sure. We'll even escort you safely out of town."

Right. She trusted Greer about as far as she could throw a cement truck. Still, she could throw other things.

Callie dug her fingernail into the fresh cut on her palm. Blood flowed. Mentally, she called up the spell she needed.

Catching EJ's eye, she hoped she projected a convincing air of capitulation. "I'm sorry, EJ. This is going to hurt some."

EJ's eyes went large with disbelief. "Callie, you promised."

She'd promised to never use magic on EJ without her consent. God, she wished she could explain. She would if they survived this.

With a hitch of guilt, Callie pushed out toward Greer's desk with her right hand while simultaneously "grabbing" EJ with her left, the thread of their connection assisting to pull her forward and to the side. Anyone else and Callie wouldn't have had the control to split forces so easily.

All three—Greer, Olive, and EJ—cried out as furniture flew. Greer's desk lifted and flipped, throwing Greer and Olive backward. A shot boomed. The bullet hit the ceiling, raining plaster down on them. Gunpowder and dust wafted in the air.

EJ and the chair hurtled forward through the doorway. Callie guided EJ to the side to avoid bowling herself over. She abruptly stopped the chair's flight just before it crashed into the secretary's desk, throwing EJ forward against her bindings with a yelp of pain. Callie slammed the door to Greer's office and threw up a hasty ward to lock it.

Callie hurried to EJ, pulling her dagger out of her coat pocket. "I'm sorry. Are you all right?"

EJ blinked several times, dazed by the spell and the unexpected ride. "Yeah, I suppose." She managed to focus on Callie and smiled. "That didn't hurt too much."

Callie cut the ropes that bound her to the chair. "Good. I was afraid you would believe I'd do whatever Greer wanted."

EJ rubbed her wrists once she was free. "I figured you showed up for some reason other than to watch Greer kill me.

You promised you'd never hurt me." She gave Callie a crooked grin. "I had faith you wouldn't do something like that against my will."

Never. Not only because it was against the Laws, but because this was EJ.

"You know me well." She helped EJ to her feet and gave her a quick once-over. "I don't know what sort of damage they sustained in there, and I want us to be as far away as possible when they get through that lock."

"They'll keep coming for us."

"I know, but let them come to us on our turf."

"Our turf, huh?" EJ grinned. "I love it when you talk like a tough moll."

Callie rolled her eyes. "Come on."

EJ stumbled on their way to the door. Callie caught her and had her drape her arm around Callie's shoulder.

"Next time I tell you it's not a good idea to go into a warded building, I hope you'll listen."

"Scout's honor."

"Good."

They left Greer's outer office. EJ glanced at the two men sprawled in the hallway.

"Are they dead?"

"No idea," Callie said, guiding her toward the elevator. "Don't care. They sent me a bloody towel. They had you tied to a chair. In my book, my actions were justified."

EJ grunted. "I'll bear witness at any Tribunal."

"Thanks."

"I mean, I do owe you one since you came to rescue me and all."

Callie laughed. "You can buy me a drink."

"I think we're gonna need mor than one." EJ nudged her away from the elevator. "Let's avoid being stuck in a box with no way out. Stairs."

Though she didn't expect anyone in the building to stop them, Callie paused at the stairwell door and opened it slowly. Nothing. That didn't mean there wasn't anyone waiting somewhere.

"Pretty quiet," EJ whispered.

"Let's hope it stays that way."

They passed through the door, and Callie closed it gently behind them.

They made their way down the four flights of stairs, pausing now and again for EJ to catch her breath and for Callie to listen for pursuit. On the ground floor, Callie had EJ wait by the door into the lobby while she opened it. Through the narrow gap, she saw the bank of elevators and part of the lobby. Overhead lights blazed, reflecting against the dark night beyond the main doors.

"Clear," she said and held her hand out to EJ. "Where are you parked?"

EJ grasped her hand. "To the left as we go out, about a block down."

Moving as fast as EJ's condition allowed, Callie brought up another push spell as they headed to the door,

So far, so good. No one jumped at them from behind the potted ficus; no henchmen swarmed as they exited the building. Callie breathed a sigh of relief in the chilly night air, but didn't stop. She could see EJ's car parked at the curb up ahead.

"Are you okay to drive?" she asked.

"Yeah, things are a little blurry."

Callie felt the hairs on the back of her neck rise. Instincts kicking in, she grabbed EJ and wrapped her in an embrace, hoping her shield held against—

The wall above their heads exploded, sending bits of brick and mortar flying.

"Shit!"

EJ yanked Callie down the alley, around bins of garbage. Callie tried a side door—locked. No time to concentrate on an unlock spell. Farther along, another narrow alley. Escape route or dead end?

"Keep going," EJ said.

Callie dug in her heels, stopping them. "EJ, wait."

Her heart hammered against her sternum. Her vision swam.

EJ turned to her, confusion and worry on her face. "What's wrong? We have to get the hell out of here."

She pulled EJ against the damp, cold brick, a bin and shadows offering them minimal cover. "You go. I'll hold him off."

Callie tried to escape EJ's grip, but EJ would have none of it. "Like hell I will. I'm not leaving you. We both go or we both stay."

"I used too much magic in too short a time," she said. EJ looked her over, hands rubbing up and down Callie's arms. "Preparing to come for you, holding spells at the ready. I can distract them while you get out of here, but I can't protect both of us while I do it."

Something heavy careened down the alley and bounced off the opposite wall with a crash. Callie and EJ ducked. Luckily nothing more than bits of flying muck hit them.

"Come out and play, Callie!" Laughter followed.

She recognized that braying laugh. Bert Underwood.

How had Bert slipped past them as a mage? Did Paul know? Probably. Kay? Hard to say. She had to give the little bastard credit if he was able to hide it and not flaunt his ability.

Though she didn't know every member of the Coven, she'd bet her eyeteeth he was a rogue.

"What can I do?" EJ asked. "How can I help?"

Callie swallowed hard. She was bound by the Laws not to take without consent. She was bound by ethics not to use another's blood if she didn't have to. But more blood and the boost from the bond she and EJ already shared would make her spells far more effective, especially now when she was feeling almost giddy with weakness.

"I need something powerful enough to make the spells I have prepared work better than what I can do alone."

It took half a moment for EJ to realize what she was asking. "You need my blood."

Callie squeezed her hand and nodded. "I can do it with my own, but since the night you were shot, the connection we've made on top of our relationship will give the spell more potency."

Footsteps echoed down the alley. They didn't have much time.

"Your choice. If you say no, I'll understand, but then you need to go right now."

"I'm not leaving you." She jerked her sleeve up. "I, Eileen Jordan, give you, Calliope Payne, permission to use my blood as you see fit."

Callie darted forward and kissed her hard and fast. The coppery tang from EJ's bloody lip danced on her tongue. The scent and power of EJ's blood begged her to bite down, to gather as much as she could from this singular source. EJ whimpered, sending a rush of exhilaration through her. Callie broke the kiss. She hadn't meant for that to happen. Not at all.

Blinking her vision and thoughts clear, Callie pulled her dagger out of her coat pocket and removed the sheath. The kiss was fulfilling, but she needed more. "I swear, Eileen Jordan, I will take no more than I need to protect us."

As she drew the edge lightly across EJ's forearm, Callie started invoking the spell. Crimson rose along the wound, bright against her brown skin. As Callie continued to speak of protection from and command of the elements that bound the universe, she drew the blade across her left palm. Aligning the incisions, she clasped EJ's arm.

Their blood mingled.

EJ's arm warmed under Callie's palm and grew hot. Breath hissed in and out between EJ's teeth. Callie didn't think she was hurting, but it was definitely an unusual sensation. For both of them.

Heat traveled up Callie's arm to her shoulder, her neck. Her heartbeat grew louder in her head, nearly drowning out the sound of the spell in her own ears.

"Callie?"

She spared a glance at EJ. "Get yourself behind something. Now."

She turned to face Bert Underwood, arms raised, body humming with the torrent of magic within her.

EJ's heart pounded as she watched the change come over Callie. Her hair had loosened from the pins that held it back, and her blue eyes were nearly black. No, so deep a red from what she could see of their glow that they looked black, the color of old, old blood.

Callie brought the blade of her dagger to her breast, and for a second EJ thought she'd do the unthinkable. She would rather die herself than see Callie make such a sacrifice. But she didn't harm that perfect breast. Callie swept her arms outward. Wind swirled like a tornado, whipping dirt and debris around Callie. Her hair and skirt rippled and flared.

EJ thought of how she'd looked like an avenging angel when they'd enacted the spell against Paul Underwood, but this . . . This Callie was something darker, something that sought more than justice. This Callie would exact any measure of revenge that she could. This Callie was ready to do everything in her power to protect herself and EJ, to stop whatever came at them.

And coming down the alley was Bert Underwood.

Callie's incantation grew louder. EJ felt her calling upon their shared power. Dizzy, she slumped against the brick wall. Callie moved her arms in giant circular motions. The wind around them roared like a freight train as it picked up speed. After three complete rotations, Callie gestured with both hands straight out, "pushing" at Bert.

Light streaked toward him. In the flash of brilliance, EJ saw Bert's eyes go wide as his feet flew up in front of him. The light winked out, but the sound of his body hitting the hard ground well down the alley, and the cry-grunt of pain, was loud and clear.

Callie started forward, another incantation on her lips, more intricate gestures harnessing power. An inhuman scream sounded from where Bert had landed, grew louder as some invisible force rushed toward them. What the hell was *that*?

Callie gasped and stumbled backward, half turned toward EJ. A bloody gash rent her right sleeve. Three scratches marred her perfect right cheek.

She caught EJ's eye and grinned.

EJ wasn't sure if she should be scared or proud of her love.

But there was one thing she *was* sure of.

"Bert, you are fucked."

CHAPTER TWENTY

Bricks and garbage can lids hurtled down the alley, banging and clanging against brick and pavement. With a thought and a flick of her hand, Callie made a shield of thickened air to deflect the missiles, sending them against the farthest wall. Crash! Bang! Plaster ripped off the building, scattered across Callie's shield and tumbled harmlessly to the ground.

"A shield? That's it? Getting tired, Callie?" Bert called, laughter in his voice.

Oh, if he only knew how she felt. How the addition of EJ's blood in her gestures made them almost indelible in the air around her. How the taste of EJ's blood on her lips—as accidental as that was—increased the potency of her incantations and energized her, became part of her, and thus part of her magic.

If he knew what she was truly capable of, he would turn tail, pissing himself.

"Why are you trying to kill us, Bert? We can talk this over like adults."

She had no delusion he would be open to talking it over. Hell, she didn't particularly want to talk to him either, but talking kept her from mindlessly lashing out and killing him. Talking meant letting him think she wasn't up to his magic.

"Sweet Callie. Always the soother of souls." His mocking

tone grated, but he wasn't wrong. She had preferred to work things out rather than resort to more forceful methods. "Janie always liked that about you. Said you were so easy to talk to. Said she'd tell you what I did, the weak little bitch."

Janie?

Callie went cold. "What about Janie, Bert? What did you do to her?"

Kay had indicated as much, but to hear him say it like it was no big deal?

"Nothing Dad didn't do to me. Well, maybe a few things if you know what I mean."

The shift from icy disgust to white-hot rage made her stomach flip. "You hurt her."

The words came out in a thick whisper that caught in her throat.

"We tried to toughen her up," he continued. "When she said she'd tell, well, Dad did what he always did."

Paul Underwood had lashed out, knocking her down the stairs.

The entire Underwood family was culpable. Even if Kay and Bert had also been abused by Paul, they were partially responsible for Janie's death. And Bert had confessed to abusing her. Paul was dead, but Bert would not get off so easy.

Callie let her rage burn bright. Had she been a fire mage, the very air around her would have combusted.

It took a moment after her head cleared to realize Bert was still talking. Jesus, did the Underwoods ever shut up?

"We tried talking to EJ, but she wasn't interested in our offer."

"Fuck off, Bert," EJ yelled back. "Your father's idea of an offer was shit. Like him. Like you."

"You are not helping," Callie mouthed, in case Bert had a way of amplifying sound and conversation. Eavesdropping spells were popular.

But she understood EJ's response. There were equal parts disgust and anger in her face. She hated Bert and what he'd done as much as Callie did. Even with a mage throwing spells at them, she wouldn't be intimidated. It was both endearing and frustrating.

A roaring force battered Callie's shield. She skimmed a fingernail along the cut on her palm, breaking the thin layer of coagulating cells. Swiping her finger through the blood, she drew glyphs and wards to reinforce the wall between them and Bert. That would hold off his attacks for now, but was he strong enough to weaken her defenses given enough time? If he was the mage responsible for the magic surrounding Paul's death and that of the other woman, then covering it up, he would be more than strong enough.

She had to act against him with similar force. He wouldn't show mercy. Could she come out of this with them all alive? Should she? What he was doing now, what he'd done, justified everything and anything she had to do, yet the Laws had been drummed into her: magic used to kill should be rare and prudently applied. The Tribunal—and there would be a Tribunal hearing—would ask if she could have managed to contain him.

Harm invoked . . .

"Always the classy broad, eh, EJ?" Bert barked another laugh at them. "You wouldn't deal with Dad. Now you deal with me. And I don't make deals."

"Is that why you killed Paul?" Callie was sure he had a hand in it. Only a mage with significant strength could force someone to murder another or take their own life. "He wasn't giving you what you wanted, was he? He never did."

The silence from the end of the alley spoke volumes.

"You wanted to prove to him you could take out EJ on your own," Callie continued, "but he didn't think you could. He didn't even give you a chance, did he?"

"He said EJ was too much for me, that once he got rid of

her, I could manage The Garden for him." Bert's voice cracked like a thirteen-year-old going through puberty. "Jesus fucking Christ, he talked about you all the fucking time. You got more attention at the dinner table than the damn pot roast."

"Is he blaming me for his shit home life and daddy issues?" EJ asked in an incredulous near whisper.

She started to retort, but Callie held up her hand. EJ frowned, lips pressed into an angry line.

"That explains what you did to Paul and that woman," Callie said. "I can see why you came after EJ and me. Especially EJ."

EJ gave her a look. Hell, he was already blaming EJ for his troubles. No sense in trying to defend her. He wasn't about to listen to any such thing.

"That woman, though. She had nothing to do with any of this, Bert."

"Collateral damage."

Callie could almost see him shrug it off. His callous attitude chilled her. The life of the woman, whoever she was, meant nothing to him. Janie had meant nothing to him. He was more like his father than he probably realized.

"You—none of you—ever thought I'd be more than Paul Underwood's useless kid. Even he didn't think I'd be anything more. Well, he was wrong. You're all wrong!"

Grit and papers and globs of who knew what swirled along the ground. The debris field grew larger, circled faster and faster. It rose over their heads, a malevolent cloud. Lightning crackled within the heating air. The hairs on the back of Callie's neck rose.

A bolt of electricity snaked down and struck her shield. Callie was tossed back into EJ, and they tumbled down the alley. They hit a bin, knocking it over with a crash. Another lightning strike less than five feet from them rattled Callie's teeth and made her body tingle unpleasantly.

"Cal." EJ's voice was strained. She held a hand to her left side.

No blood under the muck from the ground that Callie could sense, at least not on the outside. She laid her hand over EJ's.

"Bruised ribs," she said. "Maybe broken. Don't move."

EJ gave her a pained, wry smile. "Not planning on it."

Callie kissed her, tasting fresh blood on her lips, which danced on her tongue. She sucked in a gasping breath without breaking the connection between them. EJ made a small, pained sound, then bit her own lip and pressed her mouth hard against Callie's. More blood flowed. Callie took it in, feeling herself energized, shivering with the buildup of power, like a boiler about to blow.

EJ broke the kiss. "Go get him."

Oh, she would.

Callie stood in the middle of the alley, every nerve aware of her surroundings. She heard EJ's heart racing and vermin scattering as they sensed what was to come. The night air smelled of dank debris, the ocean a mile away, Bert's sweat. And blood. The blood of her foremothers coursing through her. The blood of her lover on her lips, touching her soul.

Her skin prickled with the still crackling electrical storm Bert had created.

She grinned, knowing Bert couldn't see her, but he would soon experience what a blood mage could do.

Callie focused on the storm overhead.

"Contain," she whispered, making gestures she instinctively knew were correct and effective. She "collected" the storm, encircling it with her own power. Bert's magic resisted her. She tugged it from him, like taking a sharp object from a toddler.

"What the fuck?" he asked with startled confusion in his voice.

Opening her hands with a quick extension of her fingers, Callie sent Bert's magical storm back at him with the addition of her own command. He had raw power, but she had more and training to boot.

"Fuck!" Bert yelled.

In the flash of lightning, Callie saw him tumble backward, ass over teakettle as Gran would say. She pushed the storm harder, never allowing him to gain his feet. He slid along the pavement, his suit tearing, his skin rubbed raw. Callie smelled his blood on the swirling air, but didn't dare allow it to affect her. She enveloped him in the cloud of debris, the lightning crackling around it like a living, deadly shell.

Bert raged. He pushed outward with his magic, attempting to break it, to regain control of what he'd created.

Callie closed her fists.

He screamed.

Part of her prayed he'd do or say something to allow her to kill him. She could let her containment spell weaken, give him the chance to make a deadly attack, which she would gladly counter ten-fold.

But she wouldn't. Because she *could* contain him rather than kill him. To purposely disregard her oath and go against the Laws in order to hurt someone would make her no better than Bert Underwood and his father.

"EJ, can you go for help?" Callie called over the roaring wind and crackling bolts.

"Yeah, let me—Ugh!"

Callie turned her head. "EJ?"

Olive Lang stood over EJ, her hand raised in a grasping claw. Sprawled on the filthy pavement, EJ's eyes bulged, her mouth agape, as she tried to loosen the invisible strangle hold.

"Let him go," Olive growled. She was disheveled from the desk overturning on her, sporting a dark bruise on her forehead. "Let him go, or I kill her."

Callie's heart stuttered as her anger burned in her chest. She squashed the immediate response of tossing Bert aside or slamming Olive in the face with a pain spell. That might get Olive to release EJ, but it could just as easily cause her to clench her fist and suffocate EJ or snap her neck.

Without releasing Bert, Callie faced Olive. "Why, Olive?"

The other woman blinked at her. "Why? Why what?"

"Is he that important to you?"

"He and Greer will be taking over Paul's organization. Bert's a powerful mage. He just needs a bit of discipline is all. He's gonna be something in this city." She narrowed her gaze at Callie. "Why wouldn't I want to be part of that?"

"Because Bert killed Paul and an innocent woman to get control of the organization." Callie noted Olive's jaw stiffen, but not with surprise. She knew about the dead woman, even if she hadn't had a direct hand in her murder. "And because you love Kay Underwood."

Olive opened her mouth to say something, but snapped it closed, lips pressed together.

"We spoke to her the other day," Callie said keeping her voice calm as she kept an eye on EJ. The second Olive caused harm she was dead. "She was confused and sad that you had broken things off."

"I didn't want to." Olive lowered her hand slightly. Had she loosened her grip on EJ? "Bert said he'd help me and Rita. Love is grand and all, but does it keep a roof over your head and food in your belly? I'm tired of working hand to mouth."

"You need to survive, more than survive," Callie said. "I understand."

Bert pushed hard against her hold on him. Callie poured more magic into the container. He cried out in pained rage.

Olive startled, as if she had remembered what she was supposed to be doing. Her hand clenched again. EJ made a strangled whimpering sound. "Let him go."

Callie's own rage boiled. Heat rose from her gut, up her chest, to her neck and face. She'd suffered a terrible fever as a child, enough to put her in the hospital, but this was beyond that. And welcome.

Whatever Olive saw in Callie's face made her eyes go wide. Her mouth gaped. She stepped back, but she didn't release EJ.

"Bert killed people, Olive. He hurt Janie when we were kids." Callie's voice didn't quite sound right in her own ears, but maybe it was from keeping herself from hitting Olive with whatever was growing inside her. "He can't get away with that, and if you help him, you will be culpable. Even if the Tribunal doesn't catch up to him, he will pay in the end, and so will you."

"You can't pin Paul and that dame on me. All I was to do was get him in the car and slip him a mickey, then leave my cigarette case behind. That's it. I didn't know about the woman until after the fact. I didn't know about Janie either." Olive licked her lips. "Harm invoked is thrice returned, Callie."

The Law was ingrained in those who followed the path. Bert hadn't been formally or even informally trained as far as Callie knew, but the Law applied even to those who didn't practice. Consequence was inevitable. Bert didn't seem to care as long as he got what he wanted. Maybe he'd care now.

"Let her go." Callie started a mental count to five. One. Two. Three. Four.

Olive relaxed her hand. EJ sucked in a ragged breath and her coloring got better, but she wasn't free from Olive yet.

"Olive . . ." Callie put the promise of vengeance into her name.

"Calliope Payne, by your oath, if I release EJ Jordan unharmed, will you leave be me and mine, content with my departure from this place?"

A request for a truce.

It wouldn't allow Callie to make a formal charge against Olive for her part in Paul Underwood's death or in that of the unidentified woman, whatever it was. If she was involved, the universe would find a way to make her pay. Callie could afford to let her be if it meant EJ was safe.

"Leave here unharmed, Olive Lang, but know this. Should

you or yours ever seek retaliation in any form or bring any sort of harm to me and mine, this agreement is null and void. And I will bring the full effect of my wrath upon you, wherever you are, however long it takes." That last bit wasn't part of any formal wording, but it was a promise. "Do you understand?"

"I understand." Olive stepped away, fully opening her hand, and gesturing in a way to dispel her magic.

EJ sucked in a breath, hand to her throat and coughing. Glaring at Olive, she sputtered out something that sounded like a string of curses.

Callie nodded, relieved to see EJ unharmed for the most part. "I promised you no harm, but I don't speak for EJ. You'd better go before she recovers. Get as far away as you can while you can."

Olive didn't hesitate. With a final glare down the alley to where Bert was pounding the barrier of the debris cell and raging, she hurried away.

Callie honestly hoped Olive and Kay would make up and find happiness together. Preferably far from Seattle.

"Are you all right?" she asked EJ. "Can you stand?"

She reached out to offer a hand, but Bert made another attempt to break out. She shored up her hold with another sketching of runes in blood on her sleeve. He was getting weaker, but she couldn't give him any chance to escape.

"I'm good." EJ's voice was raspy. She rubbed her throat as she used the wall to get herself to her feet. "Why'd you let her go? Do you really trust her?"

"Mostly," Callie admitted. "She might be a problem later, but Bert is the bigger one at the moment."

EJ looked down the alley. Beyond the swirling debris and crackling electricity, Bert pounded his fists, his face contorted with rage.

"Neat trick using his own magic against him." EJ smiled at her, and Callie grinned back. "What can I do? I mean, it won't be as nifty as what you are capable of, but maybe I can get us a coffee or something."

Callie laughed. "Are you up to calling the cops?"

EJ's jaw dropped. "You want *me* to call the cops? Me? I don't think I even know the number."

Callie laughed again, but before she could reply, she heard police sirens in the distance growing louder. "Looks like someone beat you to it."

"Thank God," EJ said, leaning against the wall. "I have a reputation to maintain, yanno."

CHAPTER TWENTY-ONE

The interview room at the police station was the way EJ remembered it from a decade ago when she'd been brought in, questioned about some rum runners, and released for lack of evidence. She glanced at the drab green walls and layer of dust on the light fixture overhead. Hell, it probably hadn't been painted or dusted since then either.

She was probably even sitting in the same rickety chair she'd occupied, behind the same scarred wooden rectangular table. Where had she carved her initials?

She started to look at the leg of the table, but Callie caught her chin, keeping her in place, and gently dabbed EJ's split lip with a cool, wet cloth. "Feeling any better?"

EJ met Callie's gaze. There was weariness in her gorgeous blue eyes, but EJ felt something else. A connection. Their connection. Callie was with her, understanding her, knowing her like no one ever had and never could.

She covered Callie's hand with her own, stopping the ministrations. "Yeah, I'm good."

Leaning forward, EJ touched her lips to Callie's. Earlier, when she had been actively bleeding, EJ had lent her blood to aid in Callie's magic. Now, she simply reveled in the touch and taste of her.

Callie moaned quietly, sending a different sort of magic through EJ.

"You make that sound again," EJ whispered, "And we're going to be terribly embarrassed when Bradford comes through that door."

Callie smiled beneath her mouth, gave her a quick peck, and sat back. "We'll have to pick up where we left off later I suppose."

Despite her own weariness, butterflies batted at EJ's belly. "I suppose."

Callie's smile turned wry as she glanced at the door. "Hmm. Not Bradford."

"How do you—"

A sharp knock sounded on the door as it swung open.

A woman younger than Callie's Gran but older than themselves stood in the doorway. Despite it being close to midnight, her gray suit was neat, the ruffles of her white blouse crisp. She turned to close the door, hesitating to stare at Lieutenant Bradford who apparently thought he was going to follow her in. From his bushy raised eyebrows in response to whatever expression the woman gave him, that wasn't on her agenda. She shut the door on him and turned around.

She set her leather briefcase on the table. "Miss Payne. Miss Jordan."

EJ frowned. "Are you a lawyer?"

Under the table, Callie rested her hand on EJ's thigh. "This is Frances Eccles from the Covenant Investigation Office." She smiled at Eccles. "Sorry you had to come out here at this hour."

Eccles shrugged and took one of the seats on the other side of the table. "Hazard of the position, I'm afraid. How are you two doing?"

"A little banged up," Callie said, "but nothing permanent."

Eccles stared at Callie as if she was trying to see more than what was being said. EJ knew little about Frances Eccles, but she knew Callie well enough to understand she wasn't about to reveal their connection to her. At least not unless she had to.

After a few moments, Eccles sat back, her shoulders more relaxed. "Good. As is standard procedure after massive magic energy has been used, and particularly in a case where unsanctioned activity is suspected, I will be questioning you both. If you'd please step out of the room, Miss Jordan—"

"No." Callie emphasized her refusal by grasping EJ's leg more firmly. As if EJ was about to move at this dame's request. "She stays here. The police already interviewed us separately. We'll answer your questions; then we want to go home."

"That isn't standard operating procedure, Miss Payne."

"I don't care, Miss Eccles. EJ is under my care and protection. She stays where I can provide that."

EJ tried to keep the smirk off her face as pride and delight bubbled in her. Sweet, quiet Callie Payne wasn't going to let this woman dictate conditions.

Then her words penetrated.

Care and protection.

EJ had thought she was the one who was supposed to protect Callie. Tonight had certainly proved otherwise. Though, depending on the threat, it made sense they each had their own way of protecting the other. The care part was pretty damn mutual. Warmth spread from EJ's gut, making her feel soft and tough all at once.

Eccles removed a notebook and pen from her bag. "As you wish. All we want are the facts and the truth."

Depending on her questions, EJ wasn't sure they'd be able to provide those.

Between the two of them, EJ and Callie relayed what had happened at Greer's office, starting with EJ going over alone. She justified her decision to Eccles with the same sincerity she had given Callie. Eccles nodded as she made notes, though EJ could all but hear the woman's thoughts that going into a warded building knowing there was magic being used was not smart and leaned heavily on the side of foolish. Callie had already given her hell for that very thing.

Lesson learned.

Eccles wrote in her notebook in shorthand or some sort of code that EJ couldn't read. There may have been notations on what she believed or disbelieved about the account. EJ really didn't give a damn anymore. She wanted to go home, get cleaned up, and go to bed. Preferably with Callie.

"Is there anything else you'd like to add?" Eccles glanced between the two of them.

EJ and Callie passed the question silently between them.

Callie turned to Eccles. "What will happen to Bert Underwood?"

The older woman capped her pen and steepled her fingers. "From your statement and those of other witnesses, Mr. Underwood has violated a number of Laws."

She meant the Laws of the Coven, not only standard laws, though EJ was pretty sure Bert had broken plenty of those, starting with the murder of his father.

"Was he registered at all?" Callie asked.

Eccles didn't respond for a few heartbeats. Her gaze steady, she shook her head.

"What does that mean?" EJ had a vague idea that being registered with the local coven was important, but so what if he wasn't?

Callie kept her eyes on Eccles. "It means he was a rogue and wasn't supposed to be practicing. It also means either he was self-taught, or someone helped him and never said anything about his ability. It means that because his magic may have been used to intentionally cause deaths, he could be corporally punished."

Silence throbbed within the small room.

EJ didn't want to ask what methods of corporal punishment witches deemed appropriate. If serious physical punishment or a death sentence was designed to deter future criminals, those who meted it out tended to go with a clear statement.

"He'll have a fair trial for the illegal use of magic and for the murders," Eccles said. "No one can speculate beyond that for now."

"Did you ever find out the identity of the woman who died with Paul Underwood?"

There was little to go on for a physical identification, and the silver cigarette case had obviously been a ruse to make everyone think it had been Olive Lang. Neither she nor Callie was going to spill about Olive, but she felt sorry for the innocent woman who had been murdered as her stand-in.

"Tessa Blake," Eccles said.

"You mentioned that name when you came to the shop," Callie said.

Eccles nodded. "She had gone missing several days before. We had been asked by her family to locate her. She had potential as a senser—a witch who could detect magic—but had an unfortunate drug problem. That's where Bert got his information about your use of a spell at The Garden, Miss Payne. Miss Blake had been there the evening before."

The night the Underwoods, Greer, and Olive had come in. No one noticed this Tessa Blake doing whatever she'd done to detect magic at The Garden.

EJ and Callie exchanged looks. That explained how Paul Underwood knew so much when he'd gone to give Callie shit. It was a relief that it hadn't been one of EJ's people.

Eccles continued. "I asked you about her as a way to cover several bases, not expecting . . . Well, apparently, she and Bert Underwood had had some sort of relationship. Whether he had engaged with her and then decided to use her in his scheme or specifically singled her out for such a sacrifice remains to be seen."

"Is he headed to Coyote Ridge?"

Even EJ knew about the Coyote Ridge holding facility. It was said to be guarded and warded by the strongest magic available, and for good reason. The worst offenders in the mage community were sent there while awaiting Tribunal courts or after being sentenced.

"He'll be transported in the morning," Eccles said. "For now, he's in a cell and muted."

"Muted?" EJ had never heard the term before.

Callie moistened her lips. "A spell to dampen his ability to do magic. Sometimes worked in conjunction with an actual physical binding. It won't hurt him, but it's the best precaution to take."

EJ wouldn't mind Bert hurting some—hell, much more than some—but she kept that to herself.

"Since it wasn't Olive Lang in the vehicle, do you know where she is?" Eccles held her steely gaze on them.

Callie squeezed EJ's leg, indicating she'd take this one. "Haven't seen her since leaving Greer's."

EJ had to hand it to her. The semi-truth flowed smoothly from her lovely lips. If Eccles suspected she was fibbing, EJ didn't see it.

"You'll both be called as witnesses for his Tribunal, so please remain in town for the time being." Eccles slid her notebook and pen into her bag and stood. "I'll be in touch."

She left the room, leaving the door ajar.

Callie rubbed her palms over her face. "I'm beat. Glad Gran was willing to wait until tomorrow to hear what happened."

Callie had called her grandmother as soon as they arrived at the police station. Though EJ couldn't hear the exact words, she could tell the older woman was relieved they were okay but champing at the bit to get details.

EJ rose and gently grasped Callie's upper arm, urging her to her feet. "Come on. I hear a hot bath and strong drinks calling our names at my place."

Callie stood. She stared at EJ for a moment, then leaned forward to kiss her. There was only the slightest of stinging from her cut lip. "I will never decline an offer like that from such a sexy woman."

EJ grasped Callie's hand and raised it to kiss her fingers. "As long as I'm the only sexy woman you accept it from."

Callie squeezed EJ's hand. "No other. Let's go."

"There's a somebody I'm longing to see . . . I hope that she . . . turns out to be . . . someone who'll watch over me . . ."

Ruth's sultry voice wafted over the dancers and diners at The Garden, her magical intonations spreading joy, contentment, and her signature sex appeal. Men and women swirled around the dance floor, dapper suits and luscious gowns creating a kaleidoscope of colors. A perfect pre-holiday Saturday night while a chill rain fell. The Y-J didn't have the Underwoods breathing down its neck, and everyone was relaxed and in a celebratory mood.

Callie sat at EJ's booth, sated by the delicious dinner they'd enjoyed together. She nursed a light gin and tonic with extra lime as she watched the dancers and caught the occasional glimpse of EJ chatting up the seated customers. It was her after-meal routine to do so, checking in with patrons and flirting a little along the way. Some would have let jealousy tarnish the joy Callie felt seeing EJ in her element, but she knew who EJ would be coming home with.

"Get you another, Miss Payne?"

Callie glanced up and smiled at Macie, the young server decked out in the standard Garden uniform of tuxedo shirt, vest, and black bow tie. "I'm good, thanks. EJ might want something when she gets back to the table."

Ruth finished her song, and the crowd applauded.

"I do," came EJ's voice from behind Macie. "Thanks."

Macie turned, nodded at EJ, and said, "Be right back."

Callie grinned up at her, admiring how the perfectly tailored tux fit EJ. The jacket lining matched the bright red rose brooch on her lapel. Callie wore a matching custom-made pendant on a gold necklace.

The band played the opening notes of "Night and Day."

EJ held out her hand. "Dance with me?"

Callie rose, taking a moment to smooth her royal blue gown and get her feet properly under her. The silk and sequined body-hugging garment had a wide V-neck with narrow straps, showing more cleavage than Gran would have approved of. It plunged to her waist at the back, flaring out slightly at the knees to allow for ease of walking and dancing. Not her usual togs, but it was a special occasion.

EJ swept her gaze up and down Callie's body, sending tingles of delight through Callie as if her hands were skimming over Callie's skin.

When their eyes met again, EJ smiled. "Beautiful. Come on."

EJ led her to the dance floor and, raising their hands overhead, twirled Callie around a few times. Callie laughed as they came together, never stopping as they smoothly transitioned into the foxtrot. EJ held Callie's right hand in her left while EJ's right hand rested on the small of her back, just north of inappropriate, the heat of her palm sinking into Callie.

Fifteen years ago, Callie never would have thought her future self would be here, dancing with a gorgeous woman, wearing a silk gown, the thrum of her heartbeat—their heartbeats—keeping time with the music. It was beyond anything she could have hoped for. Dreamed about maybe, but making it a reality? No. Her reality had been the butcher shop and being with Nate.

Safe choices. Choices that were expected and accepted.

But now she knew better.

She didn't have to stick with the safe choice, the choice others thought would be best.

EJ was *her* choice, and the best one she'd made in a long time. That came with risks, but they were risks the two of them would face. Together.

Other couples gathered on the floor as Ruth began to sing about tom-toms, clocks, and raindrops.

"It's almost hard to believe we're here like this, isn't it?" EJ asked, echoing her thoughts. Callie wasn't sure if it was their bond through her magic or merely that they were of the same mind on most things. Maybe a bit of both.

"You've done a fantastic job getting The Garden back on its feet." Callie smiled as she glanced around the room. "Everyone is happy and feeling fine."

"Good," EJ said leaning in to nuzzle Callie's ear. "So am I."

"Me too." She laid her cheek on EJ's shoulder. "What's next?"

"Another drink. Another round of glad-handing customers."

Callie gently slapped her shoulder. "Not that. I meant what's next for business. The club is doing well. You should invest in more locals. Diversify. See where you can go from there."

EJ laughed. "You sound like my accountant."

Callie tilted her head back, keeping their bodies as close as they could while dancing in public. "I want to help all I can. With Paul and Bert Underwood gone, and Kay off with Olive, there should be a number of opportunities to expand. We can keep the neighborhood flourishing and even go beyond the Y-J if we do it right. And we will, won't we?"

EJ stared at her with something like wonder in her dark eyes. "We."

Callie's face heated. "I don't mean to be presumptuous."

"No, no. I like it." EJ grinned. "I like the sound of 'we.'"

The rest of her body heated along with her cheeks. "So do I."

EJ kissed her, a mere touching of their lips, but she let the touch linger as she whispered, "I love you, Calliope Payne."

Callie smiled beneath her mouth, her heart soaring. "I love you too, Eileen Jordan."

She felt more than heard a low wanting growl come from EJ as she pressed her mouth more firmly against Callie's. Just as Callie was about to part her lips and let her in, a commotion at the front of the room pulled them apart.

Three men in dark suits with white shirts and purple ties were laughing loudly and calling for a table. The server gestured at the full house, then over to the bar where a couple of stools were still unoccupied. The larger of the men glared at the server.

"Shit. Crispin Lerner's boys." EJ nodded in their direction. "The purple ties are their thing."

"What are they doing here?" Callie didn't like the way the men stood surveying the room. Several of the patrons were starting to look nervous.

"We aren't the only ones looking to take advantage of the Underwoods being out of the picture." EJ slid her left hand into her coat pocket, where she typically kept her brass knuckles. Her right went to the small of her back where she kept her .38 holstered. "Lerner is scoping us out, sending a message."

Callie reached up to the rose pendant hanging around her neck. The custom-designed blood-red piece wasn't just pretty, wasn't just a symbol of her connection to EJ. She pricked her finger on the needle-sharp thorn. *Only a little, Callie-girl.* As her blood welled, she rubbed the warm, sticky droplets between her thumb and forefinger, muttering the key words of a spell that would protect her and EJ while repelling those against them. Magic swirled around them, flaring Callie's skirt and ruffling EJ's hair.

Taking EJ's arm, Callie started toward the intruders. "Let's send Lerner a message of our own."

ACKNOWLEDGMENTS

Many thanks to the entire Bywater Books team. EVERYONE over there rocks!

In particular:

Salem West for her encouragement and bolstering emails. Best Cheerleader Ever!

Kit Haggard for her insightful edits and questions that brought out depths of the characters and story that I hadn't realized were in there.

Ann McMan for the striking cover that inspired the purchase of a pair of kick ass Doc Martens.

Radar for fixing glitches and making my day brighter with kind words.

Thank you to all who pick up this book and give it a whirl. Having the opportunity to offer a bit of entertainment is a pleasure and an honor.

ABOUT THE AUTHOR

Cathy Pegau grew up in New York reading horror, science fiction, and fantasy novels, and playing RPGs. Writing seemed like a natural progression, adding a touch of romance to her favorite types of stories. Her science fiction romances have won RWA Fantasy, Futuristic, and Paranormal (FF&P) Chapter Best Futuristic Romance and Best of the Best Prism Awards and a Golden Crown Literary Award for Science Fiction/ Fantasy. Her writing has garnered such rave reviews as "This was a treat to read," and "I didn't hate it." She lives in Alaska with her spouse and critters, preferring to hunker down in front of the woodstove with a good book to outdoor activities.

Twitter | @CathyPegau
BlueSky | @cathypegau.bsky.social
Facebook | facebook.com/100063567667885
Website | https://cathypegau.com/

Bywater Books believes that all people have the right to read or not read what they want—and that we are all entitled to make those choices ourselves. But to ensure these freedoms, books and information must remain accessible. Any effort to eliminate or restrict these rights stands in opposition to freedom of choice.

Please join with us by opposing book bans and censorship of the LGBTQ+ and BIPOC communities.

At Bywater Books, we are all stories.

We are committed to bringing the best of contemporary literature to an expanding community of readers. Our editorial team is dedicated to finding and developing outstanding writers who create books you won't want to put down.

For more information about Bywater Books, our authors, and our titles, please visit our website.

https://bywaterbooks.com

9 781612 942834